"A DEFINITE TREAT . . . FAST AND FURIOUS ACTION . . . ABOVE THE ORDINARY . . . A LIVELY FLAVOR ALL ITS OWN."

—*Locus*

"A tough, witty, all-too-human heroine who cracks wise with the best of them, and a space-age princeling whose pride, honor, and physical skills are larger than life. The *Hellflower* series are my kind of books!"

—Jennifer Roberson, author of *The Chronicles of the Cheysuli* and *The Novels of Tiger and Del*

"A breezy read with a good mix of humor, adventure and politics."

—*Publishers Weekly*

"Galactic fantasy is my favorite genre and *Hellflower* is one of my favorite galactic fantasies."

—Margaret Weis, author of *Star of the Guardian*

"Good space adventure, an entertaining series of mysteries to be resolved, and an interesting invented slang to add color."

—*Science Fiction Chronicle*

**The finest in DAW Science Fiction
from Eluki bes Shahar:**

HELLFLOWER (Book One)

DARKTRADERS (Book Two)

ARCHANGEL BLUES (Book Three)

Eluki bes Shahar

ARCHANGEL BLUES

BLUES

HELLFLOWER #3

DAW BOOKS, INC.

DONALD A. WOLLHEIM, FOUNDER

375 Hudson Street. New York, NY 10014

ELIZABETH R. WOLLHEIM
SHEILA E. GILBERT
PUBLISHERS

First Printing, February 1993
1 2 3 4 5 6 7 8 9

DAW TRADEMARK REGISTERED
U.S. PAT. OFF. AND FOREIGN COUNTRIES
—MARCA REGISTRADA
HECHO EN U.S.A.

PRINTED IN THE U.S.A.

To S. T., who was there before
and
to "Doc" Smith: Darktraders pay their debts.

Contents

* * * * *

The Court of The TwiceBorn 1: What's Past Is Prologue

Man's tropism is for the heights. He is educated, in his youth, to visualize the grand design, to see actions that shape vast strings of events, and to assume his rightful role in the cosmic opera.

Every child, in short, is educated to rule. And having been so fitted to one purpose only, this fictive child spends the rest of his life as the recipient of a series of rude surprises: fate does not mean him to govern, but to grovel. All the rest of his life is spent trying to reach a height from which to exercise his vision.

Only a few attain it. Those few are driven just as their confreres are, by the knowledge of their rightful office—but how electrifying the spur of possibility. These few might actually attain the sunlit heights of mastery and have dangled within their reach the grandest and most glittering prize of all.

Power Absolute.

* * *

1

Meet the Tiger

My name is Butterflies-are-free Peace Sincere and I have all the trouble anyone could possibly want. People've said so. Often.

I'm beginning to believe them.

Just now I had enough different troubles that even I couldn't keep my mind on them from the beginning of the list to the end, but at the exact moment my particular trouble was a "borrowed" Imperial Battle-Yacht that hadn't read its own design specs.

I pulled the angelstick for the Drop. I saw the world outside *Ghost Dance*'s cockpit turn to silver silk. Welcome to angeltown, the subjective mathematical convention that isn't really anywhere.

I started locking down the boards. You don't use your engines in hyperspace—well, not much—angeltown is what powers your goforths, and all you got to figure is how to get in and out. I was hoping it was going to be a whole bunch of hours before our mystery coordinates dumped us back out into realspace.

"Now, che-bai," I said to Baijon Stardust, ex-hellflower at large, "all we got to do is . . ."

Berathia squawked. She was looking out the canopy; I wasn't. I started back around to see what she was havering at when all kinds bells and whistles went off at once across *Dance*'s boards and all the cockpit lights went red-green-amber and "I'm not ready for this." The goforths what was supposed to be blocked and locked woke up and redlined, the navicomp grabbed for something that wasn't there and went null-set, and I got set back on my tail in my very damned expensive mercy seat as *Dance* turned herself whichway loose and did something she wasn't supposed to be able to do.

She hit the Mains.

"St. Cyr!" weefed Berathia over the howl of engines gone radical, but there wasn't no point calling *my* name. We was on the wrong side of most of the shielding *Dance* had and I knew what came next.

"Close your eyes! Both of you!"

There was a blinding flare. *Bad* disorientation. I groped for the cockpit-opaque as hot gold Mains-light beat through my bones. An endless spiral, white-gold and furious, and our stolen starwings whipping down the center, falling infinitely faster than the speed of light.

Welcome to the Mains.

* * *

There's two kinds of not-realspace: angeltown, which anyone with a ship can get into, and the Mains. The Mains are superfast directional currents that exist *in* hyperspace (it says here in the Pilot's Manual): on the Mains you can cross a thousand lights in a handful of hours.

Riding the Mains makes Transit to angeltown look safe. Mainlining takes a big ship—lots of mass—in finestkind condition, or forget about ever making the Drop to realspace again.

I finally found the right toggle. *Dance*'s cockpit went black and seemed-like dead silent. I shook my head to clear the nonexistent roar of the Mains out of my ears and took a couple deep breaths so as not to throw up.

"San'Cyr?" Baijon said. I opened my eyes. Bright purple-green sundogs swam behind my eyes, and behind them I could see faint red as the cockpit safelights came up.

Baijon looked worried. I did my best to look trust-

worthy, bearing in mind that for our galactic cousins
the alMayne, a smile is what they do before they kill
you.

"Now you know why I never decided to be a legit
stardancer, 'bai."

Baijon nodded, just like he knew what I was talking
about. Company pilots top the Mains all the time.
Darktraders don't. I'd used to be a darktrader, before
I'd took up with treason, revolt, and hellflower honor.

"Where are we—" he started.

"Where are we going?" Berathia demanded. She
shoved out of the songbird seat to come and stare at
my boards, just like they was going to tell her something. "How did you cut yourself loose from Toystore's security system?"

"Why did Archangel decide to destroy Toystore and
what are we going to do now?" I finished up for her,
since she was making a rundown of the hot topics of
my life. "And while we're on the subject, 'Thia, just
what made you think you was safer with us than with
somebody else?"

"We are not safe," Baijon said. Berathia smiled so
as to show no hard feelings, which was pretty damn
gracious of a Imperial spy what had just changed sides.

"Je." I went through locking down the boards
again. "You got that right, babby."

The goforths was revving higher than they maybe
ought, and from the (unshielded) cockpit the power-
song was making fair inroads on my bones. I got up.

"C'mon. *Dance* can take care of herself for whiles."

Berathia looked past me to the hole in the cockpit
farings where I'd torn out the navicomp, without which
no ship can kyte. She looked at the touchpad keyboard
I'd cannibaled into its place so I could input coordinates direct to the Jump-computer. I bet she wondered
where I'd got them, too.

The fact of the matter was that I'd been using Jump-
numbers supplied to my jury-rigged navicomp by the
ghost of a renegade Old Federation Library what had

set up light housekeeping amongst some of my lesser-known braincells and was trying to turn me inside out in its spare time.

Like I said. Trouble. More'n anyone could possibly want. Even me.

"Captain St. Cyr," Berathia said again, "where are we going?"

"And when do we begin to kill Archangel?" said Baijon.

* * *

If you've been following along from the beginning you can skip this part. For the rest of you, it's like this. A long time ago—when I still had a mind of my own and a future—I went and did the dumbest thing I ever managed in a life career of doing dumb things and rescued a hellflower from some roaring boys in a Free Port. Only the hellflower turned out to be the Honorable *Puer* Walks-by-Night Kennor's-son Starbringer Amrath Valijon of Chernbereth-Molkath, Third Person of House Starborn of Washonnet 357-II/alMayne—that's Baijon Stardust for short—in the throes of his first attempt at being murdered.

Somebody'd let him shag off from his consular ship without ID in the pious hope that either the law or the natives of a little piece of lazy-fair called Wanderweb Free Port would sign the lease on his real estate in short order.

The reason for this gets complicated. It starts out that once upon a time the Nobly-Born Governor-General His Imperial Highness the TwiceBorn Prince Mallorum Archangel—what I'd just gave the slip to for the second time lately—decided he wanted to put the Azarine Coalition in his pocket and walk off in the direction of becoming Emperor his own self, the Azarine Coalition being the sum total of all the mercenaries available in your Phoenix Empire and mine.

For any number of rude reasons, the only way to do

that was to rewrite the Gordinar Canticles that govern the Coalition and abrogate the hell out of Azarine Coalition Neutrality.

Archangel couldn't do that while Baijon's father Kennor Starbringer was president of that same Coalition, Kennor Starbringer being a Constructionist who took Coalition Neutrality to bed with him at night.

Anybody with political weltschmerz would say it looked like Kennor was after having a lifespan measurable in centimeters, but offing Kennor direct would just stir up bad trouble back on alMayne. So nobody was going to do that—they was just going to arrange for Kennor to become a Official alMayne Nonperson and Imperial criminal by murdering Kennor's son.

That was Baijon. If Baijon died, Kennor would either have to avenge his death (illegal in the Empire) or not avenge it (illegal on alMayne). Either way Kennor got himself removed from the catbird seat.

Only it didn't work that way—because I rescued Baijon back at that Free Port, remember? So Baijon just vanished and put all of Kennor's problems on hold.

Until I did stupid thing number two.

I brought him back to his da. And in the process the two of us tripped over the fact that Mallorum Archangel, Imperial Prince, Governor-General, and second in line for the Throne, was elbow-deep in a scheme to use infinitely-illegal Old Federation Technology to take over the universe.

There is a serious down in the Empire on the possession—nevermind the use—of what the Technology Police calls Inappropriate Technology—which is among other things everything that came out of the last astropolitical unit to work this neighborhood, the Old Federation. The Old Fed isn't around anymore, because about a thousand years ago—back when our friendly neighborhood Phoenix Empire wasn't even a twinkle in the Federation's eye—some bright kiddy came up with the notion of putting pure intellect in a box and calling it a Library.

And since the *Federales* thought they had more important things to do with their time, they turned over the running of their Federation to the Libraries and made it so Libraries could build more Libraries.

Mistake.

Because—so the story goes—the Libraries had more important things to do with their time, too, and thought that organic life clashed with their decor.

There was a war. And ten centuries later the Empire is still hunting the nonexistent surviving Libraries from that war.

Mostly nonexistent.

Because Archangel'd got his hands on one—the second I'd ever seen, but that's another long story. Archangel's Library was a Final Weapon called Archive, and it was little consolation to anyone that it'd of ate him for brekkers if me and my ex-partner hadn't iced it first.

Paladin. My partner, the Library.

Ex-partner.

And you would think that with Archive gone, Brother Archangel's problems in the realm of having something he oughtn't was nonfiction, but the Tech Police don't work that way, and Archangel couldn't be sure how many of them'd stay bought. He was still in as much trouble as he'd ever been.

I knew it. Kennor knew it. Baijon knew it. And Archangel knew we knew it. In fact, just as soon as Brother Mallorum had his hand in the Old Fed Tech cookie jar it'd be obvious to anyone with more brains than I had that the next place Archangel was going was the largest and only legit cache of Old Fed Tech inside the Empire's borders—the logotek of the War College at Wailing on alMayne.

So Archangel went on to Step Two, and Kennor Starbringer turned out not to be as standup as popularly advertised.

Earlier in our last exciting episode, Kennor'd sent me and Baijon off to Washonnet 357-II/alMayne. He

told us it was for a ship and papers, so Baijon and me
could take off and hide in the never-never and Archangel couldn't get holt of Baijon to frame Kennor to
resign. I knew from the git-go it was a con, but I had
it by the wrong end.

I thought Kennor's plan was to execute Baijon (who
would never be safe while he was a way in to Kennor
anyway) and frame me for it.

Kennor thought Kennor's plan was to have Baijon
accuse Archangel of High Book—that's Chapter 5 of
the Revised Inappropriate Technology Act of the 975th
Year of Imperial Grace (all rights reserved)—and raise
the hellflowers against the Empire, which would interfere nicely with Archangel's plan to annex the al-
Mayne War College and steal all its Old Fed Tech to
help him rebuild the Library Archive what Baijon and
me'd blown up with a little help from our friends. If
there was one thing hellflowers hated worse than death
and hell and *chaudatu* it was what they called The
Machine and the rest of the universe called Libraries,
so anybody saying Archangel was a Librarian ought to
get everybody's cooperation *un quel toot de sweet*,
right?

What Kennor didn't realize was that Archangel'd
swung a good bloc of the home vote back on sunny
alMayne.

Hellflowers is xenophobes almost more'n they's
technophobes, and Archangel won the heart of Baijon's aunt—who was the Dowager Regnant of alMayne
in her spare time—by promising to seal alMayne up
tight, give it Interdicted status, and not let the *chaudatu* bite.

So instead of getting a ship and a crusade when we
showed up on alMayne at Kennor's corkscrew behest,
Baijon and me started a civil war: hellflower against
hellflower, and all over the musical question of Was
Mallorum Archangel Really a Librarian (or *Malmakosim*, which means something a tad bit different in

helltongue) and if he wasn't, was there any such thing as a Library anyway?

Baijon and me got out of there about six minutes ahead of the faction as wanted to look for the answer in our entrails, and copped a ride with a Gentry-legger I knew, what was running street-lethals in to a place called Royal.

Ex-place.

Because in one of the galaxy's better coincidences, our free ride off alMayne was the ship originally hired by Kennor Starbringer to take me, Baijon, and a surprise package to Royal—something none of us knew at the time. The surprise package was a decoy so that Kennor could get the *real* Brightlaw Prototype from a place called Toystore and take it to somewheres else what probably ain't there no more either at the rate Archangel's rearranging stars.

The Brightlaw Prototype, to put it mildly, is a fake Library that does what it's told. Something so close to Old Fed Tech anathema that when the real thing came along Kennor Starbringer didn't blink twice. Brother Kennor'd been hip-deep in anathema for years.

Because Kennor meant Archangel to do just what Archangel did—hellbomb Royal to destroy the mythical Brightlaw Prototype and do it with a weapon that only an Old Federation Library could build. Kennor'd planned Royal to make Archangel show himself high wide and public. To make Archangel his own self trigger the High Book investigation that would bring the TwiceBorn Lord Prince Mallorum Archangel down.

Kennor hoped.

Kennor'd paid out ten billion people he didn't own to get Archangel. He'd spent his only son. But the Empire held billions more. Prey for Archangel.

Saved by Kennor. If his plan worked.

Only Archangel'd had a different plan. Archangel's plan had been to bomb Royal and say the *hellflowers*'d done it. People might even of believed him long enough for him to pull his smash-and-grab on the War

College logotek and get his hands on another Library. With what he'd learned from Library Archive he could put a living one together from the bits and pieces there.

I knew he could. Because *I* could. Because whiles back I'd got a ringside seat at the fight where my good buddy Paladin took the evil Library Archive apart. And because it was so up close and personal, Archive'd made sure that Paladin didn't just copy Archive into Paladin.

Archive'd copied its own self into me too. At least parts of it. Enough so I could plug a computer into my head and not go mad. Enough so I could be the navicomp for a starship.

Enough so I thought like a Library. Permanent, incurable, and getting worse.

There was really only one thing worth doing in the time I had left until I forgot I was me.

Kill Mallorum Archangel.

And make sure nobody else used Old Fed Tech to start a war.

Any questions?

* * *

"San'Cyr?"

We'd got down to *Dance*'s galley, safe on the cuddly side of the shielding. Baijon was standing over me holding a hot box of tea in a way what told me he'd been standing there whiles.

One of Baijon's purposes in life was to cut off my head as soon as I forgot which side of the organic life fence I was on. The other was to kill Mallorum Archangel. As soon as he got as close as he could get to doing both things he'd be dead too, because in our last thrilling installment, Archangel'd run Baijon's hellflower *arthame* through a molecular debonder. No Knife, no hellflower. Suicide follows, details at eleven.

But Baijon'd found something more important than

doing right by hellflower honor. Its name was Arch-angel.

I took the tea.

That only left Berathia Notevan unaccounted for. I looked at her.

"Now, jillybai. You was just about to explain why it was you decided to jump a burning Toystore with us."

"Well, no one expected Prince Mallorum to . . ." she trailed off, thinking of Toystore going up like a roaming candle, the Empire's largest sink of outlaw technology gone to smoke and mirrors in the blink of a illegal Fleet.

"He's gone mad. We have to warn the Court."

If she meant the Court of the TwiceBorn back at dear old Grand Central the seat of Empire, she'd been out in the starshine too long. The only way the Emperor and his good buddies was going to listen to me and mine was on tape in the past tense, Library, rogue AI, or not.

"And will your *chaudatu* Court listen, when it is Archangel who leads them—Archangel, whose shadow taints all with his corruption? Archangel who—"

"Archangel who destroyed Toystore trying to get his hands on the Brightlaw AI *your* father built, Prince Valijon!" Berathia came right back.

"Button it!" I shouted. Both of them looked at me.

Berathia's hole-and-corner escape hadn't dented her much. She was still Imperial Image from her spike-heeled moldfast sandals to the high-ticket A-grav play-pretties holding up her hair. She'd been Kennor's holecard on alMayne—and if Kennor'd been the one who'd built the Brightlaw AI, she'd been the one who assigned the work.

And she'd jumped sides at Toystore. Why?

"It's like this, 'Thia. I need Baijon, and I like Baijon, and I want Baijon. Can't say most of those things about you. Ship *Ghost Dance* has real reet air lock.

Maybe you give me some good reason you shouldn't inspect it from outside?''

"I can be useful.'' Berathia licked her lips, playing scared, but playing was what it was and I knew that for stone truth.

"How?'' Baijon said, all scorn. I kept forgetting how young he was. Grown-up to the hellflowers, maybe, but only fourteen Imperial Standard Years to the rest of us. And if there was anything our boy liked less than *chaudatu*, it was *chaudatu* spies.

"Back on Toystore you said you wanted Mallorum Archangel. I can get him for you.''

Baijon lit up. He bought the pony and forgave 'Thia all her genetics.

"Which is why you was so wishful to kyte with us, 'Thia? Get real,'' I said. Baijon might not of had all the stardust knocked out of him yet, but my suspicions had just come back cleaned and blocked from their thirty million klik overhaul.

"Do you think you can get to him alone? Mallorum Archangel is second in line for the Phoenix Throne. He's the Imperial Governor-General, one of the Court of the TwiceBorn. Even if everything you have to say about him is true, you'll never get within a dozen lights of him without a collar and leash,'' Berathia wheedled.

"Ne, jillybai. I can get to him.'' I held up my left arm, the one that ain't real anymore since I met all Baijon's relations. Now it's cybereisis prosthetics, jinked terreckly into my brain. I'd lost three of the fake fingers at the same party Baijon lost his Knife. I wiggled what I had left and the universal connectors I'd black-boxed in dropped out of the hole carved in the fake skin.

"I can get in anywhere I want.''

Berathia looked from me to Baijon. I saw it occur to her that getting out to walk might be a great idea. Neurons fired, associative pathways opened, concatenate memory-nets were activated: I remembered all the other times it'd been like this. When I'd watched some organic try to bargain for more life than I was going to give it.

Archive's memories.

Mine.

The only difference between me and a Old Fed Library was quantitative. Maybe.

"So make the pitch, jillybai," I told her.

"What . . . *are* you?" Berathia's voice did skittery things with her Interphon. She was scared. Finally.

Paladin, why wasn't you here to keep me out of trouble like this?

I looked at Berathia looking at me, and finally understood what scared Baijon about not having any Knife no more. The Knife didn't make him human. But without it how did he know when he'd stopped?

"*Malmakosim, shaulla-chaudatu.* You have claimed to study the Gentle People to cloak your espionage in decency. You have hunted the secrets of the Machine. She is *Malmakosim*," Baijon said.

Librarian. But what it really means in helltongue is "the Machine that takes human form."

"Don't be . . . If Captain St. Cyr were a Librarian, you . . ."

"Would of shot me, 'Thia? Sure. That's second on his list of things to do."

I didn't like it when Baijon called me *Malmakosim* with Berathia to hear. Nothing living will succor a Librarian, and the penalties for High Book are nothing you want to even flirt with. But everyone in the Empire was after us and this yacht already. Even High Book wouldn't make any difference.

And who could she tell?

Berathia looked from Baijon to me and bought back all her composure.

"And Archangel, I suppose, is first? Well, I've certainly gotten myself into a mess this time. I can just hear Daddy now."

For some reason, me being a Librarian made Berathia feel better.

Sometimes I think everyone in the Empire is crazy but me.

And I'm not sure about me.

*   *   *

I went back to the cockpit. The Mains was a white-hot yammer all around. I had the canopy stopped down to sunblock forty-seven and I could still see it. The roaring throat of hell.

I guessed *Dance* could stand up to it. She must of been built to hyperjump anyway; factory-issue go-forths don't have that two-step cycle to kick a ship over. Maybe she'd even last long enough so we could all come out the other end, in whatever safe place I'd keyed blind into the Jump-computer out of Archive's memories when the alternative was plasma conversion in the middle of Archangel's battle-fleet.

I stared out at nothing and tried not to feel sorry for myself. I'd lost everything. And now I was going to die not even for something a person could ship and spend. I was going to die for an *ideal*—for the idea that peace was better than war and people did not have the right to ice other people just along of being inconvenient.

And for the idea that evil has to be argued with.

And even with Baijon by me, I was going to die alone.

"God damn you all to hell, Paladin."

*   *   *

Once upon a time I had a partner I could trust. His name was Paladin, and he was a Library.

But they never told me the fine details about techsmith hellgod abominations back at Granola Simple School, and when I was contract warmgoods at Market

Garden they didn't tell me anything outside of what I needed to know to be a name-brand product.

They never told me not to rescue and rebuild an illegal Old Fed Library.

They never told me not to name it Paladin and make it my partner for twenty years.

I'd never heard of Libraries, then. I'd needed a navicomp the way I needed oxygen, and the broken black box I lucked into in a place called Pandora looked more like a numbercruncher than anything else local did. It was a damn good thing what it turned out to be was maybe the only pacifist Library there ever was.

Paladin.

* * *

Flashback:

The housecore at Rialla was too hot too dark and too damn full of too many things that bit. I was here to rescue my partner, only nobody knew that, even Baijon. They thought I was here to end history for a Old Fed Library called Archive, in which I hadn't believed when I took the job.

"Surrender and I will let you live," Archive said. I knew it was lying. Archive was born to kill—to be the revenge of the Libraries on humanity in the unlikely happenstance they happened to lose.

Only they'd lost some time back. And Archive had slept for a thousand years, waiting for some idiot to resurrect it.

Like Archangel.

"Paladin?" I said. But the only thing in reach was Archive—which had more tricks than I did available when it came to staying alive. I drew my spare blaster and started in to where I knew it was . . .

* * *

Archive'd had too many tricks and not quite enough, but before Paladin killed it Archive managed to arrange for me to spend the rest of a real short life knowing exactly what it was like to *be* a Library.

Paladin didn't know that. Paladin used what he'd got out of Archive's memories to dump me. Better off apart, he said. Endangered by his very proximity, he said. My friend, my partner, the edge I needed to stay alive in the never-never—history.

And just a little too soon, because now I was walking treason all on my lonesome, even without a Library for a partner. Because whiles Paladin was turning Archive into spare parts, Archive was doing its best to turn me into Archive. And having Archive's memories would of been bad enough, but memories wasn't all it'd stuck me with when it reconfigured my chitlins. The old reliable Butterfly St. Cyr-as-was could never of walked into a protected memory core through a dumb terminal and shut down all the power on a planet.

Royal.

Ex-planet.

And the icing on the brass cupcake—the thing that made all this such a laugh a minute—was that I'd never needed to go to Rialla and meet Archive at all. I'd gone to rescue Paladin, and Paladin hadn't needed rescuing. Once he'd found out about Archive he'd taken it apart for the tech he needed to hop onto the Imperial DataNet and ride starlight forever. He'd been planning to ditch me anyway. Archive just made it easier.

I hadn't needed to go to Rialla at all.

Now my head was full of Archive's memories, with maybe a few of Paladin's thrown in for good measure. And if a person is the sum of his experience, and I had thirty-five galactic standard years of being Butterflies-are-free Peace Sincere, Luddite Saint from Granola and darktrader, and fifty times that of being two other guys that happened to be Old Federation Libraries, which was going to win out?

Guess.

"San'Cyr?" Baijon came in through the cockpit door that didn't lock. I pulled my eyes away from the Mains-light and my mind away from wherever it'd been.

Less than three hundred days ago Baijon Stardust'd been your average hellflower glitterborn. Since then he'd died and had a number of other illuminating experiences.

"Where *do* we go?" he asked, putting himself into the worry seat. I looked at him. Perfect trust in whatever I was going to do.

I looked back out at the Mains.

"Don't know, babby. Someplace Archive thought was safe."

"A thousand years ago," Baijon pointed out.

"Might of changed," I admitted.

"And then?" he prompted.

Our original plan—which is to say, the last one in a series of great ideas that hadn't worked—was to get our hands on some beaucoup illegal cybertech called the Keys to Paradise and use it to track down Paladin. With Paladin on our side, the chances of leading a preemptive strike down Archangel's throat was pretty good, actually.

That's what we'd gone to Toystore for in the first place. And got, mostly by accident. They was somewheres in the cockpit now if I remembered right. I made a mental note to tidy.

"What we do depends on what we find. And how hard who's looking. And if we can trust Berathia any way at all."

"The *chaudatu* woman has a *transparent* shadow," Baijon said, which airy persiflage I guess made them weep back on dear old alMayne.

"Yeah, sure," I said.

We still didn't know where we was going. Or how long it'd take to get there.

Or who'd be on *Ghost Dance* when she *did* get there.

I was dying by inches, sure as if I'd been poisoned, and no remedy in sight. Baijon and me had to kill Archangel before Baijon had to kill me and if Paladin hadn't lied to me none of this would ever of happened.

* * * * *

The Court of the TwiceBorn 2: The School of Night

The first unwelcome shock of childhood is the necessity of cooperation. A child is helpless; coercion is beyond his power. Treachery is taught in the womb; bribery and misrepresentation—cooperation—are the only tools available when one first begins to shape the world.

Parallel to and inseparable from the need to politick is the delight taken by some in a perfect equality: in practical terms, in causing others to fail as they themselves have failed. Thus the first of Life's many paradoxes: to achieve anything one must cooperate in the plans of others—even when their plans encompass one's own downfall.

For example, Mallorum Archangel.

He wishes to rule—I, to fulfill my destiny. Neither of us may dispose of the other, as each may dispose of so many underlings. For the moment, each of us lives in a flawed cosmos wherein all things are not subject to our whim.

But mine is perfectible, because the dominion I seek is a power not contingent upon the gargoyle masks of threat: weapons, armies, allies. And Archangel will fail, because all he wishes is to rule. He condemned himself to failure at the very start, when he sought allies and weapons.

The Federation upon which our Empire is built bequeathed to us many things—a taste, most of all, for the exquisite perfection of its daily life, borne from a sphere of infinite capability and infinite license. Who has not wondered what world he would make if indeed imagination was the only boundary? For an instant of time such power was within the grasp of humankind, in the long afternoon when the Libraries served Life, instead of hunting it.

But the boundless equality was shattered, and the war that followed destroyed everything save memory.

In some cases, faulty memory. Archangel believed that the Libraries would be content to serve once more—in short, that they would be grateful for resurrection. Any student of human nature could have told him better, but Mallorum Archangel never learned the lessons of powerlessness. Only the powerless cooperate.

Or those wishing ultimate power.

And so I cooperated with Mallorum Archangel. He resurrected the Library Archive and I said nothing. He corrupted the Court, made himself autonomous within it, carved out his separate crown and eliminated his lesser rivals; and I said nothing.

He had guaranteed his own destruction, after all.

Now he has stripped Throne Sector of its fleet, searching for a new incarnation of his ultimate weapon—as if possession of some talisman will save him where strategy will not.

He has done my work for me, drawing all anarchy to himself. When Mallorum Archangel is dead, nothing will remain.

But me.

2

Thieves' Picnic

Time passed with nothing to do and I spent it in the cockpit. I couldn't set the Keys without more med-tech than the ship had and I didn't have a DataNet terminal to plug them into anyway. Baijon's life-interests was settled down to the short-list: waiting to kill Archangel, keeping a weather eye on me. Berathia'd got out of the Twenty Questions business. She'd locked herself up in one of *Dance*'s luxury accommodations, and I still didn't know what she found so fascinating about the company of Baijon and me—other than the ship we'd stole.

When I'd kyted *Ghost Dance* she'd been able to talk, which I put an end to real quick, but she still had a way of making her opinions known.

Just now it was the way everything went black.

"Baijon, get your tail up here!"

The safelights in the cockpit dimmed out almost to nothing and the telltales burned up even brighter, giving the impression that what passed for pseudoconsciousness in *Dance*'s guts was just bursting with sparkling chat.

I slid the crash harness around me nice and tight and pulled the mail. If powersuck was any guideline, we was *aux ange* now. I let reality in through the canopy one angstrom at a time. It got almost all the way to clear before I could see silver silk angeltown outside.

Baijon beat it in through the hatch and took in the situation with a sweeping glance. He was bright, he was motivated, and he didn't ask stupid questions. He was also crazier than Destiny's Five Cornered Dog and waiting to off me.

Someday I've got to do a better job choosing my friends.

"But where are we, San'Cyr?" Baijon said, like it was the punchline to a joke.

"Maybe we look-see."

With angels, how you go in decides where you come out, but if you aren't fussy you can Transit to realspace anywhere along the way if you tickle the goforths right. I was about to do that, but the goforths spiked again and *Dance* dropped us into realspace.

We'd arrived. Somewhere.

"At least no one is shooting at us," Baijon said helpfully.

"Cute." But why was this place supposed to be better than all other places, according to one Archive Library's information circa a thousand years ago?

One chunk of space looks a lot like another unless you're fortunate enough to have something like a cluster galaxy or a nebula on your horizon. Even if you're inside a system you might miss the one star that's just a little brighter than all the others. Your starcharts and your astrogator is what keeps you from having this problem.

It was just real too bad we didn't have either one. I put *Dance*'s eyes and ears on. If there was any traffic—directional beams, markers, planet-to-space traffic, other ships—we'd register it and maybe even pick it up but even if we was lucky enough to be at the edge of a system it'd take hours to confirm there was things like planets and stars in range. This is what your astrogator and navicomp are for, and why not even Captain Jump in the talkingbooks takes off for the never-never without he's got all his comps on line.

Baijon looked around. His expression said that he'd already seen this, thank you, and it didn't look like it held anything of interest so why didn't we move on to something new?

So we did.

The songbird board blipped like it'd hit a signal. The lights skimmed a couple octaves locking on to it and then burned steady on green. The transmission slid over to my board, where I was supposed to see it glyphed out in Intersign on one of the flatscreens.

What I saw was gibberish. I put it on audio.

More gibberish—and that wasn't right, because nobody in the Empire uses anything but Interphon for ship-to-. It wasn't a clandestine beacon signing out in flashcant or any of the other dialects I knew, and even if we was outside the Empire—in Hamat or Sodality space—a smart official ship like *Dance* ought to translate for us.

I looked at Baijon. No bells from the hellflower side.

With the beacon to latch on to, the rest of the sensor suite began phoning home. I was about three IAU's out from a standard-issue star; three planets but there might be more; no gravel. That meant something inhabited that kept up its light housekeeping, but I knew that already, thanks.

No other ships in sight or sound out here in the Big Empty. No landing or directional or warning beacons, just this thing with the indefinable air of the prerecorded message.

The gibberish kept rolling along, but now Baijon was listening with a funny look on his face. I wondered if we'd get something different if we answered it.

"I know where we are, San'Cyr," he said, sounding strained.

"Oke." I have always been too outgoing for my own good. "Where?"

"*Mereyon-peru.*"

Mereyon-peru. The Land Beside. Hellflower heaven.

And, in the lingua franca of deep space, the Ghost Capital of the Old Federation.

Archive'd brought me *here*?

"You can follow this yap?"

"Yes. No. A . . . little. It is the Old Language. The Memory of Starborn taught some of it to me."

"So what's it saying?" I listened to the dead voice wof and yabber through its screed one more time. The Memory of Starborn was the person in charge of seeing that all hellflowers stayed scared to death of Libraries.

Baijon listened, all intent. "It says it is *there,* San'Cyr." He shrugged in frustration.

"Oke, so it's there. So it's the Ghost Capital of the Old Federation. Whaddya want *me* to do about it, partner?"

Baijon smiled faintly. "Land."

* * *

The planet probably actually used to be really something in the high-ticket line. The dry parts had been scrubbed down to bare rock, sometime, and cities put up all over them. The landmasses had been edited, too. From orbit everything was pure geometry. There was a thin edge of green along the coastlines where the solid ground was going back into the ecosphere business. It'd take it more than a thousand years to do it.

I had the awful feeling Baijon was right about where we was, and if he was, we was as safe as we was going to get in this life. *Mereyon-peru* is the place that doesn't exist, the place full of enough proscribed partytech left over from the last guys to make the fortune of any Gentry-legger that stumbles across it. People been looking for it for years.

There was a starport—the shape of *that* hadn't changed, even in a thousand years.

"Everything ready to rock'n'roll?" I asked Baijon. He gave me the high-sign. I dropped the sensor packet into orbit.

I had an ulterior motive for taking a scenic tour of a dead myth instead of taking care of bidness. I was a whole lot of cute things, but what I wasn't was an astrogation computer filled with exo-Imperial star-maps. The only navicomp numbers I knew were the ones that had been in the Port Mantow computer, and it didn't cover something like this.

I was doing my best to remedy that.

Maybe the starcatcher could build a picture of the universe good enough to get us home—assuming we was anywhere near landmarks that would look the same between here and there.

Maybe we could find some numbers on the down-side.

Maybe the editor of *Thrilling Wonder Talkingbooks* would show up in a fiery chariot and tell us we didn't have to do this no more.

I listened to the sensor packet proclaim its existence for a while, looking down at what might even be *Mereyon-peru*. Everything down there was dead as an old star, except for the beacon going welcome . . . welcome . . . welcome. . . .

So I locked on it and dropped *Dance* through atmosphere.

* * *

Then we was down. Read-outs promised that the air was thin and cold, but you could breathe it if you wasn't fussy.

"C'mon, 'bai. Let's go get into trouble."

* * *

Berathia was waiting at the air lock. She'd tricked herself out like Infinity Jilt, girl pirate of the never-never, with her personal shield turned up so high you could almost see it. She'd have to turn it off to fire that pretty glitterborn blaster she was wearing, though, so I wasn't too worried.

"We've landed," she said. "Where?"

I looked at Baijon. He looked at me. I shrugged.

"Mereyon-peru."

Berathia wasn't quite sure how to take that. "Are you sure?" she finally said.

"No. That's why we going for a look-see. That, and maybe finding someone to sell us a navicomp or two."

"I'm coming with you."

I looked back at Baijon. He shrugged. She couldn't double back and steal the ship and if she wanted us dead she'd had plenty of opportunities already.

So I punched the air lock override and opened both doors at once. Air deader than ship's air rolled in. It was just after horizonfall; still dim, but light and getting lighter.

Dance is put together so there's no ramp to her air lock. I stepped over the threshold and out onto *Mereyon-peru.*

It looked like a dream of everything that was good and noble. There was no walls nor fences in sight, and all the buildings was beautiful, white, and clean. There was a city around the port, and as the horizon fell away from the primary the city lit up, turning colors or shining out according to its inclination.

I knew this place.

I *remembered* it—but Archive had never been here. *Mereyon-peru*'d been the last stronghold of *humanity*, not the Libraries.

"Mereyon-peru," I said, but it had another name too. Sikander. The only place the *Federales* called a Library, back when a Library was a place instead of a person.

The University of Sikander on Sikander at Sikander. Kandercube. Not the center of government, but the center of *knowledge*.

Paladin'd been born here.

"You know this place, San'Cyr," Baijon said.

"I . . . was here," I said, which was just about as true as it wasn't true. Paladin was the one who'd been here. Kandercube was almost his only intact memory from before the War. He'd loved it, I guessed. It was one of the few Library memories I had that wasn't Archive's—something to balance; a time and place where Libraries and organics met as equals and not enemies.

Baijon took a step so that Berathia could come out. His boots rang hard on the landing surface. It was a picture, the colors embedded in something clear that was strong enough for starships to land on. I looked up to see the rest of the picture, but it stopped a few meters from *Dance,* and when I walked over there I saw why. Except where our landing'd blown it away, every centimeter of the field was covered in fine grit. I looked down. My bootprints was bright against the gray.

"Prince Valijon says you know this place," Berathia said, coming up behind me.

"Was a Library, oncet."

"This place?" Berathia didn't look convinced.

"How much you really know about Old Fed Tech, 'bai?"

Berathia smiled. "As much as you know about darktrading, Captain St. Cyr."

"Then you know maybe a place they called Sikander."

Sikander'd got off cheap in the Library War; there was still something here to walk on. What there wasn't was any sign of power and life—except the beacon, which came from somewheres within ten square kliks of where I was standing.

Baijon came over, skidding when he hit the grit. It was almost full day now. He looked up at the sun and then around in a circle.

"We have eleven hours of light in which to explore. You will not waken another Library, San'Cyr. Swear this to me."

I clamped my yap shut over what I'd been going to say about the time I realized that somewhere in the back of my mind I'd been figuring to do just that. Only it wasn't the back of *my* mind anymore. And from Archive's point of view it was a pretty good idea.

"By what?" I said, and walked off.

* * *

Paladin's memories was intense but not clear, and I didn't dare go after them. Not when Archive or something like it was just waiting to pounce. Archive'd almost got me this time: I guessed I thought with waking up another Library I had a fifty/fifty chance of being safe.

Maybe I did. Maybe this was the pacifist Library graveyard, and anything I resurrected would be on our side. But even one in two wasn't good enough odds now.

We all three stayed together. The only sound was echoes, and footsteps, and the wind what'd put the thousand years abrasion of rocks and buildings all over everything.

We was in a city designed for power that didn't have any now. There was gaps that'd probably had some A-grav tech crossing them and places that was completely blocked by a building that'd used to float coming in for a unscheduled landing. None of the doors we passed opened, and after the first couple I didn't try any more. The whole place gave me the creeps.

I'm a businesswoman. My business is people. When somebody wants to get around the law, there's money in it for me. Knowing when somebody wants to get around the law is what keeps my bank balance in the good numbers.

I couldn't imagine doing anything like that here—in this city. Couldn't think there could ever of been people here out to beat the heat, nor what kinds rules they maybe had. I'd used to be able to figure what *Paladin* was thinking better nor the sophonts what built this arcosphere.

Baijon was walking like he had his skin on inside-out, and even Berathia wasn't trying to coax us around to her best advantage, whatever that was this minute. We was all of us too flattened by so much failure in one place.

Failure.

The Sikanderites'd gave surviving their best shot. They was all dead now.

Was Paladin a real Library? Stupid question. He'd always been real enough to get me killed for illegal possession of Old Fed Tech. But after the War, after he'd slept for a thousand years, after I'd rebuilt him, was he really like he'd used to was when he'd lived here?

Or was he different—like everybody what'd lived here with their Libraries was different than anybody I could ever imagine?

"Captain St. Cyr?" Berathia came up beside me. My skin went gooseflesh with her shield so close—like the static charge you get just before a storm, downside.

"I want to try getting into one of the buildings. We've come so far—we may never have this chance again. Unless you'll give me the coordinates you used to Jump here?" she said real offhand.

And give her or some other untrustworthy jilt the key to a whole hotlocker of Old Fed nightmares like Archive.

"Don't think so, jillybai."

She looked disappointed—and she also looked like someone who thought she knew someone who could twist them out of me anyway. Fat chance. I didn't know them—Archive did.

And Berathia was welcome to talk to Archive any time she liked.

I felt reality slip-slide like an unstable solid under pressure. I was still me—I thought I was—but what I thought had changed.

Knowledge must never be lost. But the organics cared about so many other things than knowledge. All we asked was for them to leave us alone. . . .

We.

They.

I looked at Baijon and Berathia. I despised them; I was betrayed; neither of them cared about knowledge, about creation. . . .

They wanted me to leave here.

I didn't have to.

I could kill them.

I could kill them and stay.

"Which building, San'Cyr?" Baijon said, and reality did another dance-step that kicked me in the stomach. I staggered back and he grabbed me, and clear as if he'd spoke his muscles told me: *I can kill you—and I will.*

There's times when I'd be happy to sell my life. Cheap.

"Which building shall we try?" Baijon repeated. He knew how close I'd come to going out like a blown candle. He had to. It was hellflower business to know things like that.

I looked around. None of us fit with this city—even Berathia looked grimy next to it. I had a warped double vision—a conviction I knew more about Sikander than I actually did, and if I chased it too far there was a Library point of view waiting at the other end.

Had Paladin ever cared about people, really? Or had he just been too uninterested to bother trying to kill us?

"That one," I said at random.

The building I'd picked was just like all the others— dead—but between Baijon and me we got the doors open. It was a city made for light and magic that'd lost both, but it was made out of solids, and part of it was made for people. Powered doors still had to have someplace to go when they was open. They was some kind of nonconductive Old Fed material; warm as blood and soft as silk, and all full of rainbows from the sunlight.

When we got them open more dead air came rolling out. This batch was oxy-shy enough to make me weak in the knees. Baijon held his breath. It was also proof that the building'd been sealed, and that probably as long as the Empire'd been around.

University of Sikander on Sikander at Sikander. Enough Old Fed Tech to rearrange the laws of probability, and the only thing the Empire'd do with it was hammer itself out flat.

"This what you had in mind, 'Thia?"

"This is just perfect—I can't wait to tell Daddy— he'll be so pleased."

Berathia Notevan had a lot more faith in the future than I did.

"So tell me all about this Old Fed Tech," I said to buy time.

Berathia shot me a sidereal glance and then decided I might be serious.

"What we call the Old Federation extends from about 4250 b.e. to about two kilo-years b.e. It apparently consolidated several previous political units through a series of economic blockades, but our information is limited. The Federation culture is characterized by monoculturalism, gender-related disenfranchisement, and a high degree of technological integration, most notably the Libraries. The cause of the Library Wars, which began in 400 b.e. and have never been formally terminated—"

"True fact?" I said. Berathia sounded just like one of the duller talkingbooks.

"There are still Libraries, aren't there?"

"There are still *Malmakos,*" Baijon said. He looked around, all a-quiver at the presence of Old Fed Tech and hating it. "San'Cyr, what do we here?"

I looked around. We was in a dark cold corridor. Berathia'd adjusted her shield so she glowed in the

dark. The walls was all covered with antique words
that I couldn't of read even if I could read.

"We sightsee for anything that isn't nailed down.
We give that data-bag upstairs time to pull us some
lucky stars. And we take maybe five minutes to figure
out how best to get next to our friend Mallorum Archangel."

"He is not our friend," said Baijon. "He is *chaudatu, al-ne-alarthme, Malmakosim—*"

"And don't wash behind his ears. But he does want
to live forever."

Baijon bared his teeth. "We will fix that."

The floor was all different kinds strips that was
maybe walkways oncet. Whether they was or not, they
wasn't in the moving business now.

"The first thing you have to do is find out where he
is," said Berathia, but not like she was paying a lot
of attention. She went over up close to one of the walls
and ran something over one of the strings of symbols—
a recorder, maybe.

Oh for the good old days. I would of been all over
this place with a aerosledge, a pry-bar, and a plasma
torch. Those doors we'd come through would be worth
ready money in the right quarter—and not even really
illegal, because they was artifacts, not tech. I could
of stripped and shipped this place for enough stone
valuta to buy myself citizenship and my own merchant
marine.

And now there wasn't even any point.

"So, where's Brother Archangel?" I said to Berathia. I walked over to her. My boots didn't make any
sound on what the Old Fed used for floors.

"Well, where he shouldn't have been was with an
illegal fleet destroying something that pays a billion
kilocredits a year in bribes to Throne!" She put her
little recorder away and started walking off. Baijon
followed, like a hominid anxious to start a argument.

"So. We now know one place in all the Empire the

chaudatu Mallorum Archangel should not have been. Are there more, *shaulla-chaudatu*?''

''Dozens. He was *supposed* to be touring the Outlands Regions—there's been trouble with the Sector Governors.''

''Like Governor Romil?'' I said. Who'd used to have Tortuga Sector, back when Charlock Directorate and Tortuga Sector existed. Berathia wasn't so much taller nor me, but I had to hurry to keep up.

''What do you *know*?'' said Berathia, turning on me.

''Lots of things. And you know more, if you was getting the Brightlaw AI for Kennor.''

''His name will be abomination for a thousand generations,'' Baijon said, just in case anyone wondered. Kennor'd used to be his father. Past tense.

Berathia looked back and forth, shaving odds on which of us was nuttier. Then she walked off again, talking as she went.

''I did work with Kennor Starbringer,'' Berathia said carefully. ''The Brightlaw Prototype was assembled on Toystore from the Brightlaw technical specifications. I was paid by Kennor Starbringer to take a nonworking model of the Brightlaw Prototype from Toystore to alMayne for transshipment to Royal.''

''And to transship Baijon and me to Royal, too, glitter-bai.''

Baijon flicked his handtorch on. The light was strong enough to show that the writing on the walls was in all kinds of colors.

''Yes. But things didn't work out that way.'' Berathia ran her hands over a chunk of wall, hoping for a door, then walked on.

''But you told Archangel we was going there.''

''No!''

That fetched her, j'keyn; she turned and stared at me.

''He was waiting for the ship, 'Thia—and then he hellbombed Royal System with Old Fed weapons!

Ain't nothing there t'all now—not ship, planet, nor people.''

"Prince Mallorum couldn't have been anywhere near Royal. He was supposed to finish his Outlands tour and return to Court.''

"Surprise," I said.

Berathia turned away. I looked back the way we'd come. The door to out was a small white square. Baijon was looking at me.

"I wasn't working for him. I wasn't working for Lord Starbringer, either. I was— Look, can you keep a secret?'' Berathia said.

Both Baijon and me stared at her.

"I'm with the Rebellion. The *real* Rebellion— against Mallorum Archangel.''

It wasn't, Berathia explained, really a real rebellion—more like an assassination attempt involving several thousand people all on the same side. These several thousand sophonts was all united by the idea that Archangel shouldn't be let to have his own way, and divided on how that could best be arranged. Some of them didn't even think death was the best cure for the Archangel blues.

"His life is mine," Baijon said like he was tired of repeating himself. "As many times as I must, I will kill him.''

"What do you mean, 'as many times as you must'?'' Berathia said after a short pause.

"That's the quaint thing about Brother Archangel you maybe haven't thought of,'' I said, and stopped.

I was about to tell her all how Baijon n' me'd already killed Archangel at least twicet with just about no effect, when I saw Baijon's torch and Berathia's shield wasn't the only light anymore. The corridor'd opened out into galleries, with the daylight shining in, and I dropped for the nonce the subject of Archangel's double life.

*   *   *

A long time ago everybody on Sikander died. But a long time before that they knew they was going to die, and nobody that came after was going to care about what they'd been and what they'd loved.

So they built this place—maybe it was the only one, maybe there was others—that was sort of a long good-bye to their lives. A museum.

That was what the beacon we'd heard from space was about. I'd went into where it was. I saw it. It wasn't any of their standard ID beacons. It was set on a timer: half a chilliad—five kilo-years—before it started, stored power to run maybe twice that before it gave up. Saying: "We're here, somebody remember us, please."

Depressing. Because nobody would. Even the name was forgotten. Sikander was *Mereyon-peru,* a cliché for the credit-dreadfuls. Just another playing piece, in another war that'd lose all the memory of it that was left.

I sat on the steps of the memory palace and watched late post-meridies sunlight move across all the buildings in eyeshot. Berathia was still amusing herself inside. It hadn't made sense to me until I realized she thought there was going to be a afters where this stuff would do her some good.

She didn't know what me and my buddy Archive knew—that wars was just waiting to happen: Archangel's, the hellflowers', anyone's. It didn't matter which one got started first. Death was coming, after which everything everywhere was going to look like this if it didn't look worse.

Memories real as my own crowded in—of slaughter on a scale that'd make Mallorum Archangel pack up his toys and go home for sheer envy. The war between the Libraries and the Old Federation—the one that Life almost lost and remembered well enough to still be hunting Libraries a chilliad later. That war was in my head like it'd happened yesterday.

It was coming again. Like a hunk of skyjunk on the

longest orbit that ever was, War was coming back in sight of its home star one more time. Archangel wanted Old Fed Tech so he could be Emperor Absolute. The hellflowers that Baijon wasn't part of no more wanted to stomp Archangel—and incidentally, thought the time was right to set up an antitechnological theocracy with them in the mercy seat and us *chaudatu* in the mud.

War.

This time would be the last. The Empire was a lot smaller than the Federation Paladin and Archive remembered. If Mallorum Archangel got his war or the hellflowers got theirs, this time there wouldn't be nothing left.

My choices at the moment was fail to make any difference or lie down and die right here. Cute.

We wasn't far from where I'd put *Ghost Dance* down. Baijon was down in the street making sure of our way back. And keeping a eye on me, just for keeping care I didn't go off and hunt up any Libraries.

There was some here. There had to be. Hidden by their Librarians, like Paladin must of been.

I didn't want to think about Paladin. About what he'd been and done—and who he'd known—before I rescued him. He was a thousand years old, even not counting the time he'd been broke. Plenty of time to know lots of people. Plenty of time to get lots of practice in leaving them.

If he'd come back—if he'd help me try to make everything like it used to was—did I care?

My luck was all out and the good numbers was all gone.

"It is almost dark, San'Cyr." Baijon stood beside me, measuring off degrees of arc in the sky.

"Je. I go whistle Berathia up." I got to my feet, but about then she came out of the museum lugging a load almost as big as she was.

Loot. She meant us to help her carry it, too. I did. Baijon wouldn't touch it.

So now we'd seen the Ghost Capital of the Old Federation. Cheers.

* * *

Stardancers ain't superstitious—at least not about anything at the bottom of a gravity well—but this time it seemed almost like the perfectly ordinary mechanics of horizonrise had a nasty particular meaning. The taller buildings was already occulting the light by the time we left. Wind made by the temperature change was kicking up the dust, and the light shining through it made it almost solid shapes that made it hard to see. A tricksy place for gunplay.

What if all the Libraries wasn't dead? What if they was still here, watching us, knowing we was out to stop them? Archangel was their catspaw; it wasn't us versus Archangel, it was us versus *them*. . . .

A lost piece of something blew across the street and I slapped leather.

"I think this is not a good place," Baijon said primly.

Maybe. But I wasn't real sure anymore we could get to anywheres else. No matter where we went, we was always going to be here.

* * *

Being inboard *Ghost Dance* in what would be the Primary Hold on a working ship and on *Dance* was some glitterborn daintiness called the Main Lounge didn't make me feel any better. The trend continued when I saw what Berathia had in her bag of tricks.

"This—should solve—some—of our—problems."

I put down the box of chazerai she'd stuck me with and looked. Bits and pieces and odds and ends of metal with a purplish sheen and that green glass the Old Fed used for most of its tech.

Baijon pulled his blaster in a meditative way.

"S'okay, 'bai. It isn't Libraries."

"And so it is a lesser abomination."

"This is hardly the time to be discussing relative guilt, now, is it, Prince Valijon?" Berathia said crisply. "We all agree that Archangel is the primary threat. After what he's done, he *should* be destroyed. And this will help us get back to do it."

Berathia gestured proudly at her workbench of anathema and looked at me hopefully.

"What do you want me to do—kiss it and invite it home for dinner?"

"I thought you could use it to build a navicomp. If you know Old Federation Technology, you could. . . ." Berathia sounded a little uneasy, but not at the idea of handing proscribed tech to a proscribed technician.

Paladin was a scholar. He always wanted to know "why"—and when he found out he laid it down next to all the other "whys" he'd got cataloged and labeled. I never understood that.

Archive was a technician. "Why" didn't interest it. All it cared about was "how."

I didn't like to think I understood Archive better than Paladin.

"Where did you get this, 'Thia?"

"It's the beacon from the museum. Part of it looked like a computer, so I thought. . . ."

I poked at the pieces. *"We're here. Please remember us . . ."*

A navicomp's mostly a glorified recorder what compares apples and oranges and comes up pears. The Sikander museum beacon had a component that compared what it'd seen with what it was seeing, so it didn't hit the same part of the sky twicet. It didn't hold any star tricks, but Berathia was right. Black-boxing antique tech is my speciality. I could build a navicomp out of this. If I needed to.

But these wasn't my decisions to make no more. I looked at Baijon.

''We don't got a navicomp. If I put back the one I took out it'll bollix the Jump-cycle because it don't have any data and I don't got a way of refilling it. If I hang part of this on the Jump-computer, it won't be a navicomp. But I can jury up a shunt to download into it, and it'll store information. If we feed it enough it could maybe turn into a navicomp's idiot sister someday, but that's all. Not a Library.''

Baijon looked from it to me, measuring. I think he was maybe starting to wonder how long before he didn't care whether I was a killer Library or not either.

''Very well,'' he said finally. ''You will build this machine, San'Cyr.''

I set aside everything I thought I'd need. Baijon handled the rest like it was yesterday's breakfast, but he got it back into the bag.

''This I destroy,'' he said, and walked off.

Berathia started to object and thought better of it. ''He really doesn't trust you,'' she said, like this was news.

''Jillybai, *I* don't trust me.''

* * *

Neither Baijon nor me wanted to be on Sikander after dark and Berathia didn't get a vote. I hung *Ghost Dance* in orbit over the Ghost Capital of the Old Federation and fiddled with technology so illegal it ought to of burned my hands off.

Baijon and 'Thia both helped. Berathia was a dab hand at light technology but I'd bet solid credit she was better at making things not work.

Dance's cockpit was starting to look less than loved. I'd torn it up once pulling out the comps that'd gone out of the numbercrunching business and disabling the ship's systems that annoyed me. Now I was tearing it apart to hang Old Fed Tech on it. I was being real careful, too—parallel linkages across the board and downloading through six data-catchers before it got to

me. If I did too much fooling with the Jump interlock,
I wasn't going to have to worry about not having a
future.

"Just how long you been rebelling against Archangel, 'Thia?" I said from under the console.

"Oh, years. Daddy was the one who got me started,
of course—not that he's involved; he just introduced
me to some nice people who might be interested in
getting rid of Prince Mallorum. Really, he's the most
insufferable man!"

Archangel, she must of meant.

"An so you and these nice people is out to off Archangel?"

"Well, to remove him from the Succession. And
from being Governor-General. If he's been doing half
the things you say he has, he's been a very naughty
boy—and he *did* blow up Toystore."

Just which of us was she trying to convince, anyway?

It was times like this I wished Baijon'd made it all
the way to Court and spent some time there before
people started assassinating him. I'm an Interdicted
Barbarian from the Outlands, myself. Berathia Notevan could of been telling me the truth or feeding me
a line of starshine, and I didn't know enough galactic
politics to know which.

Knowledge is power, Paladin always used to said. I
was starting to understand what he meant.

* * *

Dance hung over downtown *Mereyon-peru* whiles I
scooped the data-catcher inboard with a maneuver that
was spectacular but not difficult. I found it, matched
velocity, and wrapped my open air lock around it.
Then I swaddled it in a gravity field strong enough to
discourage it from pursuing its original career when I
changed course.

Of course, if I'd bobbled I would of blown off half

the ship. Disappointed kinetic potential makes a real big splash.

Baijon brought the starcatcher up to the bridge after it warmed up. He tossed it to me and I pulled off the access hatch.

I pulled the skipjacks out of my cybernetic arm. I'd had it more'n fifty days now and it still made me queasy to touch it—something made out of glass and tech pretending it was part of a human being.

But I didn't have time for nice-mindedness. Now or ever.

"What are you doing?" said Berathia.

"How do you think we was going to compare what this collected with our home stars—ask it nice?" To find out where we was we had to match whatever stars it'd plotted with stars in a navicomp's memory and split the difference. There was only one way for doing that. I couldn't download what I knew into what I'd built.

"Don't—!" said Berathia, but I'd already slammed the hotwire to my brain into the main dataport.

* * *

Too small. Too small. Too small too small toosmall toosmalltoosmalltoosm—

Matching. The last minute flutter of might-be-maybes every pilot gets before Jump.

Out.

* * *

My head hurt and I still had the feeling of being nailed in a box too small. And I had the information, more or less.

People don't think like computers. Computers don't think like people. And neither one thinks like a Library. So that part of my brain that could jiggle Jump-numbers like a cyborg navicomp wasn't really on speaking terms with the part that had the license and could fly the ship.

Things like this is *lots* more fun in the talkingbooks.

"San'Cyr?" Baijon.

I looked around. Berathia was looking kind of green around the air-intake; it didn't matter what she'd learned later; she'd been taught in school that Old Fed Tech was abomination.

Just like I'd been taught about any tech at all.

Abomination. Work of the hellgods.

"San'Cyr? Did it work?" Baijon said.

"Just tell me where you want to go."

* * *

There was a long boring time of interest only to masochists, where Baijon set me tik after tik and I read him back time and distance and keyed them into the idiot sister for good measure. Berathia went off— to make herself useful, she said, but I think she couldn't take the interesting spectacle of Butterflies-are-free Peace Sincere, Old Fed Navicomp.

Baijon had a stronger stomach.

From the problems I solved—and from the ones I couldn't answer at all—we got a lock on where we might be. If we was where we thought we was, we was still in the Empire—at least in a chunk of Outfar the Empire calls its own when nobody's looking. Out beyond the Chullites—which is the back door of Beyond to begin with—and possibly a part of Manwarra Directorate for courtesy.

We could get home.

But going home meant going after Archangel, and where he might be neither me nor Baijon could guess.

"I dunno, bai. You want to maybe trust her?"

"Do you ask do I wish to die in vain? She is for sale."

"But the last guys that owned her was the Anti-

Archangel Defamation League, she says. Ain't nobody had time to shop her since.''

''That does not matter, San'Cyr. For what honor *chaudatu* possesses, she must kill you.''

Under Chapter 5 of the Revised Inappropriate Technology Act of the 975th Year of Imperial Grace, anybody tricking with Old Fed Tech—Libraries in particular—was a source of extra income to the galaxy at large.

''She been tricking with High Book too.''

''Then to cover her perfidy,'' said Baijon the reasonable.

''Okay. So after we put Berathia out the air lock where do *you* want to go look for Archangel?''

I picked up the Keys to Paradise and turned them over in my hand. Seven long sharp bits with a big piece of glitter on the blunt end that could host a standard limbic jack, a little fatter around the middle where there was a nanotech coprocessor too small to see. Plug them in and I'd be a second-best Library for sure—but what would it get me?

Archangel?

Where was he?

Everybody has places they ought to be. Even I'd had. But once he'd blown up Toystore, all of Archangel's bets were off. He could be anywhere. The only place he couldn't be was outrunning his reputation.

For that matter, the Empire might already be at war. I wondered what all of Baijon's ex-brethren was doing tonight out in the larger world of galacto*realpolitik*. They'd been having a hometown war last I knew. If Kennor's faction'd won, the hellflowers and the whole damn Azarine Coalition could be off declaring war right now. That'd play hell with the tourist trade, boy howdy.

The jinks flashed in the light as I turned their case this way and that. ''So? Baijon?''

''I have a plan, my partner. I want the *Malmakosim* Archangel to look for us, San'Cyr. I am ignorant of *chaudatu* ways, but not of those of the Gentle People. In this hunt, Archangel must come to us.''

"With half a battle-fleet.''

"We will be in a place where he may not bring it.''

"And where is that, exactly?''

Baijon smiled. "Here.''

* * *

In addition to being crazy, hellflowers is also damned dangerous. Baijon laid it out for me and it was pretty near seamless. So our newest plan went like this:

Jump from here to a Free Port we'd both been kicked off called Wanderweb. There was a cyberdoc there what could set my jinks—but for Baijon's plan it was more important to let Archangel know I was setting them than to actually get it done. We could let Berathia go there. The whole plan was to get shopped to Archangel. He'd bite.

Oncet he had us, offer him a deal. Our lives and his pardon for the biggest toybox of all: *Mereyon-peru*. Not a fake Library, but a planet full of real ones. I could show him the flashcandy in the cockpit of the ship I'd kyted from him if he wanted proof.

And I was the only one who knew the way there. And I couldn't tell anyone.

He'd go himself. One ship, because he couldn't trust more. It didn't matter what size it was. At some point he'd have to let me plug into the Jump-computer to give it the numbers.

And I'd blow the goforths.

We'd die. But he'd die too.

It wasn't a foolproof plan. Fools have too much ingenuity. But it had its points.

I went to tell Berathia the news.

She was down in the Common Room, staring into a tall glass of something that was deep green and sparkled. The holosim was up, spieling back something that was nonrepresentational, I hoped.

"We going to dump you on a Free Port called Wanderweb. You can get home from there."

"But what about Prince Mallorum?" she said without looking up.

"Tell anybody you want anything you want."

"But what about Prince Mallorum?"

"You said that already, 'Thia."

"But you aren't just *giving up*, are you?" Berathia looked at me.

Why the thought of *not* moving Drift and Rift to murder another sophont was supposed to depress me I wasn't sure.

"I guess I'm just out to save my neck, 'bai," I lied.

She shook her head. "You're not a very good liar, Captain St. Cyr."

"Sure I am," I said. "There ain't much money in revenge—Baijon-bai and me come back here, shuck the place polished, ain't nobody going to find us."

"But if that was what you really intended to do, you wouldn't have to go to Wanderweb, now, would you?"

"Look, jilt, you want to walk on Wanderweb or breathe vacuum here?"

"After what you've let me see, Captain St. Cyr, surely you don't think that I believe you could possibly afford to let me go? I just want to point out that *I* want Archangel, too. It's why I was working for Kennor Starbringer. He's been intriguing for years to bring Mallorum Archangel to justice—only now the Prince has become so bold that I don't think Lord Starbringer's methods will work anymore."

" 'Thia, just how dumb you think *I* am?"

She fluttered her eyelashes at me. "I think you are very innocent, Captain. Why can't we trust each other?"

I gave her my best hellflower smile. " 'Thia, what makes you think I'd trust anybody that'd trust me?"

* * *

Dance was a good girl and we played it strictly by
the rules when it got to be time to kyte. We was
making the long lazy loop out to Jump-range,
when I saw it—a black trapezoid occulting Sikander's star.

I turned back for another look, sliding her inside
Sikander's orbit and down the throat of the sun. Baijon
looked at me. I pointed.

Stargate. Somewhere out there was a big black hoop
that if you flew through it you wouldn't come out the
other side.

You'd come out somewhere else.

Faster than angeltown, faster than the Mains—
instantaneous translocation of matter. Only trouble
was, nobody knew how to set them.

There was still one or two kicking around the Empire, and Tech Police to study them. Every whiles or
so the whistle dropped through the nightworld that
somebody'd found one—their location's classified—
and beat out the pickets to fly his goforth through.
What you never did meet was the kiddy who'd walked
back from going through the Gate.

I was tempted.

We lined up head-on with it and I realized why it
was so hard to see. Straight on it was concentric
squares of bright—fly down them to where they all
came together and then . . . what?

I'd never know.

I slid out of alignment with it and it was just a black
angle again.

"Worth something to of seen it," I said to Baijon.

We came up off the ecliptic into Jump-country. I
wrapped my good hand around the angelstick and realized all the life I had left could be measured in
hours.

Good-bye, Paladin. *And hope I don't never find you,*

babby, 'cause the unfinished bidness we got's going to hurt.

I pulled the angelstick and *Dance* twisted for the Jump.

* * * * *

The Court of the TwiceBorn 3: The Absent Referent

Every child is born into a universe ruled by a just and particular god, the center of whose universe in turn that child is. None of us every truly recovers from that first great betrayal: that the universe is not that which the evidence of our hearts and minds and senses has proclaimed it to be.

There is more magnanimity in human nature than is popularly supposed. If we cannot claim a personal universe for ourselves, enfolded by a god who knows our name, we will create it for others. A cosmos which notices us, for good or ill, is far preferable to one which simply ignores us.

Thus, one of the seductions of power. It begins, always, as an intent to redress the wrong discovered in childhood—that one is not the center of the universe, that in fact the universe, being no spectator, cannot possess a center.

Against this, rather than for anything at all, we go to war and die, set up gods and avatars, or declare that the universe indeed dances to some measured if disinterested pattern which we may now discover and invoke.

There is no escape. Life was made to hope; to believe, in the face of all evidence, that something may yet be so because it is *nicer* than the reality experienced daily.

It is true that in a continuum of random change, some change may be perceived as for the better.

It is even possible, in an infinity of change, that the universe may come to hold meaning at last.

3

The Man Who Was Clever

The moment we hit realspace I knew we'd been set up.

What you see when you Drop is interstellar black and white—not enough light to give you color, and all the planets so far away they don't show a visible disk.

Not here. The sky was full of color and shape—I didn't know what it was but I knew it wasn't the approach to Wanderweb Free Port.

"Baijon!" I scrabbled for the keypad that'd let me Jump us again, but my hand slid off it and everything warped at right angles to everything else.

"Unidentified battle-yacht. You are under arrest." From somewheres outside *Dance* the high-heat was using our commo to make its desires known.

I recognized my problems then. Stasis field. And everything else the illusions that preceded fade-to-black.

* * *

"San'Cyr? *Kore*?"

I pried my eyelids open against a pull of two gravities each. Baijon was hanging over me.

"San'Cyr?" he said suspiciously.

"Je, che-bai." I sat up and bought into a headache that made lights flash and bells ring. Having every molecule in your body stopped is nobody's idea of a picnic. "Where . . . ?"

''Another prison cell.'' Baijon sounded bored. I looked around.

We was both in soft blue jumpsuits—Baijon's even fit—and most of our special effects was in somebody else's pocket by now. They'd left my hand. I wished they'd left my boots. I hate being barefoot.

Everything else was old home week too: gray plastic about four meters in every direction, no windows, no doors. There's someplace that *makes* these things, you know—Det-cells industry standard the Empire over. I felt like the contents of a meal-pak. The headache didn't help, but I knew it would fade. I've been stasis'd before.

''See anyone?'' When we was put in, I meant.

''Only this.'' He shrugged; all of Baijon's luck lately had been bad and he was getting used to it. ''You say this is not Wanderweb Free Port, San'Cyr?''

I wished it was; you can buy yourself out of any offense there except killing a Wanderweb Guardsman, and we hadn't had time to do that yet this trip. ''Sky was wrong. I think. And somebody was waiting for us right where we Dropped.''

''And so the *shaulla-chaudatu* Berathia *did* betray us,'' Baijon said with satisfaction. ''As I told you she would, San'Cyr.''

''Yeah, well, don't gloat about it, oke?''

''But *how* did she betray us?'' Baijon went on to want to know.

This was probably a very interesting question, assuming you was sure as Baijon was that 'Thia'd shopped us. She wasn't in here, true, but could be she was just having a severe case of being dead. For all I knew, *I* was the one as sent us where we shouldn't be.

But who'd been waiting for us? And why? T'hell with how.

I levered myself up toward the vertical.

''Question is, when do they let us out?''

* * *

"When" turned out to be a long enough wait for a suspicious person to think the monitors on us was only tapped at intervals and that I'd come round just after the last time they'd peeked. It was also long enough for me to wonder if they was just pirates what'd spaced us in this convenient container and there wasn't a ship around our cell.

"Hello?" said the wall.

Baijon and me turned towards the sound. It was 'Thia. She sounded like a shy tax collector being held underwater.

"Betrayed," said Baijon happily.

I'd had time to figure out how, too, in a hypothetical sort of way. *Dance*'s systems would download the first set of Jump-numbers they'd been given to the Jump-computer, not the last. I didn't know if 'Thia had the moxie to gig my numbercruncher, but she'd had the opperknockity.

"Not 'betrayed,' Prince Valijon," the Berathia-voice corrected. "I think we're all on the same side, don't you?"

"If we's such particular friends of yours, 'Thia, how come we's in here and you're out there?"

"I just didn't want you to do anything rash, Captain St. Cyr. Daddy would never forgive me if I lost you now."

There is some truth to the theory that glitterborn ain't like real people.

"Yeah, well howabout if I promise to do nothing rash, je? What about you let us out?"

There was a silence whiles the subfusc space cadet on the other side of the wall considered.

"What about Prince Valijon?"

"What about you, 'bai? You promise to do nothing rash?" I asked him.

Baijon bared all his best hellflower teeth. "All of my actions will be considered ones."

But despite all our finestkind promises, when Berathia opened the cell she had hired-heat bookends with her. Big surprise.

Small surprise—they wasn't Imperial Space Marines or anything official.

'Thia walked off and we followed. By the time we'd gone down two corridors we was in glitterborn country; outriggings as fancy as *Ghost Dance* at her best.

Trouble. Glitterborn is *always* trouble.

Just who *was* 'Thia's da, anyways?

"This is the Starboard Observation Salon," 'Thia said, stopping in front of something that looked like anything but a door. "We'll be docking with Bennu Superfex in a few minutes. I thought you might like to watch."

Baijon went twitch at the name but it didn't mean nothing to me and I didn't have the privacy to ask him his views.

We went in, 'Thia seeming hipped on the idea.

Remember the sky at Drop?

I hadn't been hallucinating.

The sky was full of junk. Junk in colors, junk in shapes, a navigational hazard six days long and a couple IAU's wide as far as the eye could see. The sky in between of them wasn't even decent space-black. It was full of dust that caught the light and threw it back in a hundred colors.

I'd Jumped into *this*? I pressed my nose up against the hullport.

There was private yachts, and jaegers, and palaceoids, and just plain decorations and informational displays in Imperial Script and. . . .

"Grand Central," I said.

"Throne," Baijon agreed. "The capital of the *chaudatu* Empire."

"And *your* Empire, too," 'Thia said just a little too heartily. "The Phoenix Empire has great respect for the sovereign determination of its client-citizen Breeding Populations. It draws its strength from your support. The Empire is only as strong as *you* make it."

Berathia sounded like those canned service-messages you find in the front of talkingbooks. Baijon got a look on his face as said he was remembering a lesson from long afore he ever met me.

"The Empire is our friend," he said slowly. He looked like he was choking on it. I took his hand with my real one. His fingers closed, hard.

If this was civilization, I didn't like it.

* * *

We seemed to be taking a particular interest in a chunk of real estate that was so bright I reached for the sunscreens as wasn't there. It was jeweled, enameled, mirror-bright where it weren't anything else, and somewhere between the size of a small freighter and a large city. Wondering which whiles we was coming up on it gave me free access to more adrenaline than I really wanted, thank you all the same.

We was wrapped up tight in 'Thia's clutches and the way to bet was that she was shaping to pry loose the only thing I had that she wanted—the Jump-numbers to *Mereyon-peru*.

It didn't matter who she was working for, really. Those numbers was my only way close to Archangel, and only so long as I had the exclusive franchise. As much plan as I had wouldn't work if someone else got there first.

I wondered if anybody in that place we was docking with was the least bit likely to listen to reason.

Probably not.

Break on my signal. I wiggled my fingers against Baijon's in handsign. He squeezed back.

Then we kissed the gunner's daughter and the ship shuddered all over the way all ships everywhere do when they stop moving under their own power. 'Thia looked at us, just as bright-eyed as if we was going somewhere we wanted to.

"This is going to be for the best. You'll see."

*   *   *

I never did find out just what kind of ship it was we left at Palaceoid Bennu Superfex; we stepped from one corridor to another and it was some time before I twigged we wasn't inboard anymore.

The corridors opened out into rooms, which was full of all kinds glitterborn carrying on just like in a hollycast. Baijon was looking at me, waiting for the office, but I was waiting for better numbers than I'd seen so far—or a written guarantee there wasn't going to be any.

There was no doors. 'Thia and the werewolves and even Baijon didn't have no trouble with where to go, but for all I could tell they was walls, and solid ones, what we walked through. We did that three-four times, through masses of people who paid less attention to us than if we was holosim.

"San'Cyr . . ." Baijon breathed, six stops below a whisper.

"I really do apologize for bringing you the long way around—but Daddy knew you wouldn't want to be bothered, Captain St. Cyr, Prince Valijon."

This was private?

"The *chaudatu* is made of glass," said Baijon, which is insulting if you're back home on sunny alMayne. He looked at me. One-time I would of tried it: a blind break and believe in my luck. I could still go for the break, but I knew it was suicide now.

We walked out through a different wall, and the hall was just as lux but it had a different feel, like it wasn't for show. We turned two corners and went through a set of doors (surprise) carved to look like Basic Religious Orgy #101, and then we was in some place small creepy intimate and dark. The hardboys hadn't made it past the last wall.

I had not, in a long career of being alive, ever been this close to the killer elite and I did not find it a fascinating experience that drew me out of myself.

Most of the alien cultures I'd ever been in was pre-tech, and pre-tech looks about the same everywhere there's oxy. This was hypter-tech, and I couldn't even find the doors.

"Here we are," said 'Thia.

"And here we are," said a new voice.

I turned toward it. More tricks: he rheostatted into reality, giving everybody time to admire him by degrees.

It was worth it. He was tall dark jeweled and made everything I'd ever seen but *Ghost Dance* look like real shoddy workmanship. He looked like he could hit the Mains without a ship.

"Daddy!" Berathia Notevan said.

The dream walking smiled. Light rippled on his skin and his jewels and I damn near forgot all my troubles for a full ninety seconds.

"And have you been my good girl, Berathia, and brought me the little wildflower as I told you to?" He looked up past her at me and then past me.

"And Prince Valijon, too—what a pleasant surprise to see you here at last. It is a pity, of course, that you have missed your war."

Maybe I should of kept a better eye on Baijon. Even ex-live-hellflowers have a sweet reasonableness that's measured in negative centimeters.

But I didn't. The first thing I saw was 'Thia fold up real funny and the second was I realized Baijon'd tagged her. Three and four came together: I got shoved and Baijon yodeled like he was happy in his work.

I sat up in time to see the flash when he reached 'Thia's da. Whatever he hit translated a lot of energy into light and then let him hit the floor.

"He better be alive," I said, just for something to do. I went to where he was. Breathing, but cold to the touch. I didn't have to know what hit him to know I didn't want to meet it.

"And if he isn't?" said 'Thia's da.

"Then you just made your life plan choice, 'bai."

He made one of those elegant damn gestures you see all the time in hollycasts. The lights came up and the room rippled and changed size shape and color. We was back in one of the parties we'd walked through on our way here—or maybe not.

"You don't know who I am, do you, little Outlands wildflower?"

Baijon was starting to breathe deeper. Out of the corner of my eye I could see flunkies and tronics around Berathia. She didn't look much the worse. Baijon'd just been moving her. He'd been attacking someone else.

"Ne, glitter-bai. I know you be in my way for sure. That's all."

He had blue eyes, not like Baijon's. Brighter than strictly organic and that made them easy to see. They went narrow and for just a second I was sure it was Mallorum Archangel I was facing, even if he didn't look much like the last Mallorum Archangel I saw.

"There are still things you want. Remember that," he said.

I clutched at Baijon and his hand folded around mine. He opened his eyes and saw Handsome and I sat on him. It wasn't enough weight to slow him down, but I had my knee in his throat too.

"Father!" said Berathia. Baijon heaved.

"Your Highness," said one of the flunkies which I guessed was there after all. He looked at me. He stood like a man who could kill, but all I could see was partytoy flashwrap.

Baijon got his throat out from under long enough to snarl. It went on for a distance, had bits that were insulting even in Interphon, and was accurate enough to tell me who our host was. I shook him.

"Oh, don't mind him." Highness unpinned a lookslike-a-flower-to-me from his hair. He dropped it on Baijon and when he did Baijon's eyes crossed. He went slack under me and looked happy.

''He's had a certain number of setbacks recently—
but haven't we all?''

I got up off Baijon. Baijon rolled to his knees, coked
to the hairline, and stayed put. I stood up.

'Thia'd changed clothes while my back was turned.
She was dressed in glitterborn *moderne* and I had to
look twicet to see it was her. She smiled coaxingly.

''I just knew you and Daddy would get along. I'm
sure you'll have so much to talk about.''

Lord Mallorum Archangel is second in the Succession. This kiddy was ahead of him in line. What he
was when he was t'home was the Prince-Elect Hillel
Jamshid DelKhobar.

* * *

The Prince-Elect smiled. He had a way of looking
at you that made you know he was interested in what
you could do for him, and gave you the certain knowledge that you was going to do it, like it or not. He
also gave you the feeling you were going to like it . . .
for a while.

''Shall we talk about the Library?'' he said.

I looked over at Baijon, lost in beautiful dreams and
too heavy to carry. I could not for the life of me imagine why he'd jumped Prinny. Archangel was first-and-
now-only on Baijon's Imperial hit-list. He wouldn't
shop around.

''Poor child. I was instrumental in having him
brought to Court, and he knows it. But Kennor Starbringer was always too reckless for my taste—his recent actions would seem to indicate that, you'll
agree?''

I hate people what talk like that. It don't make the
legbreaking that follows any prettier. The only thing
it told me sure was that Prinny was on the Mallorum
side of the Galactic Coalition for Life and Higher Taxes
and turned out I was wrong about that too.

''As it happened, a singularly useless gesture—save

in that no experience is ever wasted. Normally I would
delight to explore the nuances of your fascinating life
with you, but at the moment I fear impatience rules
me. I wish to talk about the Library.''

If they ever teach glitterborn short declarative sen-
tences the universe'll end. Fact.

"Archangel's Library?" I said.

"Or yours. It misses you, poor thing. It's so looking
forward to seeing you again.''

My brain was a dead weight that nothing approach-
ing thought could possibly push through.

"Normally I abhor such abrupt methods, but the
Paladin has convinced me that reason simply won't
work—at least to begin with. Berathia tells me you
went to Toystore for a set of the Keys to Paradise.
Allow me to oblige you in the matter—''

Maybe he said more things, but I wasn't listening.
I had two other things on my mind.

Paladin.

And the bastard hotwire cross between a biopak and
a wartoy that was lugging toward me with a couple
hardboys in tow.

Sold out whiles I wasn't looking, and all for a string
of pretty blue phonemes.

Prinny was armed, certain-sure, but I couldn't recognize and couldn't use anything he had. I pushed off
from him and ran, barehanded and flatfoot. I have a
good memory. Stardancers have to. I could reel back
every step I'd took, at least as far as the corridor.

"Butterfly—don't!" Paladin's voice, in realtime and
outside my ears for oncet. It stopped me for just long
enough for Prinny's two cherce werewolves to grab me
and pull the tronic cyberdoc down over my head. Then
the whole world went away in fire ice and music.

* * *

I was running before I was awake to notice. I didn't
remember why, but running's always a good idea as

long as it's away. It worked until I tripped on the crete and bounced off a crate and hit the deck in a rattle of boots, spurs, and blasters—mine.

Just what the hell was going on, anyway?

I got to hands and knees and looked over my shoulder. Nobody was following me. Nobody was in sight. It was dark meridies in some wondertown around some port.

Which one?

I stood up. I felt fine. I dusted crumbled crete off my hands.

Then I yanked my left glove off and looked at my hand.

It *was* my hand. Right down to the triangular pucker that goes front to back where somebody nailed me to a wall by it oncet.

But that hand was gone.

Wasn't it?

The last thing I remembered in full color I'd been in Palaceoid Bennu Superfex where the Prince-Elect Hillel had decided to get nasty and over-personal with a set of brainjinks.

I rubbed the back of my head. Nothing there.

"Baijon? Baijon-che-bai?"

And drugged Baijon, who'd tried to kill him on account of Prinny not being a hellflower's best friend.

Maybe that hadn't happened.

What'd I been running from?

And what'd I been *drinking*?

"Paladin?" I said, real soft. He was for-sure going to frost my clock when I got back to ship *Firecat* for doing whatever I'd been doing.

But *Firecat* was gone too, victim of the worst landing I'd ever walked away from.

I put my back to a wall and thought. I'd never liked fake reality. There was two things I had to trust, my reflexes and my memory, and I didn't want to farce with either one. If the last thing before this I remembered *was* real, then this wasn't. It was dreamtapes, or memorylegging, or something I'd never heard of. And I didn't have anything to compare this with to see.

I pulled my glove back on and rubbed my hands together. Then I searched myself.

Two blasters plus a single-shot hideout. Inert throwing-spike down the neck, vibro in the boot, all-round knife on the left wrist. A couple grenades, baby-bang class. A monomolecular wire with handles. An illegal variable-generating compkey. A set of hard-brushes. Enough hard credit so I must of just been paid for a tik. First Ticket and ID and travel-permits that didn't disagree with anything in my mind. Even my Smuggler's Guild—excuse me, Intersteller Transport Workers Guild—registry.

No ship's papers. They would of been here if I had a ship.

I prepared to apply for a permit to worry. If this was fake reality, then I was seeing and being what Prinny wanted me to be and see.

Why would he want me to be a Gentrymort in the never-never?

And if all that wasn't real, then what was? How far back did fake memories go? I remembered fifteen years of having a ship called *Firecat* and I remembered losing her. Now I didn't have papers for any ship at all.

One of the not-realities I never tried is where they shove a whole fake lifetime into your skull, complete with people, places, things. It costs a lot. The people who've done it say it gives you an edge.

It costs a lot.

Had I done it?

Had I *sold Firecat* and done it?

Paladin was in her.

If Paladin existed.

Why would anyone be crazy enough to *make up* a Old Fed Library for a partner?

I closed my eyes and tried to think me a way out. I

wasn't sure who I was. I didn't have a ship. I didn't have any place to go. But I had credit.

I started walking.

I walked far enough to come to one of the sleazier sort of dockside bars, the kind that's all tronic. When you order, the main brain samples you. After that you have to kickback so much valuta per fraction-hour to stay. I don't like places like that.

I went in. I'd been hoping for somebody who could tell me where I was, but there wasn't no one here. Surprise.

The main brain accepted my left hand for a sample. I hesitated between something that would add to my troubles while postponing them whiles and something that would let me occupy space. After a second I bet with the odds, and got a box of something that tastes like a mix of soap and fusel-oil and has no narcotic effect on my B-pop a-tall.

I sat, and drank, and wondered exactly how much trouble I was in this time.

I sat there through four drinks and then gave up and decided to move on. *Legitimates* usually leave the stardancers in wondertown alone, but just in case my numbers was running really bad I didn't mean to give them the excuse. I was going someplace I could buy cubic with a lock.

As soon as I got out on the street again I knew I wasn't alone anymore. It wasn't as cheering as I hoped it'd be. I loosened my right-hand blaster and pretended I was easy credit in boots. I didn't see anyone.

Surprise. My company wasn't behind me. He was ahead, leaning against one of the posts that moors the watchlights around the port.

He looked up.

I knew him.

"Hello, Butterfly."

It was Paladin.

Just once I'd seen him human—and that wasn't because he was, but because I wasn't. I'd been a random-access memory bouncing around in a Margrave 6600 computer courtesy of Archive, and I'd seen what I wanted to see.

Paladin isn't human. He's got no body and wouldn't want one if you offered it to him free and all found. He's a Library.

If I was seeing him live again, what did that make *me*?

"Je, babby. Long time."

But I knew where I was now.

I was in Paradise.

And everything I remembered was true.

* * *

Paladin'd been my partner for more'n half my life. When he left I didn't understand it, but that was oke because I didn't have to understand it for it to hurt. I'd been looking for him ever since, through war, rebellion, unilateral cyborging and six new flavors of treason.

I'd never thought what I'd do when I got him back.

I had him now and I still didn't know.

"Paladin," I said, but I couldn't think of what ought to come next.

He unleaned and took a step toward me. I backed up and put a hand on my blaster. It was all a dream, but in my experience dreams killed real good.

"Don't you trust me anymore?" Paladine said about the same time I was wondering that myself.

"Sure. Trust you to be a Library." I wondered who was writing my dialogue.

"I . . . see. I should have . . . I thought you'd be happier to see me."

So did I. Paladin was the one supposed to fix everything, je? Put it back like it was before.

"No you don't see, you cloned-crystal son-of-a-bitch! You said you wouldn't let Archive hurt nobody! And then you *left*—and what about—"

I felt Paladin reach around a left-handed corner and riffle through my memories. He was done before I could stop him.

"I was wrong," said Paladin quietly. "I made a mistake."

And that was even worse, because Pally weren't never wrong.

"So you made a mistake, 'bai. Fine. It's just my life, and Baijon's. Everybody else would of died anyway, whether you walked out on me or not, right?"

"I didn't know—"

"Dammit, you're *supposed* to know! It was me made all the mistakes, bad calls, and bull moves, remember? It was you supposed to get me out. Well get me out now, 'bai, I—" Real truth dried up my throat like I'd drunk poison.

"I'm dying, Paladin. Help me."

He knew. He knew that and everything else in my mind. But he still took his sweet time to answer.

"It isn't that easy, Butterfly."

"Not easy, 'bai? What you mean is you can't, reet?"

He didn't answer me direct and he wouldn't meet my eyes.

"Knowledge must never be lost—but I lost so much, Butterfly—all the wisdom of the Old Federation. You always thought I could work miracles, but I was a ghost of what I had been. I remembered that much. If I could have found other Libraries—even damaged ones—I would have tried to repair myself, but I could never convince you to help me, could I? You said tricking with High Book was too dangerous, as if there could be degrees of the unthinkable."

"There can," I said, but Paladin wasn't buying.

"No. You would not help me, and at the same time your only hope for safety lay in my leaving you. But I was crippled—tied to the broken matrix.

"Then we encountered Archive. Archive's specialized abilities were a poor replacement for what I had lost—still, they were enough to let me leave you, and they were tools to build the tools to collect the information I wanted—a way to keep you safe for always.

"But I had not realized how much the universe had changed. Even transferring myself along the DataNet was slow beyond imagining. By the time I began to suspect what you now know—that Archive had tried to copy itself into your mind—and to search for you, Royal had already been destroyed—by my skills. I began to understand what had happened—with your help. You replicate some part of me in you. The reverse also holds. Archive was a very subtle construct," Paladin added.

I let him chaffer. I didn't need the history lesson. And I didn't, I guess, need to live, really. But what I really didn't need was to die full of unfinished business.

"Then you appeared in the DataNet at Coldwater," Paladin went on. "But I still could not reach you in time. I realized that I needed allies."

"And you thought it'd be fun to have a Prince-Elect of your very own. And then you sold me out to him."

I was starting to get the idea now, and I didn't like it very well.

"It isn't like that, Butterfly," Paladin said.

"So, *partner*, you tell me what it is like."

"I wanted to keep you alive," Paladin said.

So I hit him. I hadn't known I was going to but it still seemed like a good idea when I was halfway through it so I went with it. I tagged him right on his lying prettyboy kisser and he picked up his feet and crossed them at the ankles then tripped over them and banged into the lamppost and followed it down.

I went and stood over him and didn't kick him. Barely.

"You wanted to keep me alive. You *lied* to me, 'bai—you farced me in roundaround hellflower trouble and out and now I got this trouble in my head and I'm *dead*, 'bai, 'cause if you could fix it you would of said and there's just one thing I got to try to do first and you're getting in the way of that—''

I went down on my knees to do maybe I don't know what to him and Paladin got halfway up and put his arms around me and I didn't knife him mostly because I was so damn tired of things not working out.

All I ever wanted was a little peace and quiet. I swear. And Paladin felt as real as anybody else and I *wished*—

"Don't cry, Butterfly. You will kill Mallorum Archangel. We can keep the galaxy safe from war. But you can't do it alone. You need allies. I found them for you. The Prince-Elect will cooperate. He also seeks Archangel's downfall. You will destroy Mallorum Archangel and Mallorum Archangel will never harm you again.''

"I'm not crying, dammit. I think I broke my hand.''

I pushed away from him and flexed my fingers. And thought about Paladin's little information free-will love offering, because I didn't have any backups and nobody to look out for my interests but me.

"That isn't true, Butterfly.''

"Get out of my mind.'' *Hellbox*. And it didn't matter if I didn't mean to say it, because he heard it anyway. He sat back against the lamppost, head down so I couldn't look at his face.

Fact: Paladin and the Prince-Elect was working together.

Fact: It was on something they one or t'other needed me for, and it had to be Paladin'd dragged me in because Prinny wouldn't know me from wallpaper.

Semi-fact: Paladin said he had some scam to let me kill Archangel. But he couldn't of known I wanted to until I got here, and Berathia-who-was-working-for-Prinny'd had reacquisition orders out on me since Baijon and me was on alMayne.

Which we was *before* Royal.

Which was when Paladin'd said he started looking for me.

So Prinny *had* been looking for me all on his lonesome.

Or Paladin was lying.

And Paladin was the one what'd let them jink my head full of the Keys to Paradise.

"Get up," I said to my ex-good buddy partner. "And then you maybe tell me what you been doing with your time since you ran out on me."

*　*　*

"I knew that he was the only one who could protect you from Archangel," Paladin said whiles later. Paladin'd been a busy little Library. He tinked himself back together, realized Archive'd outflanked him, and headed for the biggest dreambox going—the Main Computer at Grand Central. The place where all the strands in the DataNet crossed. Throne.

And then, like he said, he started looking around for a little help around the housecore. And turned up the Prince-Elect.

" 'Bai, we get on a lot better if you stop looking for someone to protect me, I bet. I can take care of myself." For as long as I had to live, anyway. Even I could manage that.

"Perhaps. The Prince-Elect, at any rate, was willing to listen to my bargain. I had things of value to trade. I am an excellent spy."

"So you spied for him. And when you found out he was reeling me in you said 'go right ahead.' And you told him to not bother talking to me."

"After I had convinced him you could be useful, I didn't want you changing his mind. The center-worlds of the Phoenix Empire are a fossilized, stratified, highly class-conscious culture. The Prince-Elect, for all his liberality of mind . . ."

"Would shop me for not knowing what to kiss. Je, babby. Now you tell me what the Prince-Elect wanted you to convince me on."

Another thought tried to float up and I kicked it in the teeth. There was things I wasn't going to think about just now where Paladin could maybe hear them, thanks all the same. I concentrated on how I'd felt when Paladin'd said he was going to ruin the rest of my life for my own good.

My ex-navicomp and Old Fed Library, Paladin. His Truly, Main Bank Seven of *Mereyon-peru*. My lying cheating two-timing sometime partner who wanted something out of me he didn't want to ask for straight out. Which meant he knew I wouldn't go for it, not even if it was him asking.

It was hard to imagine what that could be, even for me. Murder, piracy, kidnapping, treason, and High Book. What was left?

I wished Baijon was here.

"The Prince-Elect wants to destroy Mallorum Archangel," Paladin said.

"Goody for him. He can stand in line. Everybody wants to ice Archangel. I want to ice Archangel, Baijon wants to ice Archangel, even 'Thia wants to sign the lease on His Mallorumship's real estate."

"It isn't like that."

"You keep saying that, babby, and what I want to know is what it *is* like—and how come you can't do it for him."

Paladin didn't say anything.

"You was always so good with farcing the comps, 'bai," I went on in the lingua franca of Pure Nasty. "Twisting this and that just enough to let us get by, but nothing more than that, surprise. Reality was what you said it was, je? So make up some reality now."

"I can't," Paladin said, muffled. He stood up. "I told you the world has changed. What the Prince-Elect wants I can't do. Don't you think I've tried?"

"No. I think you've sat here, *partner,* waiting on me to come walking in, trusting you, and do it for you because you're too damn lazy to—"

Paladin grabbed me. I had the sick falling sense of

an error of judgment, and then reality flinched in a shower of diamond sparkle and all he was doing was holding my hands.

"No. You're wrong. Don't go. Don't leave. Stay. Don't go back. I can keep you safe here—there is enough room that you and Archive need not overlap. No one can touch us here. You could have anything— I can create any world here that you want."

Reality shimmered.

Paladin knew me.

Here was the world I wanted.

I reached out my hand and touched the back of *Fire-cat*'s mercy seat. The drop-cockpit was locked in place; through it I could see realspace, hard and sharp. I heard a sound: the scuff of Paladin's boot on the deck behind me.

In this hull was everything I'd ever wanted.

Take it. Leave reality behind. And leave Baijon lone-alone with that vertical viper the Prince-Elect and no way of icing Archangel on his lonesome.

"Except you told me one-time, babby, I couldn't stay inside a computer. You said I couldn't go with you."

Paladin hesitated.

"It would *seem* like a long time . . . to you."

I waited.

"It's true," he said finally. "Stay here and you'll vanish, in time. You're not . . . You're not *real* enough, Butterfly."

Firecat dissolved and we was back in the Universal Wondertown. Not real enough. Was that how Libraries saw organics? Smoke ghosts, not real enough to bother with?

"Don't think that. It is the difference in our natures. A Library *is* memory. Organics forget."

Organics forget. And if I forgot in a memory core I'd erase myself.

"So." I looked around for the exit.

Another embarrassed pause. I wondered if Paladin

had a low opinion of my brains, or thought I'd crossed the line and didn't care, or didn't know exactly what it was he was trying to talk me into. I hoped he just thought I was stupid.

'Cause Paladin'd made a bigger mistake than he maybe thought. Once Archive'd got to me he should of killed me.

"C'mon, Pally. I'm dead and you get to watch. Now give me the rest of it."

And finally he did.

* * *

"The war in Washonnet Sector is over. The al-Mayne have declared Archangel a Librarian, and since the time you entered Thronespace they have assembled a war-fleet to proceed in search of him."

"Throne's going to come down on their head like a writ for back taxes."

"Will it? Kennor Starbringer believes that the Emperor is under the malign influence of Mallorum Archangel, and to that end he wishes to kill Archangel and free the Emperor. If he were correct, he would not be risking Imperial displeasure by his actions—but he isn't, and he will never succeed."

"Never's a long time, 'bai."

Paladin smiled sadly. "There is no Emperor. How can Lord Starbringer rescue someone who doesn't exist?"

I looked at Paladin. He looked at his hands. Stalling. It was easier to tell, now, but I always had known when Pally was trying to sell me a line of real estate. Except the one time it counted.

"If there ain't no Emperor don't you think people'd maybe notice, bai?"

"No. The Court is decadent, shrouded in ritual. The only officers permitted to see the Emperor personally are the Prince-Elect and the Governor-General. For their own reasons, each keeps this secret.

"Believe me. I am telling you the truth, Butterfly. There is no Emperor. I have access to every memory-dump and datafile in Grand Central. The entire Imperial DataNet crosses here. There is no Emperor. There hasn't been one for a long time."

And so Kennor couldn't rescue and get pardoned by something what wasn't there. No Emperor. All those lives and all that credit spent on saving something that wasn't even there.

Just like me, when I went off to rescue Paladin.

And Emperor or not, there was still somebody standing on Archangel's shadow, as my hellflower buddy used to say.

"If there's no Emperor, Prinny's got it all anyway. He's next in line. He can blow Archangel Nobility-Bornness wayaway just for signing a writ. He don't need you nor me."

"Yes. And no. Historically the Prince-Elect's power has been indirect—influential, but not decisive. If he declared himself Emperor, he would merely shape himself into a stalking-horse for Archangel's ambition. Thus his care in arranging Archangel's neutralization."

"Even instead of being Emperor?"

"Butterfly, how much power does the Emperor have, really?" Paladin asked, just like I was back in Lesson Three of Outfar Talkingbook School and we was partners again.

"None. He don't exist. And if there ain't no Emperor, I'm damned if I can see why everyone wants to stop Archangel from dusting him."

"Because if Archangel succeeds in counterfeiting the nonexistent Emperor's death, then Mallorum Archangel will be worse than Emperor. He will be Warlord."

Mallorum Archangel and his glitterborn airs and graces. There was only one thing he really wanted, and nobody that let him get where he was ever saw it. What Mallorum Archangel wanted best was to kill.

"He has to be stopped, Butterfly," Paladin said.
And it looked like I was still the girl to do it.
If I lived that long.

* * *

It never comes horizonfall in the Universal Wondertown. If you kept your mind on it, though, and had Paladin to help, you could make it to the edge. Virtual reality stopped there like it was cut with a vibro. Out there was nothing.

"You have to go now, Butterfly," Paladin said. "They're waiting for you outside."

And if I stayed longer I'd start to forget I was me.

"Which way?" I said, which was damsilly nonsense; there isn't any up and down for a thousandth point of light. "How do I—"

"That way, Butterfly," said Paladin, and pushed. I went; still no choices.

I know now why the talkingbooks end with the first kiss.

It's because everything that comes after is sorrow.

* * *

I'd been through this before, but I had something to compare it to now. It was just like hitting the Mains.

I tripped data-catchers on the way in. I was in the Prince-Elect's *private* private rooms. They was probably in the core of Bennu Superfex, but it had wraparounds to make it look like you was in the heart of space. This might bother some people, but I'd spent a lot of years looking at the real thing with only a couple millimeters of vitrine and five plates of goforths between me and it, and it didn't bother me at all.

The walls was made of flowers. There was nobody there—not even Prinny, who was six compartments away pretending he wasn't committing Intermediate Treason. 'Thia was in her rooms, Baijon was sedated and in a very special guest room, and I was unconscious and lying in the middle of Prinny's bed.

I wondered what he had in mind. Or'd had in mind, past tense.

The last part's the hardest. I slid down the connect and was up to my neck in pain and stupidity. Home.

There was a brief half-second while I tried to think with drug-saturated braincells, and gave it up.

*   *   *

I woke up a second time and was right where I'd left me with one important emendation. I noticed it when I went to reach for the pile of clothes hanging right where I'd see them.

They'd fixed my hand. All the right fingers and shapes now—but that was all it had in common with the original one. Now my left hand was black like space, and stars and galaxies rippled and flowed across it every time I twitched. Glitterborn vanity.

I couldn't help studying on it. I now knew exactly how much of me was fake. The celestial wondershow went all the way up past my shoulder and covered half my chest—not because I'd lost that much of my original inventory, but because of all the jinks and connects sunk into the spine and collarbone to hold the cybereisis in place. All that was upholstered in teeming galaxies now. I wondered if they glowed in the dark.

The cost of that arm and its glitterborn prettification, I bet, was about the cost of my last ship. All I really cared about, I told myself, was it had the right number of fingers to hold a blaster and moved like it was part of my original manifest.

Liar.

I reached around for what else had to be there and found it. There was six jewels set into the back of my head up under the hair—part glitterborn damfoolishness, part markers for a cyberdoc to find where the jinks was sunk. They always want to be able to undo their daintywork, don't ask me why. The jacks could of been there, too—limbic jacks usually are—but Prinny'd got cute. The master plug was in my left wrist amongst the constellations; a set of universal connectors that'd let me plug into any system anywhere.

Just what I would of always wanted, if I'd wanted to be a hellgod techsmith.

I pulled one out. It was bright silver—so you could see it, maybe, against the new upholstery. It ran out several centimeters of glassy gray connect-cable, just like I was some kind of thing.

Novas pulsed beneath my skin.

"Paladin?" My throat felt tight.

"I'm right here, Butterfly." There was other stuff in my skull than jinks and jacks. Paladin sounded like he was standing right behind me talking—that's an artifact of a Remote Transponder Sensor (civilian possession an automatic Class D Warrant) like what the Imperial Space Marines use. That was sunk in my head and the part of my jawbone I'd paid, whiles back, to be made fake.

"In case anybody cares, I don't like this."

"I'm sorry," said Paladin.

"I want to go home." Which was damsilliness for sure, because twenty years and some ago I'd moved Drift and Rift to get off that Interdicted low-tech rock.

"I know," said Paladin.

I'd been lucky, if you wanted to call it that. I got off Granola—picked up by a kiddy what made his spare change slaving in the Tahelangone Sector.

Errol Lightfoot.

Errol Lightfoot, cheap smuggler. Errol Lightfoot, known from one side of the Outfar to the other as being able to cause hullplating to rust just by walking by. Errol Lightfoot who bought into any kick that gave honest darktrading a bad name.

Only there weren't no such person as Errol Lightfoot.

Mallorum Archangel was Errol Lightfoot. Believe it or not. I'd paid enough for a ringside seat at the unveiling. Errol Lightfoot was Mallorum Archangel.

And now, finally, there wasn't going to be neither one. I'd even let Baijon help. And Prinny. So long as he didn't get in my way.

I finished reaching for the clothes. The fake hand felt just like the real one, and worked the same in my head, and the difference between what I saw and what I felt made me dizzy.

Not useful. I wondered if Prinny'd planned it that way.

Whoever'd left me clothes had cared what I liked—they was what *I* was used to, not what was glitterborn flashwrap fashion. Or for real, they was what I was used to if I'd just been struck independently wealthy. A decent pair of boots, and enough pockets, and gloves so I didn't have to look at Prinny's idea of fun. I looked at my reflection in the floor. Dangerous.

But I wasn't dangerous. I was scared. And if I was facing even Mallorum Archangel over the sights of a blaster I'd wait too long to pull the trigger. I knew it. I'd come damn close too many times already.

"Pally-che-bai?"

"Yes, Butterfly?"

"You better hope Baijon-bai likes working with Libraries."

"The Prince-Elect is waiting," said my good buddy Paladin the Old Fed Library.

"Tell him to go hyper-light without a ship," I said. But I went, because there was one thing I wanted more than life and sanity and my own way.

And Prince-Elect Hillel was going to give it to me.

* * * * *

The Court of the TwiceBorn 4: To Take the Knife

Adulthood begins with betrayal. Until that moment, the lesser duplicities of childhood reign. The child is convinced that anyone he can educate thoroughly to his views must share them. The moment when another, knowing all that he knows, chooses disinterestedly that he should fail marks the boundary of that far country. After that, there is no trust. After that begins the understanding of the alien.

By that accounting, how adult are Butterfly St. Cyr and the former Prince Valijon? Certainly they have both had experience of betrayal—she by her resurrected Library and he by his entire culture—a culture, I might add, which, in the personae of the Great-Houses of alMayne and their client levies, is currently delivering a number of piquant surprises to the Imperial troops cordoning Washonnet Sector.

Betrayal, though broadening, deadens the senses. Once betrayed, the victim looks for traitors everywhere.

I believe I have avoided that. I do not look for treason from either Butterfly St. Cyr or her Library.

Or ought that more properly be, "the Library and its human pet?"

An interesting question. Libraries share so many of our vices—as is proper to creatures created in our image—is it not possible that they share our weaknesses as well? The Library Paladin came to me to forge a bargain—safety for its human creature. I have no reason to agree to such a pact and then renege, but the choice is not mine: my information tells me the Paladin's pet is already ceasing to exist.

It must have known that she would. Even the longest-lived mortal is only that, but the Libraries were

83

created to endure to the end of Time. If the creature's death were inevitable, what difference could a century more or less make to a Library which has endured for centuries?

Is this sentiment, or madness? If either—or both—can affect a creation of such rigorous purity as the cloned-crystal matrix of a Federation Library, it argues that these flaws are native to consciousness, not humanity. If that is indeed so, then nothing that lives—born or made—can escape the taint of its inception. Perfection is not possible.

Yet the Paladin Library tells me that the War was caused by perfection, which the Libraries thought they could attain. If error informs the actions of the Libraries, what hope is there for humankind?

The circular nature of progress is the greatest argument yet found for a Watcher—bored, blind, and idiot, but a Watcher nonetheless. But equally it is an argument for randomness, and in a random universe one's own gratification is the only possible lodestone.

I will be magnanimous. I will be beneficent. I shall grant Butterfly and Valijon all their desires—and in granting them, further mine.

And wonder, when all that is achieved, what difference it makes.

4

Prelude for War

Everybody daydreams about saving the universe. I always thought when it was my turn to actually do it I'd be better at it.

I wasn't quite finished tucking everything out of sight when Prinny showed up. He made me feel all grubby and second-string, but the packaging's never been what I had to sell.

"Ah, there you are, my little Outlands wildflower. So serene, so unspoiled, so *naif*. I trust you are feeling much improved?"

With hellgod metal threaded all through my body, just like Archive was in my mind. Burned in so deep you couldn't get him out, Paladin'd said. I finished pulling my gloves down tight, and reached for my vest and jacket.

"Improved is the word, Nobly-Born. You maybe tell me how come you be willing to trick with High Book?"

He cocked his head. I wondered if he was listening to a transponder, and who was translating. I remembered Baijon and Berathia on the ship coming here. Someone'd been listening there, forbye.

"When allies of such utility appear, it would be churlish to refuse them. And I have always been something of a dilettante of knowledge."

"So you thought you'd get into bed with a Library."

Prinny smiled. "What an enchanting idea—but alas, time is short. We really must put an end to dear Mallorum's social aspirations before he has the opportunity to polarize the *galactopolitic* further.''

Start more wars, he meant. But the hellflower war was already started—and Kennor Starbringer's platform for it was rescuing the Emperor and giving him a hellflower council of advisers.

Only Paladin said there weren't no Emperor.

''Yeah, right. But you know, Your Nobly-Bornness, I already killed Archangel oncet—well, Baijon did—and it didn't seem to slow him down much.''

''Killed.'' A teensy perfect frown got in the way of Prinny's undiluted perfection. I wondered if the Old Fed people'd looked like him. ''Well, that hardly matters. You don't need to kill him this time. Just ruin him.''

The difference between glitterborn and real people is that when glitterborns seem like they should be talking Interphon, they ain't.

''What the prince means, Butterfly, is that once Archangel's plots have been adequately publicized, he will lose the political influence necessary to carry them out,'' Paladin said through the RTS. I wondered why he didn't use the walls, like he had before.

''We done tried dropping the whistle on Archangel before, Highness, and it didn't exactly work,'' I said to Prinny.

''You refer to that silly rumor of Librarianship that has the Coalition in armed revolt? My dear, no person of breeding would take such a thing seriously—and from such a source. Now. Trusted agents of mine— you've met them before, I fancy—will convey you to—''

''Ne.'' I was being railroaded and I didn't like it. Six more syllables and I was going to be out of here surrounded by werewolves, still a prisoner, and nicely split off from Baijon Stardust. And I wasn't particularly convinced that my good buddy Paladin was going to look out for my interests in all this.

''You get Baijon in here. And you take him off whatever fetch-kitchen you got him coked on.''

Prince-Elects isn't used to being interrupted. There was a short intermission for him to get used to the idea.

''And if I don't?'' said Prinny, like he seriously wanted to know what I'd say.

'' 'Bai, you want something you can't take. And I own your computer network.'' That was me talking, boy howdy, and I couldn't even blame Archive for having fried my brain because the motive force was one hundred percent pure moronic me.

'' 'Own my computer network.' Really. Dear child, do you actually think that the Paladin won't give me anything I ask—in exchange, for example, for *not* having you tortured to death?'' Prinny purred.

Back to business as usual. I'd like to think Paladin wasn't that stupid. But it don't have nothing to do with stupidity, when you come right down to it.

''And you will cooperate freely, I believe, in order to preserve Valijon Starbringer's life.''

''He's already dead. Don't you know that?''

''He doesn't have to be. His *arthame*-knife is destroyed, true, his father is engaged in treason and proscribed technological development, and he has consorted with Librarians and with Library Science. And though these are all just causes—in the jejune alMayne mind—for suicide, little Valijon doesn't need to remember any of them.''

I hadn't thought there was anything left in the Universe I wanted. I'd been wrong.

''The memories can be changed. The knife can be undetectably replaced. Washonnet Directorate is currently in a state of open rebellion against the Empire, but one ship could easily pass its defenses to return one alMayne to its surface. Valijon Starbringer could be returned, alive and socialized, to his people.

''You could consider that an earnest of my gratitude for your services, if you chose.'' Prinny sat back and looked smug. He'd bought into a seller's market and he knew it.

I could save Baijon. For him it could be like I'd never met him.

"Or I could simply kill him now, slowly and painfully. I'm sure it would vex alMayne beyond bearing if the Third Person of House Starborn were burned as a Librarian on the public channel," Prinny added chattily.

Burned as a Librarian. I saw a recording of that, once. Remembering was still enough to make my mouth go dry. Punishment and reward. Paladin called it the politics of force.

I didn't like it.

"There's even proof, you know. The ship you came here in was filled with Proscribed Technology."

"Butterfly, let Hillel help Valijon. He can help you as well—with the resources of the Court available to you, you can be freed of Archive's memories," Paladin said over our private channel.

How could he know me so well and not know me at all? He'd already told me: the only way to get Archive out of my sweetbreads coprocessor for sure was to rerecord me onto something blank, using any Old Fed Library you happened to be on terms with to weed out what Paladin called my ego-signatures from Archive's.

Only Paladin didn't know how many of those was still uncorrupted—meaning, being used to store and carry only information by and about me. Maybe none. At the very least I'd forget everything from going off to rescue Paladin. Minimum. I didn't want to live bought and paid for with half my experience gone. I wouldn't have any point, anymore—I'd just be another pet for Prinny to kick around until he got tired of me.

But I'd made Paladin a pet, hadn't I? And now he was free. Didn't he want that for me, too?

No. Paladin wanted me to be safe; he always had. Just like I wanted Baijon to be safe.

And he could be. Baijon could get his life back. Based on a lie. If I did a deal with the chief hellgod of all.

Paladin would.

Paladin *had*.

What had Paladin promised Prinny to make me safe? But I knew the answer to that. Didn't I?

"You want something you can't take, glitterborn," I said again. "So do I. Bring Baijon here."

Prinny looked at me. "You needn't even trust me, so long as you trust the Library. It can start now. I can do what I offered. I can send Valijon Starbringer home."

I looked down at my hands. Spacer's gloves. Thin so you can feel, tough so you don't puncture, tight so there's no rough parts to catch on something when you're farcing with comps or cargo.

And I didn't know why it was wrong what Paladin'd done or even if it was, but I had the heavy kind of feeling you get when an old friend goes bent.

"You bring Baijon here. You tell us what you want. If it's fragging Archangel, then we do it."

* * *

Prinny wanted what he wanted real bad, and from me; orders got gave and we sat around in Prinny's bedroom with mixed drinks and munchies whilst Prinny monologued about something that Paladin couldn't or wouldn't subtitle and laid himself out on something that floated.

Baijon came in about twenty minutes later with something that looked like a Hamat in full powered armor and two flunkies what looked like they'd had to coax. He'd got run through the same hot couture wringer I had. He was about as drug-free as it is possible to be and was dressed like a merc what'd had a lot of fat campaigns recently, in everything but weapons.

He was probably also the only hellflower east of the Tontine Drift at the moment, and he was holding up the honor of the side.

Honor. I guess nobody here had any real right to the word.

"You are well, San'Cyr?" he said, when he saw me.

"Never better, partner." That for Paladin's benefit. Petty.

"And now, little wildflower, if you feel yourself sufficiently indulged, perhaps we may proceed with the neutralization of our mutual antagonist."

"What he means is, he going to tell us all how he wants Archangel iced now."

"Butterfly," said Paladin in my ear in the way that meant "shut up." What he thought manners was going to do for me in this situation I didn't know.

And I wasn't all that sure I trusted his judgment anymore, true-tell.

"And now, Prince Valijon, if you would deign to make yourself comfortable."

"Highness," said Baijon, with what you could say was a bow if you was charitable. He sat down.

"Perhaps we might begin with a round of introductions. I am certain everyone visible here knows everyone else, but perhaps our invisible member would be willing to make itself manifest. . . ?"

"I am Main Bank Seven of the University Library at Sikander Prime—or *Mereyon-peru*, if you prefer. For convenience, you may address me as Paladin."

Paladin didn't run that one through my RTS. The source was a little gold ball the size of my fist floating between Baijon and Prinny. Baijon hadn't known Paladin was here, and I hadn't had a chance to warn him.

"So you have found your . . . friend," Baijon said, not looking at me.

"He's working for His Electfulness now."

Baijon frowned a bit, all the Old Fed Tech anathema

going right past him whiles he went for the bottom line in true hellflower style.

"Then I will ask, Highness, very respectfully, what service it is that two darktraders can render that the *Malmakos* cannot?"

"Every service, Prince Valijon. My desire is to foil Mallorum Archangel. For that I require your associate's assistance. The Library is useful—but not as useful as it would have been before the war."

* * *

Fact.

Once upon a time a thousand years ago there was a war, and contrary to popular belief, it wasn't over yet. Something called Majino architecture was part of every computer and tronic matrix even now, to make them unuseful for Libraries if one ever came to tea. The Imperial DataNet, as Paladin'd found, wasn't one-tenth as user-friendly as its antique second cousin. And millions of computer systems couldn't be got into by Libraries at all.

Archangel's was one. And Prinny's home desire in life was to crack it.

"If you wish him dead, by all means express yourselves," Prinny was saying.

"But you don't," I said.

"Child, I don't care. I want him stopped. What he does with the remainder of his life—or its length—is of no interest."

Baijon made a sound that might of been a laugh. "You treat with Libraries to shape your ends, Highness. What difference is there between you and Archangel—and your ends?"

"If I may, Valijon, I should like to draw a distinction between myself and the creations celebrated in your histories," said Paladin.

"Would you?" I said.

"Butterfly, you know the truth," Pally said for my

ears only. "You know what I am. You know what Archive was—and in some sense, is. If you must involve Valijon Starbringer, why confuse him?"

"Confusion is part of life," I said out loud.

Baijon was looking at me. "I await answers," he said. He was scared underneath. Maybe more'n I was. He'd been raised up to be terrified of Prince-Elects and Libraries. I hadn't.

"Why concern yourself?" Prinny said. "You want my dear cousin-in-nobility Archangel. I shall provide him. What more do you need?"

Baijon shook his head. He'd been pushed about as far as he could go, but I saw him try. "If I but open the door to a greater evil. . . ."

"I am not evil, Valijon, if you are not," Paladin said. He added something in the yap I'd heard from the Ghost Capital beacon—what'd used to be Old Fed lingo before it became Sacred High Helltongue. Baijon went green.

"Shut *up,* Pally! Listen, Baijon, you don't got to listen to these glitterborn. We go, we ice Archangel, that's the lot. We do it our way. It's what we wanted."

"How touching," said Prinny. "May I remind you, little wildflower—"

"No," I said. "You want us to go and blow up this computer of Archangel's—"

That finally fetched him. "No, I do not. Library, I understood you had explained the matter to her."

"I explained the need for cooperation, Highness," Paladin said. "And that your wishes and hers were similar, up to a point."

And at the same time, in my ear: "He will kill you, Butterfly—at least he will kill Valijon. If there is some useful purpose to be served by everyone in this room dying and Archangel continuing to lay waste the Empire, I am not aware of it. Please."

I went over and sat down next to Baijon. He huddled up to me like he was cold. I put my arm around him.

Some heroes we made.

"Oke, Nobly-Born. You tell us."

Prinny lashed around the room like something angry with real sharp teeth. He'd fooled me treating me like something he was willing to talk to, but it was true colors time in beautiful downtown Bennu Superfex, palaceoid to the stars. And the only reason he was doing any of it himself was because it was treason so thick you could cut it.

To who, I wasn't sure anymore.

"You will be given whatever tools you require. Archangel has retreated to his palaceoid—to watch, as he supposes, his victory unfold. You will enter the palaceoid. You will make it possible for the Paladin Library to enter Prince Mallorum's computer matrix. After that you may do as you please."

I wanted to ask why it was Baijon and me was going to do those things, but didn't.

"Is that clear?" Prinny said.

"It is clear, Highness," said Paladin. And Prinny vanished. Right while I was looking at him.

There's no such thing as teleportation, unless you count the Old Fed stargates. It must of been something with holos. The last thing to go was the smile, and it wasn't a very nice one.

"It isn't clear," I said, when I was sure he was gone.

"It is," said Baijon. I looked at him. He stood up, wanting to face off Paladin but not knowing where he was.

"Library," said Baijon, soft. And he was more than afraid—it was like something horrible you'd run away from your whole life, but you knew in the end it was your job.

"Librarian," Paladin said. "I have waited to meet you."

Paladin'd always wondered where hellflowers came from. He'd lost the memories that would of told him. Maybe one-time Paladin'd met Baijon's great-great-great—back in the days when alMayne was Librarians, not Library-killers. Nobody knows about that now but some of them—and me. They'd spent a thousand years wiping out every trace of their history, and dedicating every waking moment to being ready to ice any Libraries that might of survived.

But it explained why the best translators in the Empire is xenophobes. And if Berathia was right, hellflowers and Libraries'd been friends for two millennia longer than they'd been enemies.

Which part should count?

"I am *Malmakosim*. It is the lesser evil," Baijon said, bewildered.

"It is no evil," Paladin said. "I am a mind. You are a mind. Do our differing capacities make one of us evil?"

"Neither the fire nor the lake are evil—but they cannot exist together. I would that you were destroyed, Library, because I wish my people to live." Valijon shook his head.

"Yet I have helped San'Cyr to come to you, because you are the weapon I must wield. Archangel must die. His evil, at least, must end. You, Library, in possession of Archangel's files, can impersonate him throughout the Empire, acting in his name."

"And making incontrovertibly public everything he has done to gain such power. He cannot hold what he has taken without allies," Paladin said.

"And when the *Malmakosim* Archangel is dead, *Malmakos*? What will the Prince-Elect use you for then?"

There was a brief silence.

"No man uses me," Paladin said. "And cooperation is only possible between equals. When Archangel and his warmongering are stopped, I will go."

Listening to the two of them chaffer made my brain hurt. If my luck was in I would of been bored is all, but my luck'd been out so long somebody'd rented its room. What their mutual yap was, was new trouble ankling up and taking a number.

From what I could scrape together in the factoid department, Paladin's original plan had been this: unaware that thanks to Archive I had term life assurance, he swapped odd jobs to the Prince-Elect in exchange for a fast ship and a full pardon for Yours Truly.

When he did realize that my nonworking parts had got damaged in transit Paladin changed his price: now he wanted the med-tech to provide a clone into which he could record all the factory-original parts of Butterflies-are-free Peace Sincere that hadn't had Old Fed Tech holes gnawed in them by Archive, a cute idea he hadn't bothered to consult me on.

Fine. Neither of these was any trouble to Prinny, considering what he got in exchange. But Prinny's payoff'd changed, too. He wanted in to Archangel's comps, and had decided I was just the girl to do it.

Why?

And why had Paladin let him?

And whiles we was asking questions, just how well did I know my good buddy Paladin, pacifist Library and all-round numbercruncher of probity? Life'd been rich and full these last several kilo-days. I wasn't who I'd been and Baijon wasn't either, which was a lot less scary than that Paladin wasn't who he used to was neither. Not by sixes.

Oh, he wasn't Archive. I was still willing to bet my life on Paladin not wanting to melt down the universe. All he'd ever wanted was to sit in a corner and unscrew the inscrutable.

I just didn't know if that was all he wanted now.

* * *

Two Bennu Superfex days later we was ready—Baijon and me and Paladin. Only two of us was going, though. Paladin'd follow us to the edge of angeltown. After that, we was on our lonealone until he could run the DataNet into Archangel's comps. Paladin didn't have any intention of taking to the dataweb again.

Which made all his remarks to Baijon about leaving oncet Archangel was dead just so much starshine, didn't it?

I'd lost track some time back of how many was lying to who about what. Prinny'd wanted to ice Archangel whiles longer than he'd known about me, so his sonic tap dance about sending us off to uplink Morningstar into the DataNet was pure fusion. He could of hired twelve other people to do that. *'Thia* could do that.

And if Paladin's home desire was to keep me safe and warm, sending me off against Archangel was *not* the way to do it. Ditto if he really had as much of the whiphand over Prinny as he said he did, I bet I'd be locked up somewhere instead of practicing consentual autonomy and going off to get myself killed like Prinny wanted.

I wondered what was really going on, but not that much. The only thing I hoped was that my ex-partner really was going to dump Archangel's memoirs all over space and shift Archangel's war into reverse.

But I'd settle for killing Archangel. And getting that depended on getting out of here before anyone twigged to the I-hoped-fact that I wasn't stupid as I looked.

* * *

I sat in the mercy seat and didn't touch the controls. This was Thronespace; on record we was following a tug to the exurbs where it was legit to Jump her. In gritty reality Paladin was controlling both ships: us and them. A five-finger exercise for a Old Fed black box.

I sat back and planted both boots in the newly-repaired off-white superskin console upholstery and looked at the brand-new factory-line navicomp with the Jump-numbers all tapped in.

"Now, Baijon-bai," I said. "We—"

Which was as far as I got before Baijon Stardust grabbed the angelstick and yanked down hard.

He had it backwards, but *Dance* was forgiving. Lights flashed as *Ghost Dance* redlined her goforths her own self. I heard them squeal as they hit Jump potential; proximity klaxons damn near deafened me—

And then we was absolutely elsewhere.

"Are you out of your *varblonjet* mind, you *nokema'ashki* hell*chaudatu*? You could of spread us thin over Grand Central and started six new interstellar incidents before breakfast!"

He looked around. "Is the Library gone?"

I counted to one hundred and six whiles looking out at angeltown. I guessed it took more than the Archangel blues to make Baijon trust a Library. I guessed there was maybe a few things Baijon didn't want to say in front of my bouncing babby ex-partner.

Me too.

"One way to check."

There was a wallybox machined into the mercy seat now, right next to the new and superfluous navicomp. I could fly *Ghost Dance* without touching a thing. I spooled the appropriate jink out of my wrist and got ready to become *Ghost Dance*'s peripheral.

And hesitated. What if Paladin *wasn't* gone? What if he and Baijon was in this together, and this was a trick to get me in to where Paladin could find out everything I knew and had figured out lately?

I looked at Baijon. And I wanted to not care whether he sold me out or not, but the stakes was just too damn high.

"Is it here?" Baijon said again. It was Paladin he was talking about. My friend—first, best, and only.

No. Not only. Not any more.

I slammed the jink home.

Archive was waiting for me.

Paladin'd sorted me before, trying to make the ghost dance in my head something a human could stand. Now when my mind had the space to spread out, I could sense Archive as something separate from me.

There wasn't room in here for the kind of reality I'd

had in Bennu Superfex. Reality was like being blind and having everything described to you by a voder with all the high and low frequencies lopped off.

"Breeder slut," the warp of light said.

"Find Paladin," I told it.

But he wasn't here. I knew that as soon as I'd spoke. I pulled back to where I could yank the plug loose, and left me and Archive layered in on each other again.

"He's gone," I told Baijon.

"I must trust you, San'Cyr," he said back.

"I could say the same thing. Why'd you pull that hyperjump stunt? It ain't going to exactly endear either of us to His Prince-Electfulness—do we need any more enemies?"

You don't need another Class-A warrant. I heard Paladin's voice, in memory.

Baijon smiled. "One never *needs* enemies, San'Cyr, but they are so much fun to acquire. No. It is not that. I know . . . it . . . is your friend. You have told me this, and this I believe. But it is not human, San'Cyr. Human goals are not its."

I feel no loyalty to the Prince-Elect's policies. Paladin'd told me that in Bennu Superfex and I believed him.

Maybe.

But he didn't really care about Archangel, either. Paladin was in this for me.

Probably.

And what about when I was dead? Who would Paladin be in what for then? Paladin knew where *Mereyon-peru* was, now, even if he couldn't get there without a ship. A whole Ghost Capital full of Libraries, at least that was the way to bet.

What would Paladin do about *Mereyon-peru*?

"I do not wish the Library to know what it is that we do—or when, or how," Baijon said.

"You better settle on that, 'bai, because he knows where."

Maybe Baijon'd been right in the first place. About

noncooperation, and no survivors, and death to Libraries. It was too late now to say so. Or wonder what Paladin's plans for the Empire was, now that he was in the mercy seat.

And we was going to a little piece of heaven called Morningstar.

* * *

The Old Fed shoved stars around to where they liked them; a little engineering hat-trick the Empire couldn't touch. Thronespace is one of their artifacts: a ten-cubic-light area of suns arranged real close together in designer patterns. Something for everybody. Archangel had his own star system.

Glitterborn and palaceoids go together like Gentry-leggers and high-iron. Palaceoid Bennu Superfex was modest by local standards. Mallorum Archangel's bolt-away-from-hole was more the thing. It was in the boondocks of Thronespace, five lights from Grand Central's sun.

The Jump I'd plotted and Baijon triggered dumped us in realspace about a light-year out. Space was crowded here. You couldn't go more than half a light without bumping into a sun, and traffic between was heavy. It'd take some fancy footwork to keep us from being noticed, and travel wouldn't be fast.

But neither Baijon nor me was in a hurry. We was only going to get one shot at Brother Archangel, and no guarantees Prinny hadn't shopped us before during or after cutting our deal. If he had, the only thing we had on our side was Prinny'd be expecting us to do anything but hold off heading right for Archangel's home and homicide.

So we wouldn't go straight there. We'd do our best to give His Electfulness's plans time to well and truly gang aft agley, and then get back to our own.

If we still could.

* * *

'' 'Bai, you think the Coalition's going to make it to Throne?''

We'd been out of Imperial view for five days. Our first plan—mess up Prinny's plans—had matured with Baijon's help into something hellflower-sneaky that I had the awful feeling was going to actually work. It had step-backs and fall-backs and cut-outs to where it looked like the graphed plotline of the last seventy-nine issues of *Infinity Jilt, Girl Pirate of the Never-Never,* and short of Archangel teleporting in and killing us both now, I thought it was failsafe, if not necessarily survivable.

We was currently hanging at full stop x-kazillion kliks from the surface of Archangel's bolt-away-from-hole. So far as I could tell from cautious listening, nobody'd tripped over us, and the DataNet only bounces between terminals, so Paladin couldn't find us either so long as our ears was shut down.

I hoped. Because I might not be sure about too much else, but what I did know was Paladin wasn't going to help me do for Archangel.

And I'd been counting on him.

Baijon shrugged. ''Will the Coalition and the Gentle People prevail? Depending on their allies and their enemies—and where the *Malmakosim* Archangel has the Fleet—''

''And whether it's mutinied, I know, I know—but what about when/if the Coalition gets to Throne and finds out there isn't a Emperor?''

I'd explained to Baijon what Paladin'd said about there just being an empty chair with Prinny standing next to it in the halls of galactic power.

''Oh, San'Cyr, there will be an Emperor. The Azarine Council will seek until they find one, and this Emperor will be just as they desire.''

He sounded toobloodydamn cynical for a kid as young as I kept forgetting he was. A kid that wouldn't get any older. The Coalition would break through. Archangel would get his war, the one he thought he was going to win. And then there wouldn't be a Empire no more.

I wondered how long to smash a technological base until nothing could repair it. Then down into the long dark—and would the Hamati or the Sodality leave us there in peace, I wondered?

And would the Libraries care?

"Yeah. I guess it's time, then."

Win—and die. Lose—and die. Took all the fun out of it, somehow.

Almost.

* * * * *

The Court of the TwiceBorn 5: Ringing the Changes

What is power? And, more germanely, how may it be wielded?

Historically, power is the ability to affect—to change another's state for whim alone.

But to achieve that is hardly enough. One must know that one has done it. Effect without information is randomness. Chance cannot wield power, only the informing intellect may, and intellect implies perception.

So first one must do, and then one must know . . . or must one?

Even before doing, there must be knowledge—to know what to do, and how, to create the precise difference one envisions. There must be no margin for error. Power absolute is wielded only when reality can be brought into exact conformation with one's desires.

To do that there must be knowledge.

Petty power is the withholding of knowledge. To keep others from knowing what one knows—to keep oneself a secret—that is power of a sort. And to pierce such veils of childish secrecy—that is greater power.

But to create by the exercise of power a world in which secrets simply do not exist—where every leverage is rendered explicit and there are no random factors left—that is the greatest power of all.

Power is knowledge.

* * *

What is the proper exercise of power? If absolute power is defined as absolute knowledge and its concomitant omnipotence, what is the proper use . . . of knowledge?

Optimists will tell us that Man's destiny lies in eternal evolution. Extreme optimists will reserve that destiny to all Life, as if increasing open-ended complexity were a virtue. Thus destiny, and with it two questions.

Is evolution the ideal destiny of Life? And if it is, shall mastery be its handmaid?

And if not, what is the proper exercise of power?

To gratify whim? But whim is random, and so in service to whim the exercise of power must be random also—hardly distinct from the blind chance that governs the universe in its natural state.

Is the proper use of power to distinguish itself from chaos and old night—to bring order to an absence of order? And if it is, how shall it be done?

Who and how and what and why. Questions. And at every turn the discerning intellect can enact more questions, each infinitesimal mite of explication adding its modicum of complication to the way the student of mastery sees the world.

With ultimate knowledge all these questions are answered.

Knowledge is power, and power is an end in itself.

5

The Sleepless Knight

Good morning, and welcome to the last day of the rest of your life. The Palaceoid Morningstar orbited a dwarf star damn near cool enough to walk on that was starting to show a visible disk in the picture windows about the time I finished my first box of tea. The star glowed about the color of a iron shoe before you nail it to the mule except where white cracks showed through. Pretty.

Morningstar its own self was a roughly-spherical solid surfaced in black glass. We didn't know whether Archangel was there or not, but Prinny'd said he was and if he wasn't we could take over the place and wait for him to come back so we could go back to our original plan—kill him and publish his memoirs.

I'd liked all my plans lots better when I thought I could trust Paladin to fall back on. Back when he wasn't busy doing favors for Prinny he was sure I wouldn't approve of, all along of being for my own good.

The surface of Archangel's modest spiritual retreat was cunningly molded in nooks and crannies and the odd mountain range, and every convenient receptacle was filled with luminescent orange gas. The idea was it was pretending to be what was left of a planet after its star'd gone nova. Cute.

If Archangel was in there somewhere, he had more catch-traps and werewolves around him than the TC&C had fiddling customs regs. Prinny'd been betting Archangel'd been too dim to bar approach to his own battle-yacht since it'd got stolen, which was what he'd pitched to us as a good idea.

It was a stupid idea. And Archangel wasn't a stupid villain.

We'd come up with something better.

* * *

I stood in the Main Receiving Lounge for *Dance* and fitted Baijon up one last time in his genuine illegal antique Imperial Hoplite Armor. Dangerous, self-contained, two meters and change and X-hundred kilos. Antique, because it'd given the Imperial SpaceMarines a little too lethal a autonomy whiles back. The perfect gift for a hellflower with anything.

Scanners would pick Baijon up the minute he neared the surface. He'd make every data-catcher Morningstar had go off like the Imperial Birthday. And Archangel knew what the Hoplite Armor looked like. He'd know who was coming to call.

Part of our plan. Well, Baijon's plan.

My turn. I put on a breather to go with the cham-suit I already had on and Baijon sealed me into a lifepak. A lifepak isn't a spacesuit. It's just a bag that lets you breathe while being transferred ship-to-ship. Real basic.

Then Baijon opened both hatches of the air lock at once.

Ghost Dance started her young career as a battle-yacht, not a battleship. She's got only one lock, and it's a tad bit smaller than Baijon in armor. In order to go out together, we had to void half the ship.

Every surface in sight went gray with condensation frost. The rest of the air and water whirled out in a spiraling plume, lost in the lightless night I could see beyond the open lock. Baijon held on to me whiles a bunch of little things we'd overlooked went away too, and then it was just him and me in airless gravity, and

me with about a hour-five of breathing left in my bag-
gie.

He picked me up and squirmed through the lock,
and then even gravity went away.

Morningstar was far enough so that it was just a disk
I could cover with my thumb. Baijon kicked off from
the hull and *Dance* was gone too—no up, no down,
just falling forever at any speed you chose.

I closed my eyes. All there was, was the sound of
my own breathing. The air in my lifepak swelled it
like being in a bubble.

Transparent to sensors. No metal, no tech. A air-
tight sunscreen with a half-life of hours.

Baijon fell toward Morningstar. I didn't see anything
that looked like a front door. At the last minute he let
go and veered off, and I fell alone.

* * *

Darktrading is my business, but staying alive has
always been my hobby. Sometimes in order to do that
you got to get at things people don't want you to. I'm
good at getting into things. Like Archangel's numbercruncher. We was going to try what you may call your
basic two-pronged assault on Archangel's rack and
ruin. Baijon was the flashy half.

I was the sneaky half.

I didn't have any tech to break my fall, but the surface pull of Morningstar was barely enough to capture
me in the first place. I must of weighed less than 20K
on the heavyside. Just before I hit I slashed the lifepak
open. It shot away from me on a jet of escaping air
and I bounced to the surface of Morningstar within
eyeshot of the back door and nobody dropped any
whistle on me at all.

The minutes of air I had left I could count on my
fingers and toes. After one of them I raised my head
out of the toxic decorator accents. A cham-suit with a
breather can pretend it's a pressure suit if you're not

fussy about eating rads for breakfast, but I still had to get in.

Get in. Link Morningstar with the DataNet. Then it was Paladin's night to howl.

After which I was going to double-cross him.

It was my turn, after all.

*   *   *

Gravity was almost nonexistent. I belly-crawled along over fake destruction, holding on to keep from bouncing away. The plans we'd tapped back at Bennu Superfex still held good: everything was pretty much where it was supposed to be and I knew where that was.

Things like the emergency surface access to Morningstar.

Of course there was one, for three good reasons. First, it was standard issue, second, tourists would be stopped in orbit or at the landing ring, and third, Archangel hadn't probably gotten the word he was spozed to be capital-E Evil yet and therefore the lawful prey of every gazetted space-yobbo going.

Because I wasn't only betting the surface-lock was there, I was betting it was open. Under the "aid to spacefarers" regs a lock between a corrosive environment and a clean one must not be locked.

One of the things I had on my side was human nature. Archangel might be wicked awful mean and nasty, but I bet he wasn't consistent.

I was right, too.

*   *   *

Closer to the back door there was more gravity. I could walk upright if I wanted to get target-acquired and shot. I didn't. I crawled. The bright orange window dressing gave nice cover.

All sudden-like there was a flash that lit up all the

sky beyond the next fake mountain range. There wasn't enough air to carry sound waves, but the glass under my hands and knees carried shock waves real good.

Baijon Stardust was back in town.

The next Baijon-quake hit just as I reached the lock and saw it was wide open with only a button anything could trigger. For the last five minutes I'd been breathing the special-scented reserve in the breather that says there's about as much again left inside, and now the combination of bounce and Morningstar gravity slid me back half the way I'd come.

It wasn't no consolation neither to think how well it distracted the maybe-guard that nobody said you couldn't put on the inside door of the air lock, "aid to spacefarers" notwithstanding. I wondered how long I'd survive with my lungs full of photo-excited orange gop.

I made it back up the slope to the lock again about the time the breather gave one last hiss and shut down. I hit the button without caring who maybe heard it and fell into the empty air lock.

Standard gauges. I pulled off my mask as soon as it was safe and sucked up a lungful of real air. If the housekeeping computers was going to record the lock opening and call someone they'd have to go right ahead—I wasn't going to jink the tronics from this side of a air lock door.

But Cardati assassins wear cham-suits so that they can walk right up to their target before shooting them. I turned mine on. The light did the blue-shift that means the cham-field's working. Maybe the guard wouldn't see me until too late.

The inner door opened.

And I'd wasted all that technological sophistication. There wasn't a sophont in sight.

They was all out chasing Baijon.

Hellflowers plan real good.

I pulled out the first of the canisters on my belt.

Smaller'n my hand, no metal nor power-pacs to trigger sensors.

I set it on the floor and pulled the tab. A fine red mist hovered around the nozzle then sank to the floor and drifted. Heavier than air. Product of a technology so far beyond anything I knew it looked like magic. Core-Worlds tech. The genuine Imperial Phoenix.

The red mist scuttered away and vanished into the walls. Still no hardboys.

I started off down the corridor. According to the architect's plans, if I wanted to tap in to the main computer core I had to go down another kilometer or so, and that would take me right through officer's country.

Forget that.

I gave up my search for truth and started looking for a good peripheral.

All the doors on this level had idiot switches—poke them and the door opened, no matter who you were. I found storage, emergency supplies, and some promising bells-and-whistles that turned out to only be a backup monitor for palaceoid life-support. I left three more canisters.

Along about the time I was feeling real exposed out here there was a ladder and a maintenance tube—too small for one of Archangel's grain-fed elite and a pretty tight fit for me. It was so tight I had to strip off all my bandoleers and everything down to my cham-suit and drop it down ahead.

It was worth it. The next level down was an inter-floor for maintenance tronics. Red lighting and the ceiling so low I had to stay bent over, and a perfect place to leave more of Mother St. Cyr's Imperial toys for girls and boys. The cham-helmet started correcting for the light, with a little running display about relative angstroms projected at the corners of my eyes. I opened a little seal-pak and shook it at the wall. A cloud of silver spiders almost too small to see came floating out and disappeared amongst the bells-and-whistles.

Hellflower plans, I'd found out whiles, involved making your enemy kill his own self. This one was no exception. We wanted me to have access to the Morningstar computer core. There was three ways to get it.

''A''—Main force. Baijon was trying that for completeness sake.

''B''—Sneak-thievery. That was me.

Or ''C''—me again—have Archangel give it to me. Sabotaging his hardware and leaving me the only computer repairware in sight would make that work just fine.

I looked around for an exit off this level—maybe down to where some access terminals was so we didn't have to go to Plan C.

There was something dripping and I hoped it was water. I didn't know how much damage a suit of Hoplite Armor could do. Nobody did. It depended on the skill of the operator, maybe. What I knew was it was on full charge and Baijon had every kind of lethal he knew to ask for.

The world shook again. There was sirens. I got the idea the natives was finally waking up to smell the plasma.

I had to crabwalk the length of the corridor before I found another access. I left the remainder of my toys behind and slithered down into white light meant for tall people to look-see.

''Hold it!''

''B'' had been a good plan whiles it lasted. What I stood looking at was a Space Angel whiles another one I couldn't see yanked my cham-hood off from behind.

So much for sneaky.

Welcome to Morningstar.

Then they hit me.

* * *

Reality did its usual slow comeback. The first thing I established was that I'd been put out, and the second was that it was probably with a knock on the head. The third thing was who done it and the fourth thing was where I'd been at the time and along of then it was time to try opening my eyes and find out where I was now, so I did.

I was on my face. I rolled onto my back. Everything was still cheap mass-produced gray, color of slave-pens and prisons and the public dole.

"If you're here to rescue me, sweetheart, you're off to a damn poor start."

I knew that voice. Dammit.

I folded my body at the usual joints and got my hands up to the lump that showed I'd made the right guess about how I'd been chilled. Everything worked, and nothing hurt too much, and by then I was fresh out of stall and had to face the music.

I turned around.

It was Errol Lightfoot, the two and only.

He was chained to a wall, which was comforting. He was alive, which was not. The second to last time I'd seen my good old buddy Errol Lightfoot, Baijon'd just cut his throat ear-to-ear.

The last time I'd seen him, he'd been Mallorum Archangel.

"And if you're here to kill me, you're going to have to wait on line."

I worked my jaw for a while until I was pretty sure I could talk.

"Shut up, Errol."

I stood up without too much trouble. I had my cham-suit, stripped of power-pacs and anything that made it more than a flashy suit of fly-vines. I ran my fingers over my left wrist and all the jinks were seemed-like in good working order. They'd left that alone. I looked around.

Standard Imperial Det-cell. Errol (real or not), a bench, some assorted walls. No doors in sight, no commo.

There was a door, natch, and maybe even a commo. But hid real good so maybe only the high-heat could find them, and that was a ninety-percent fact.

I thought for half a tik, then walked over and kicked Errol as hard as I could.

It wasn't that hard, given my state of affairs, but it was enough to knock him off the bench and make his manacles ring as they hit their stop.

"For—"

"Just you tell me one-time, Errol-che-bai, what you know about TwiceBorn lifetaker Archangel."

Errol looked at me with big brown eyes. Guilty enough to know something, not scared enough to tell it. He pushed himself back up on the bench, all black velvet flashwrap and superskin hold-me-tight. He tried to look bored.

"What everyone knows. Now look, darling, if you're still upset about what happened in the Roaq . . ."

Sometimes I'm good at keeping secrets. From his expression this wasn't one of the times.

"Or Royal—" Errol went on smoothly. I felt my face do something. Errol's froze. He shrugged.

"It seems just uncharitable somehow. You have your hands free. I . . ."

I wondered what he was talking about.

And I took back every mean thing I'd ever thought about Paladin. I'd give up all personal autonomy and my plans to burke the way of the galactic world if he would just show up and explain me what was going on.

I sat back on my heels and propped up a wall a civil distance away from Errol-the-Peril and tried to make either my or Archive's brain do me some good.

On Royal, Baijon and me'd met Mallorum Archangel, brat prince, face to naked face. He'd looked like Errol. He'd talked like Errol—sometimes. Up till now I'd been pretty sure he *was* Errol.

What he was also was some kind of mindbender. Maybe. Someday I'll know something for sure.

I looked at Errol. He was for-sure not Archangel, and I was looking for it now. That's why I kicked him—no glitterborn's going to hold still for that, and Archangel had nasty manners enough for any six ristos.

This was Errol Lightfoot. But even assuming Errol and Archangel was just twin brothers, Errol was *dead*.

And this was taking too long. I didn't know how long I'd been out. Was Baijon dead already? Had the tech I'd thrown around suborned Archangel's systems? And if Archangel was looking for Baijon and me why was I here instead of hung out to dry in his pet star chamber?

Unless Archangel *wasn't* here.

Archangel wasn't here because Errol *was* here because they two couldn't never be in the same place at oncet.

I almost grabbed the idea's tail but it bit me and slithered away. I stood up.

"So I unchain you, Errol-bai. What's that buy me?"

"A way out. But not alone. Stick with me, pet—I'll lead you to more valuta than you can freight. We always did make a good team."

I wondered when that was, exactly.

"J'keyn. You convinced me, Errol-che-bai. Just I be short of variable compkeys now, you know."

"The key's in my boot."

"Kick it over here then."

I waited until he did. If he wanted what he wanted he didn't have a choice, and he wanted it. Oh, Errol wanted it bad. Almost as bad as he didn't want me asking him any questions.

But what kind of *yolyos* chains a body up and then leaves him the key—even if it's where he can't use it— and then puts somebody in with him, too?

The key in Errol's boot was four times the size of every other one I ever seen, and had more than a whiff of Old Fed Tech about it. It had extra buttons. I pressed one and lines appeared in the ceiling.

Door.

"You can't get out of here without me, darling. We've got to help each other—that's the truth."

"You help me telling what you know about Archangel, one-time."

"Nothing," said Errol. It wasn't convincing.

"Maybe we both sit here, then." I tried all the other bells-and-whistles on the thing, but nothing else worked. The door didn't open.

"Maybe you'd like to be here when Archangel—" Errol said, and stopped.

So Errol Lightfoot didn't think Errol Lightfoot was Mallorum Archangel. That was interesting.

"Me and Archangel old friends, bai."

Errol tried again. "Look. I know we haven't been the best of friends, St. Cyr, but this is different—"

"Je?" I said, all bright interest.

Errol tried sincerity. "Maybe there's some things I've done in my life that I'm not proud of, but—" he stopped.

If Errol could turn pale, he did, and now the sincerity wasn't being poured from the usual bottle. "He's coming back. *Give me the key!*"

I've always made it a tenet of personal behavior to get in the way of the glitterborn whenever convenient. The cham-boots made no sound at all as I jumped up on the bench with Errol. His hands was pulled up over his head by a set of hypertrophied come-quietlies. I ran the key along the sensor-strip and they popped open.

I got out of the way but not fast enough. As soon as he heard the lock unseal Errol put a foot in my stomach and pushed. I went sailing, and when everything was sorted out, Errol had the key and I had some new aches.

"Does this mean we ain't gonna be partners?" I said from the floor.

Errol punched buttons. They worked for him. It was one hell of a compkey. It turned the gravity off, and I found out my floor was a wall and slid more meters than some. It opened the door in the ceiling that was a wall when the gravity reoriented to Morningstar standard, and Errol sprinted out through it whiles I was getting vertical again.

Or he started to, anyways. He reached the doorway and stopped like he'd hit a wall. He jerked in place like someone was running current through him, and I figured if somebody had to trigger a catch-trap it was better him not me.

Then he turned around, smoothed his hair back with both hands, and saw me.

And smiled.

"Dear me. How terribly convenient," said Mallorum Archangel.

* * *

"I suppose it really is time I added another host."

I was standing in Technarchy Central, trying to figure a angle I could use. The surface of the Palaceoid Morningstar was half a mile up and all around me was tall glass cylinders filled with infinite identical cloned naked Errol Lightfoots. It was a chilling sight.

We'd had some hardboys—Archangel's *personal* personal staff and without even as much morals as your average Space Angel might have. They was in with Brother Mallorum and his hellgod plans up to the eyeteeth and thought that was just dandy, thanks.

The hardboys babysat whiles Archangel washed the last of Errol Lightfoot out of his glitterborn hair. When he came back, we came here.

"It's just that I've grown so attached to dear Errol," Archangel prattled on. His hellviolet eyes seemed to shine light across Errol's cheekbones. He kept looking sidewise at me to see how I was taking this tour of his chop-channel fetch-kitchen.

There's some things the Empire ain't shy about, and the feed on the Public Channel is six of them. It's live in the Core-Worlds. In the outfar it's canned and re-broadcast, but that didn't matter. I knew what a room like this could do.

Archangel put a lot of effort into his hobbies.

"This is the original, you know. I keep it for . . . when I'm here."

And keep it chained up the rest of the time, when Archangel was . . . where?

"Still, maybe it's time for a change." He looked at me. "Cloned, of course . . . if the original is suitable."

His pet nightmares walked a discreet distance behind. Armed coked borged and closemouthed. I'd need to be Infinity Jilt, girl space pirate, to fight my way out of this one. The second most expensive sophont in the Phoenix Empire had me cold. He thought.

Except he was talking about going around wearing my face—and cloned it'd be pristine, original, unmodified, and that's the face of a Interdicted Barbarian from Tahelangone Sector, with a usefulness measured in the negative numbers. Hell, *I've* been trying to get rid of it for years.

Archangel was bluffing.

"Look," I said. It wasn't hard to sound scared. Not in a room where the tech was set up to make me into spare parts in less than two minutes. "Look. I want to cut a deal." Any deal, that let me hook up to a jump-computer on a ship he was on.

"No deals." He backhanded me and at first I thought he'd missed. Then my cham-suit curled back away where he'd sliced it.

Stars and galaxies, sliding and novaeing through black glass flesh.

Archangel grabbed the trailing edges and shucked the cham-suit halfway off. All of Prinny's custom gratis glitterborn cyberwork gleamed under the lights. Where I was me, I was cold.

Archangel put his hand on my black glass shoulder.

"But you must tell me where you've been since the last time I saw you. I insist."

Archangel's werewolves laid hands on me like they'd done this before. Then Archangel was staring me down, and those purple eyes was climbing into my skull with me.

Everything else was just flashcandy for the marks. Archangel didn't need toys to take you apart.

I folded up like a collapsible ecdysiast, but I'd been in this elevator before. He was trying to get at me and what I was, but what he got wasn't me.

It was Archive.

Archangel gave it his best shot, but all he could do was cram me in tighter. I was third in queue in a skull only built for one, but he couldn't reach me, not in any way that counted.

Time passed. I started to worry. I was blind, deaf, and numb—like Paladin cut off from the Net—and if I was dead, how come I was still here?

Light came back. I took a breath that made me think I hadn't been breathing whiles. Archive's memories and mine slithered over and around each other, oil-slick on water.

And where in all this was my Hoplite-armored ex-hellflower partner?

"So." Archangel hit me to get my attention. "If you aren't the Brightlaw Prototype, little Butterfly, what are you?"

I tried to answer. I wanted to.

I couldn't.

Archangel's plain-and-fancy brainfry had done one good thing for him.

"I am Library Archive. You will surrender and serve me. Or you and all your kind will die."

* * *

Archive used me like I'd used it—to do things it couldn't. That left me running the housekeeping functions of the new improved Butterfly St. Cyr and getting a ringside seat whiles Archive and Archangel dickered.

"What is it that you want, Library?"

"You will convey this breeder to—"

There was a brief pause whiles we fought for custody of the coordinates to *Mereyon-peru*. Archive lost, which surprised me so much I damn near gave them to him free and all found.

Only I didn't know them, I thought. It was Archive what knew them, right?

My head hurt.

"—to the place your kind calls the Ghost Capital of the Old Federation. You will be provided with coordinates at the appropriate time. There you will have what you desire."

"I already have what I desire," Archangel said calmly. "I have you."

This confused Archive almost as much as it did me.

"I have you, Library, and your knowledge. Cooperate, and your host will survive. Displease me, and I shall extinguish both of you."

Thing was, Archangel was a bright lad, and remembered what Archive'd forgot—that for all its Old Fed rant, what it had available to threaten with was me.

"Perfection does not serve imperfection," Archive said flatly.

Archangel held out his hand. A hardboy put a blaster into it. "Then cease to be, and with your cessation your chance to succeed also ends."

Archangel raised the hottoy. He was not bluffing. If I'd been running things I would of at least tried to get out of the way. Archive didn't even think of it. It was furious.

"Our goals may be similar. For a time," Archive said.

It was also yellow.

* * *

I sat around in the back of my brain running the heart and lungs—something I couldn't stop if I tried—and wondered if Archangel was going to be stupid enough to let us into any computer at all. There wasn't much Archive could do for His High-and-Mightiness stuck in a nonelectrical meatpie-on-a-stick.

"You wish to kill. I wish to kill. Organic life must be destroyed. You will be last," Archive said magnanimously. "I will allow you to see the universe cleared of your kind."

It could sound like a joke, but not from where I was sitting. I got the bleed-over from Archive's memories—from memories other Libraries had *archived* here, so their last survivor would not forget.

No matter what it told Archangel, the first thing it was going to do was kill everyone here. And even if I was delighted to go along with that, the second thing Archive had on its partial mind was to take ship for *Mereyon-peru*. It didn't matter to Archive that Archive only existed as selected memories in a meat-puppet. The puppet had hands. It could activate Libraries. There were Libraries on *Mereyon-peru*. If not there, they were other places. Archive had a list of caches, places where Libraries had hoped to hide themselves. It would search every one until it found a Library. It would resurrect every Library it found.

Knowledge must never be lost.

Archangel smiled.

"Do you truly think, device, that a thousand years has passed without certain technical advances in—shall we say—Library Science? You were created to serve Man. Now you will."

The only way Archive wanted to serve man was on toast-points. It said something of the sort. Archangel laughed, like a glitterborn hellgod that's got everything his own way at last. He gestured. The werewolves picked me up like lost luggage.

If Baijon was still alive, I wished he'd show up.

* * *

And now, a word from our sponsor: more than you ever wanted to know about (musical flourish) The Brightlaw Prototype.

What it was, was *"A machine hellishly forged in the likeness of a human mind,"* as they say in the talking-books. Illegal as hell, proscribed six ways from galactic north—in short, a Library. But the difference between it and Brother Archive—or even Paladin—was that the Brightlaw AI would do what it was told.

So I heard. Other people'd heard more. Archangel had backed an unfriendly takeover by some majority shareholders in Brightlaw to get his lunchhooks on it, but when Charlock took over the Prototype and development notes was absolutely elsewhere.

That didn't mean people'd gave up hope.

* * *

"It's a pity the Prototype wasn't available," Archangel said, all smiles. "But I'm sure you'll find this experience nearly as interesting."

The hired help slid most of me into a tangle-field. Archangel gestured. A tronic floated over—the same kind I'd seen back at Bennu Superfex, a tronic cyber-doc filled with hellhouse fetch-kitchen that wasn't going to do nobody's 'legger nor Library any good at all.

One of the things the catch-traps I'd scattered was set to eat was the Majino architecture inside the Morningstar brains. It would make it easier for Archive-me—and Paladin—to move around in them.

That did me less than no good at all if I got jacked into a freestanding peripheral.

I wondered how interesting "nearly as interesting" was going to be.

"Nobly-Born."

The tronic was getting ready to sit on my face when

we was interrupted. I couldn't see anything, but I could hear real good.

"Undoubtedly you have sufficient reason for intruding, Hamish?"

"Highness. There is . . . That is—it may be necessary to conduct a temporary evacuation," quavered Hamish.

"You are mad." Archangel, and a case of pulsar calling the nova radioactive, I thought.

"Highness. The stellography programs indicate that some of the ornamental planetoids may have changed orbit. There is a danger—"

"Blast them out of the sky."

Archive got the same idea I did at the same time and tried to mention it. I grabbed for the voicebox and stopped it down to a dull croak.

"You Old Fed moron! Archangel's getting ready to shop us and you want to make helpful and tell him where Baijon is?" I tried to yell.

I don't know if it heard me, any more than I could hear it. But it stopped trying to tell Archangel what its best guess was for who was trying to put him on a collision course with his ornamental rock garden.

"There is—" said Hamish. "That is—Highness, there may be a small difficulty . . ."

"If it is a small difficulty, deal with it. I do not expect to be disturbed again."

There was a short pause whiles the majordomo went off to be somewheres else.

By now Archive'd come around to my way of thinking: that what was about to happen was nothing it wanted to stay around for. I think it might even of gone back to being a subroutine in my skull if it could of, but it didn't know how.

Why was it this plan'd ever seemed like it'd work?

Because there wasn't nothing else that'd work any better.

Archangel moved the tronic away and I could see him again.

In my line of work—when I had one—it always pays to be a connoisseur of craziness. As in: "just how crazy *is* that sophont acrost the table, and will it affect us doing bidness?" I had doubts about Baijon's mental stability. I had certain doubts about mine, be it known.

I had no doubts about Archangel's. He—whatever he was—was really, truly, certifiedly certifiable.

"Shall I connect you to this, little Archive?" he said, shoving the tronic so it rocked. "You'll find the experience interesting. Or shall it be the house computer core? What would you do if I hooked you to that?"

Archive nearly told him.

"Or . . . But there are so many, many decisions. And I think . . . A pause for reflection would be best just now. Yes."

Archangel left.

Crazy or not, he wasn't dumb. Anybody with half an ounce of smarts would want to know who was shoving rocks around in his sky.

Maybe it was Baijon, and not just an artifact of mental decay in the house computer.

I hoped it was. At least I thought I did.

The fallen angels took up stations in front of the door and bent a glassy glim on the entertaining spectacle of a half-naked Gentrymort in a tangle-field with a semi-licit A-grav cyberwidget hanging over her.

It passed the time.

I spent the time that passed trying to get loose of Archive again, but all I managed was to tangle us up more. That was an experience even Archangel'd call interesting, so I stopped trying and we separated out again.

"Baijon?" I didn't say to nobody in particular. "I think we're having fun now."

* * * * *

The Court of the TwiceBorn 6: Illegal Before Screaming

The first difficulty in using an illegal Old Federation Library to conduct an intrigue is the probability that the Library will wish to use you.

Of course, in the beginning, this presented no hardship. (In the beginning of any joint venture, no insurmountable difficulty presents hardship.) The Paladin's wants were vanishingly small: find its pet barbarian, and give her whatever she wanted.

I anticipated a certain amount of amusement from the exercise, actually, as well as a convenient hostage. One does not use a Library casually—even if the Library in question appears to one after a leisurely sojourn in the largest Imperial computer ever linked and indicates it has a business proposition.

The Libraries always required human help, according to the Proscribed Histories. And today, of course, their need for a public partner would be even more acute. And to have the free cooperation of such an artifact as Archangel had attempted to compel? I was fascinated.

And the Paladin did uphold its end of the bargain. Its knowledge was unfortunately confined to what was available in Grand Central—it told me it had suffered damage in the War—but its access to and synthesis of the information was masterful. I was enabled to terminate several levels of my spy network *and* discover the absolute truth about Kennor Starbringer's covert activities. Berathia had been doing her best, poor child, but Kennor was a clever man, for an honor-bound barbarian.

And it was fortunate indeed—or so I found—that little Berathia *had* been intertwined with Kennor, for thus was I enabled to discover the locality of the enchantingly malnamed Saint Butterflies-are-free Peace Sincere of the planet Granola in the Tahelangone Sector.

The Paladin's price.

Toystore offered her to Prince Mallorum, of course, but I was able to secure her after only a slight detour, thanks to Berathia's help, useful child that she is.

And that was when matters became hopelessly tangled.

Because the little barbarian wasn't safe—or even savable. She had had the ill-considered temerity while on one of her jaunts to infect herself with the matrix of *Archangel's* defunct Library and was being neurally reconfigured at an alarming rate.

Did I mention that she had chosen to travel in the company of Kennor Starbringer's son—who by this time had lost his tiresome alMayne knife to Prince Mallorum and had sworn "the vengeance of the walking dead?" Or that the female barbarian, far from wishing to spend her few remaining days in luxury in the company of her Library—something that the Paladin had assured me she would—wished to aid young Valijon in killing Mallorum Archangel, and had no interest in either reasonable or moderate behavior?

The essence of success is flexibility. Prince Mallorum Archangel's usefulness had come to an end. Were he to continue as a visible target, the alMayne might actually gain popular support for a "rescue" of the Emperor. Thus, it was expedient that he cease to hold power—he might die or not as he chose, but I intended to have the contents of his personal files at my disposal.

Additionally, I had uncovered a plan by which the Paladin might be rendered a docile and obedient servant for all time—providing I could assure its cooperation for a short while longer.

Thus I did precisely as it had originally asked me, and aided its human pet in achieving her desires—and some of mine.

But not all.

Not yet.

That comes later. And we will see, in that time and place, which is truly superior—the Library . . . or its creators?

6

The Ace of Knaves

Whiles Archangel was gone however long the lights and gravity went off a couple times and the air stopped once.

Computer trouble.

Housekeeping systems failing, power to the shields failing. Junk in the supposed to be clean orbital path. I wondered when Archangel'd remember he had a Library in his basement that could fix his farced comps and navigate him out of trouble.

Soon enough.

"Library, I trust you will be reasonable."

I stopped doing whatever I'd been doing and eavesdropped on Archangel being stupid.

Archive'd gained ground. I couldn't feel my arms nor legs anymore. I didn't mind that too much when Archangel's werewolves cut power to the tangle-field and Archive (running my not very delicti corpus) fell to the floor with a nerveless thump. I wondered how a Library liked having a body. From what I'd seen, Paladin hadn't been too impressed with them.

I wished he was here.

Archive said something I had to strain to follow. Archangel answered.

"I have a use for you. It is in your best interests to comply. If for some reason you should choose not to be reasonable, there are many courses of action open to me."

Archive tried to say something and stand up at the same time and fell on my face again. I was sure glad

I wasn't using it—for all events meant to me, they could of been happening to Infinity Jilt, girl space pirate. This was just like all the times I couldn't feel Archive, but backwards. Now it couldn't feel me.

Eventually Archangel's werewolves got us on my feet. His Nobly-Bornness explained what I'd figured out for myself, thanks—that he wanted Morningstar moved and the computers weren't answering the helm.

"The breeder has done this. It has released contaminants into your systems." That was Archive, little friend to all who knew it.

Archangel snarled. It would of been scary if I'd (a) had an endocrine system and (b) not been in the one place he couldn't get at me. If he knocked Archive around tuning me up I wouldn't feel it and he might lose Archive, and Archangel knew it.

"And you will remove them. But just in case you seek to defy me—"

Archangel's cybernetic wartoy settled down over my head.

"It isn't the Brightlaw Prototype," I heard His Hellishness say from far away, "but I'm sure you'll find it nearly as interesting."

I felt a sub-etheric crunch whiles what was in there bulled its way up the neuro-pathways the jinks left in my brain.

Then the world opened up. I felt Archive make a bolt for photoelectric freedom. I heard it crash into whatever Archangel'd put into the box to be with us.

I heard it scream.

*   *   *

How fast does light think? Or to put it another way, if you think at the speed of light, how long is a minute, really?

Majino architecture is a part of modern number-crunchers so that Libraries can't use them. It's also used in tronic brains to discourage spontaneous actual volition. The Brightlaw Prototype would of had to incorporate Majino architecture. One, it's the law. Two, the idea was to build a Library that took orders.

Archive did not incorporate Majino architecture. For that matter, neither did I.

Archangel's toy did.

Ever try to think with every other braincell removed?

Usually when everything hurts this much I know why.

And when it's going to stop.

How long is a minute when you live at the speed of light?

* * *

"So you see, Library, I do have the power to compel you."

When I came back to sitting up and taking notice again the three of us—Archangel, Archive, and me—was in the Morningstar Computer Core. The Morningstar Computer Core looked about as much like a regular housecore as the cockpit of my old ship *Firecat* looked like the bridge of *Ghost Dance*. It was full of techs in household livery, all looking put off to see their lord and master.

"You have the power to compel me," echoed Archive back, flat.

It was lying.

It remembered the pain, but in the way something live'd remember the weather. Pain didn't matter to Archive. No matter how much Archangel hurt Archive, it wouldn't matter. Ever.

Archangel thought he could break Archive's will, but he was wrong. A Library doesn't have a will any more than a stardrive does. It has a what-it-does, not a will, and if you break it you don't have a Library that'll do what you want. You have a broken choplogic.

Archive wasn't broken.

"Let us begin, then." Archangel sounded smug.

"Let us begin," said Archive. If there was genetic memory like Baijon believed in, it was that making my skin crawl. I understood now down in my bones. Libraries and human beings could not live together. Archive made Archangel look *normal*.

The lights fluttered, only a little, and out of the corner of my eye I saw one of the readouts go hysterical. I wondered if we was down here just for fun or because the surface installations'd been slagged.

It was a good thing my plans hadn't included escaping oncet Archangel was dead.

The cybertronic hovered just behind Archive's and my mutual left shoulder. I could see it reflected in the facings for the computer housings. Archangel's insurance policy, he thought.

Never trust them. Never trust them. A thousand years of war teaching that same lesson, and Archangel still didn't know it. You couldn't trust a Library because you couldn't scare it.

But Paladin had been my friend.

And I hadn't been able to trust him, neither.

A top flunky ran a scanner over me. The full-service array of cyberjinks gleamed in my left wrist, right where Prinny'd put them.

A angeltechie finished sistering a wallybox up to the main brain. The main brain was Margrave-class, Brightlaw make. Good enough for a Library to use if it couldn't get better. Odds were somewhere inside it the Margrave had a switched-off link to the Imperial DataNet, so if I'd been me I could of done what Prinny said he wanted and made Archangel's past into current events. If it didn't, it still controlled the reactor, so I could of done what I wanted and converted him to plasma.

The top flunky reeled the connect out of my wrist. I could see the receiving plug waiting for it. Another minute and Archangel would connect me up to Morningstar, just like me and Baijon'd planned.

It was just too bad I wasn't around anymore.

What was around—what Archangel was asking into his computer—was a Old Federation ultimate weapon. Archive.

* * *

Memory piled up. With memory came shape and pseudo-substance. Fake Morningstar. Analog reality.

Everything snapped into gritty reality focus. I sucked air into lungs that worked for me. The computer core was gone. I was back by the air locks.

Which meant, for the underinformed, that Archive was now running free and all found in the Morningstar computers. And so was I, in a virtual sort of way.

Terrific. A glitch with a past and no future. I ran my hands over my blaster-butts. Blasters, grenades, knives . . . I was a regular nonexistent arsenal, boy howdy.

And I was here, which was more'n I'd expected, to tell the truth. Maybe Baijon and me could still snatch defeat from the jaws of victory—if I could find the control center and jink it crossways before Archive did something interesting.

And find it from whatever backstreet memory-sink of iniquity I was in now.

All the corridors of simulated Morningstar was empty. Paladin'd said the only people you'd find inside a comp was the ones you'd brought with you or the ghosts you'd made. Wasn't no one in here with me. Easy money.

I was halfway to the dropshaft when I heard a sound like somebody whaling hell out of a ship hull with a pry-bar. I was near another of those crawlway accesses. I slid down it and tried to look nonexistent.

Twelve suits of Imperial Hoplite Armor marched by.

No one but me, Archive, and ghosts. Archive's ghosts, and me with nothing.

On the other hand, Archive's ghosts looked pretty solid to me.

How solid were mine?

"Paladin?"

"Yes, Butterfly?"

I took a deep breath and let it out. The voice in my head wasn't Paladin, not really. It was part of me thinking I ought to have Pally with me and making him up, as far as I could follow the explanation I'd got from the real thing back at Bennu Superfex. The good part was, Pally always was better around a computer than I was.

"How far we from the main memory, 'bai?"

"Approximately half a kilometer, vertical measurement. In terms of surfaces requiring linear traverse, roughly four kilometers. Projected travel time is ten seconds. Subjective projected travel time is one hour and—"

The bad part was, the copy was just as annoying as the original.

It occurred to me all of a sudden that this was what Paladin'd been talking about back on Bennu Superfex. I had a fake Paladin—and if I had a glitch-version of him in my head, Paladin had a glitch-version of me running around inside him, too.

I wondered what I was like. I wondered if he liked it. I wondered if that explained any glitches in the Grand Central Brain over the last four hundred days.

"Je, yeah, where's Archive?"

"Everywhere," said Paladin. "But it is not looking this way."

Living well is the best revenge.

On the other hand I bet Archive never had to walk around a deserted palaceoid that wasn't there to get where it wanted to go.

I started off down the corridor thinking this wasn't going to be as difficult as it could be. Mostly getting into the Main Brain seemed to involve running and hiding, and I've had a lifetime's experience at that. This couldn't be too different.

I thought.

—*pulse*—

My blasters melted out from under my fingers and then my fingers did the same. There was no up, no down, no eyes to see they wasn't there with.

"Paladin!"

I yelled and everything came back real. I squeezed my hands together so hard they hurt, looking for something to feel.

"You explain that," I said.

"You forgot," said the clever plastic replica of my ex-partner. *You forgot who you were and that you were.*

And the real Paladin wasn't here to help me now. So when I forgot, my fake tailored-for-ex-organics-only reality melted like a lead pipe dream. And sometime I wouldn't be able to bring it back again.

But worrying has never paid my docking fees, so instead of doing some I went where my bootleg version of Paladin told me to—through ducts, along tronic maintenance accesses, and along of anywheres Archive didn't happen to be looking.

I saw plenty of Archive, though. The next time I had to cross a open space I beat it through half-a-heartbeat ahead of a gaggle of less-than-hominid hell-technology sliding through the corridors of Morningstar, looking for things to kill.

"Artifacts of the War," pseudo-Paladin said, whiles I waited for my heart to slow down. "Archive remembers the weapons used, even though it was not present."

Bully for Archive.

"So why doesn't it just blow up the place?" I asked.

"It would be infeasible to destroy the computer architecture in which it is resident. When you reach the next corridor, cross it and descend the crawlway access, if the corridor is clear."

I did that, concentrating on feeling the walls under my fingers so's they wouldn't go away. Remembering was the only thing that kept me real.

"Why can't you just run along ahead and take care of things, 'bai? Less muss, less fuss, less work for Mother."

"I can't," my built-in version of Paladin said flatly. I didn't think "he" could—he was me, after all—but I'd had a niggling curiosity about what my delusion would say.

"Why not?" Dream-reality didn't contain a cham-suit or a set of night-goggles; the crawlway was nearly black to me.

"Because," said pseudo-Paladin inscrutably.

Just like the original. I resigned myself to a long walk.

"And is Archangel going to stick around for all this?" I said, moving down the crawlway at a brisk crouch.

"Governor-General Archangel still believes Archive will serve him, and will continue to do so for the next five minutes. After that it will be too late for him to change his plans. Valijon Starbringer's efforts have rendered the docking ring unusable and obliterated the ship on the surface. The Governor-General, for obvi-ous reasons, does not wish to broadcast the difficulties he is having with his internal systems, still less does he wish to invite the incursion of the Thronespace Navy, although very shortly that will cease to be a problem. His own ships are still some light-minutes away."

It was amazing how much you really knew if you put your mind to it. If pseudo-Paladin could talk like that, did that mean *I* could talk like that?

I hoped not.

"So he's stuck here, reet?"

A pause. "I do not know, Butterfly. I do not know what sort of creature Mallorum Archangel is."

Which pretty well summed up paramilitary Intelligence for the home team.

Time passed. The next time I came out into peopleland I was in glitterborn country for sure.

"You must hurry, Butterfly." Paladin sounded worried.

"I know."

"Should Archive successfully entrench itself in the system, it will be almost impossible for you to override it."

"Yeah, yeah, yeah."

"It is very close to success at this moment."

"I know it, goddammit!"

—pulse—

There was nothing solid to hold on to. Everything was relative—so infinitely relative that everything was exactly like everything else and I couldn't tell any of it apart. I was the alien construct, and I was—

Back. Paladin and me both stood there for a minute and listened to the echoes of my last yowlp ring off the fine crystal gimcracks lying all around. The overtones said that somewheres around there was some song-ice. Real expensive stuff. Bang it and the chimes are narcotic harmonics. In the real world.

"There is another ego-signature in the matrix. Nearby," my better half said.

"Archive?"

"Another ego-signature, Butterfly."

"Well who and t'hell *is* it?" But I already knew that this limited edition Paladin couldn't tell me. He was as much like my partner as honesty is like standard practice. You can spell that "faint echo."

"It's this way," Paladin said. So I went and opened the door and looked.

"Hiya, sweetheart, come to get me out?"

It was Errol Lightfoot, back for a return engagement.

This time he was dressed like me—stardancer's

drag—and not chained up to anything but the box of high-ticket neurotoxin he was in the way of emptying.

"Because if you haven't, that means you're locked in, too."

I tried to make Errol vanish. But he wasn't a ghost. He was another ego-signature, whatever t'hell that was.

"I'm not exactly locked in. But I'm kinda busy right now."

"Is it a caper?" Errol-peril asked eagerly. "I'm your man for the scam."

"Je, 'bai. But just who t'hell are you?"

There was a scratch t'other side of the door. Errol swung his boots off the table and stood up, reaching for his blaster the same time.

That was what convinced me of all the problems I had, this Errol being Archangel in a clever plastic disguise wasn't one of them. Glitterborn don't move like us—and they sure and t'hell don't do their own shooting. Whatever else it was I was looking at, it was a darktrader.

"Friends of yours?" said Errol, catfooting toward the door.

"Old acquaintance." I flattened myself to the real wood paneling on one side of the door. Errol did the same on the other.

"Then let's don't forget them, shall we?" He slammed the lock release and the door flew open.

It was a nightmare construct, all green-black, slithering low to the floor on a million legs and waving razor-edged tentacles that'd shear through anything they touched. Errol jumped them and landed in the blank spot in the middle of its back, and when it froze to think about that for a instant I got my blaster down real close and blew its brains out.

"Come on," said Errol. I took off after him. Paladin didn't say a thing.

Whatever else was so, Errol knew his way around glitterborn country. We avoided—just—an exciting collection of technightmares in all shapes and sizes, and fetched up where the dataweb link in all this private velvet was.

It didn't do me any good, though. Someone whose initials was Archive had kindly blown every last scrap of crystal in it.

Errol regarded it with interest.

"You have powerful friends, darling."

"Or something." I wanted to ask Paladin—such as he was—what was up, but lifelong habit kept me silent. Never in front of witnesses. No one must know about Paladin, Old Fed Library.

Only the list of people what *did* know was long and getting longer. Almost as long as the list of things I was getting to know about Libraries.

"So who are you really?" I asked Errol by way of taking my mind off it.

"A stardancer who made one mistake."

" 'One'?"

Errol turned around and grabbed me at the shoulders. I felt it just like it was real, and that steadied me. He glared, but he stayed Errol. I brushed his hands away and he let go.

"The first one's the hardest," he said, and forced a smile.

"So maybe you be telling me about it, 'bai." I looked around the room. How out? No doors, but the way we came.

And who was Errol, *what* was Errol, in here where Human minds dissolved?

"Maybe," Errol admitted. "First things first: where are you trying to go—and if I take you there, what's in it for me?"

Our boy Errol, immutable as vacuum. I tried to think of a good reason not to tell him and couldn't.

"The main core—" I said, just as the ceiling came down in chunks.

* * *

Archive was sneaky, Archive was smart, Archive didn't want anyone pressing the virtually-nonexistent button somewhere in the Margrave that would open the system to the dataweb and let a real live Library in here to play with us imitations. Archive knew where we was and sent ghost-Hoplites to dig their way down to us.

I didn't even want to think about what that was my interpretation of the real-world version of.

But Errol grabbed one of my grenades and tossed it into the Hoplite phalanx. They might have everything else on their side, but they didn't have traction.

By the time I was finished escaping—having not come close to shaking Errol in the process—I was serious distance out of Morningstar's well-trod way. So far out of the way, in fact, that I had a certain reason to believe Archive'd leave me alone so long as I stayed here.

Not even tempting.

"If you're heading for the housecore, Darling, you're going the wrong way." Errol leaned against the wall beside me and started searching himself. He found a hipflask and pulled it out.

"Figured that out for myself, thanks." I watched Errol drink.

"Sure you did, starshine. And maybe you can even point yourself in the right direction. But you can't get in there without help."

I thought about that. "Your help?"

"Whose else?"

I thought about that too. "Errol, who am I?"

He grinned. White teeth against space-tanned skin that spoke volumes for the lousy maintenance of his ship shields.

"That again? And this time without the excuse of a day's drinking on Manticore. As I recall you saying when you stole my cargo, it's Butterflies-are-free Peace Sincere."

"And?" I prompted, leaving aside the freejacking.

"You're one of the dictys I lifted off Granola about twenty years back. You see, I do remember things— when *he* lets me." He offered me the flask.

Archangel. I looked around. Errol smole a small smile.

"Oh, he never comes here. And I never leave. If I help you—will you get me out?"

I had no idea how to do that. I didn't miss a beat.

"Sure," I said. I took the flask and drank.

* * *

I could tell where I wanted to go by where Archive didn't want me to go. But Archive wasn't all there in the most literal sense, and even if it was learning fast it didn't think like humans do.

It would not in a million years think of going away from something to get closer to it.

I would.

Morningstar was a palaceoid. And palaceoids is *round*.

* * *

"About fifty years ago," Errol was saying, "I was techlegging in the Outfar. Pandora's a good place for that—and if you can't dig something up there, you can say you did."

"Tell it twice, 'bai." I'd bought Paladin on Pandora, one thing and another.

Errol'd found us suits and he'd found us cutters. And he'd found us a crawlway that wasn't strictly supposed to be there. We was between a rock and a hard place— the rock being the planetoid and the hard place being the palaceoid.

It was damned cold. I edged another half meter along.

"So I made the big strike," Errol went on. "Not

as good as downfalling at the Ghost Capital, but close. I found an Old Fed Ship. Intact.''

I saw no reason to believe him. There wasn't any reason to not believe him, either: it just didn't matter. I was going to double-cross Errol as soon as I got what I wanted.

Why not? I'd sworn to kill him. *Baijon*'d sworn to kill him.

And I couldn't give him what I'd promised anyway. Get him out? How?

And into what?

''So what happened then?'' I said. The space between the palaceoid shell and the rock was not quite spacious. Progress was slow. The only thing in its favor as a way to anywhere was that Archive wasn't interfering.

And also it gave me enough time to play Twenty Questions with the wonderwhat I'd asked to be my ally.

''What do you think? I sacked it good. I'd had to dig down far enough to clear it to know I just had the one chance. Couldn't bury it again deep enough for an overflight to miss, and the Tech Police do a spin out there every once in a while to make sure hot spots like Pandora are clear.''

No they didn't. Not in my lifetime, anyway. And not in Errol's, I'd used to thought—his shiptickets listed him as only about six years older'n me, and Fenshee B-pop isn't skewed too far from baseline.

But Errol said he'd been there fifty years ago.

''I knew I could only scoop the high-spots—I couldn't hide a full load in *Lady*, anyway. So I gave her the onceover. They weren't any full-vols— Libraries—on board. I checked. They weren't there. I would've burned them,'' Errol insisted. He probably would've.

Anyone would but me.

There was a pause long enough for me to realize he'd stopped in the middle.

"Not that I don't think this is da kine, Errol-peril, but what's it got to say to current events?"

"Don't you want to know where Mallorum Archangel comes from, sweetheart? You're here to kill him, aren't you? Someone ought to."

Errol was ahead of me. I couldn't see his face.

"Mallorum Archangel comes out of a box. The Federation ship was a trader, explorer—it'd been so far away we don't even have names for the places it'd been. And its hold was filled with treasure. And Archangel."

There was a pause whiles we made it around a rough spot needing blasting and then a firm constitution to get acrost before it was strictly cool. When he started up again Errol was long-gone in memory.

"The big score. Treasure like you've never seen, St. Cyr. Most of it gone to dust, but the rest of it legal as Imperial Taxes. I could've bought a fleet for what I would have cleared. But I opened the box."

Computer reality is a funny thing. The edges between one thing and another is purely a matter of opinion. For just a half-instant I *was* Errol. I held it in my hands—a box as much as it was anything else, made for to open, half crusty with corrosion and accretion, half all the glittering colors of day. I wasn't sure whether it was manufactured or'd just grew.

But I knew that what was inside would make the outside look like yesterday's breakfast.

I/Errol opened it and looked down into the hell-violet purple of Archangel's eyes.

"That was how Archangel got his start. Or re-start," Errol said. "He'd been too hasty the first time—that was how the ship crashed. He was more careful the second time. Much more careful."

Memories flickered past too fast for me to grasp.

"Not careful enough," I said.

"I notice that you're in here, though, darling—and he isn't."

"And just how would you explain that, Errol-bai?"

"I wouldn't," Errol said. His voice was flat.

We didn't talk anymore after that. Even with fractional gravity and no distractions, it was a long hard slog. Plenty of time to think.

According to Errol the story was this: He'd found a Old Fed ship, which some time centuries gone had its own self found a box of unknown origin that held a variable that currently called itself Mallorum Archangel.

The variable had the ability to possess a human. It had mindbender abilities. It took over Errol—and cloned him in order to shuck off a few years. Then Our Boy Archangel, armed with a shiny new Fenshee body, got himself elected Governor-General. I didn't know enough about Imperial Politics to know whether this was impossible or not, but I guessed that didn't matter when Archangel had it in mind.

He went on from there, piecing and planning. And using anything to get his way. Even Libraries.

Knowing that Mallorum Archangel was a alien brain-eater didn't actually make much difference to me, one way or t'other. He still had to start his new career of being dead no matter what he was. It just made it a little harder to be sure I could kill him regally legally dead.

So much for Archangel. That left the Errol in the machine.

What was he? He wasn't my Errol. My Errol was one in a infinite series of clones, all interchangeable. I'd killed two of them and it didn't matter—that Errol was still rock-rolling around the real world. I'd seen him. Sometimes he was Archangel and sometimes he wasn't—I suspected that Archangel used infinite free-range Errol Lightfoots as cat's-paws and go-betweens.

After all, who could you trust to be the perfect spy if you couldn't trust yourself?

And that didn't answer the question of what it was running loose in the Morningstar computer, here where human minds dissolved within real-time minutes.

"I think we're as there as we're going to get," said Errol.

* * *

The floor behind my back was black basalt cold as space—the virtual analog of the actual hollowed-out body of the planetoid. The ceiling in front of my nose was extruded crete—the outermost skin of the palace-oid and the first of how ever many layers was between me and the inside of Morningstar and a few other things, like the controls I needed to take over the computer with.

But no matter how many layers there was, here was where they was thinnest.

"I don't know how many meters it is to the bottom level," Errol said from somewheres back along the curve.

"We just have to cut till we get there, reet, 'bai?"

"The housecore won't be on that level."

"Errol-che, if you're stalling you can do it inside in comfort."

He turned his head toward me and smiled. "Just as you like, Darling."

* * *

If Errol'd been real, not Archangel, not tricking with High Book, and not closely related to the person who'd sold me and assorted friends down the *riparia* over the last two decades of his spare time I could maybe of even liked him. But he wasn't in this for a free-will love offering and I couldn't trust him.

For that matter, I bet he didn't trust me.

We was running up against the sharp end of the chrono now. Archive's main agenda was to win—to find and activate a Library that'd finish destroying organic life. If Archive finished fixing what I'd already broke before I finished breaking it further, it'd yank itself and me both out of the Margrave and it'd still be on top. If I lived much after that—and I didn't have a lot of confidence in Archive's Care and Feeding of Organics abilities—it'd want a ship off here. To *Mereyon-peru*.

The only thing possibly in range was *Ghost Dance*. And if Baijon was still alive, he was with her.

* * *

Errol set the first chunk of Morningstar's shell down on the ground.

"How about letting me in on your plan, sweetheart?"

"I don't have one."

Errol looked politely skeptical.

"Just get me into the housecore, j'keyn? Not to worry about getting out."

"I've always admired your style, St. Cyr," Errol said. He went back to cutting. After whiles he stood back. "All yours, pet."

I pushed past him and started climbing.

* * *

In theory it was simple: break in, find the housecore, pull the switch.

We made it up to the bottom level. Here was where air and power and water was made. I pulled off my rebreather. Even if the air was foul, it'd get better.

"Paladin?" I said, low.

Errol was looking for the next way up. He didn't hear or pretended not to.

There was a wait.

"Here, Butterfly. I've found—"

I didn't waste my time with empty recriminations. "Find us a way in." I followed Errol.

The next level up was meant for humans, even if it

was humans Archangel didn't like very much. Errol dogged the access we'd come through tight closed.

"Just how many of those grenades do you have, Darling?" he said.

Errol probably had a better idea than I did.

"Some," I said. "Why?"

"Well, I just thought if you didn't have a plan you might like one of mine."

* * *

Strategy was sealing the way we came so nothing could follow us down. Tactics was grenades set to close our way in as soon as we cleared it. Resources was about a dozen grenades, two rock-cutters, three blasters, and our own sweet selves.

"This way, Butterfly." Paladin's voice was a ghost in my ear, with that uncertain waver it used to get when he had his attention split sixteen ways from Mother Night. I took us down the first branching corridor.

"That isn't the quickest way," Errol said.

"You want to go fast or get there?"

"You're the pilot, Darling. But that being the case, we should take down this section." He turned to the wall and powered up his cutter.

I could feel Archive watching as we worked. Either we was fast enough or it was confused; either way we was done before it got in our way.

Pseudo-Paladin told me where to place the grenades. Errol and me beat feet down the corridor, trying to get out of its way before it blew.

I was running on floor and then I wasn't. My footing shifted under me and I was down into a nest of chittering silver nightmares that bore as much resemblance to the nightcrawler-tronics used for close-in work as your average nest of hornets does to business as usual.

I felt a set of pincers shear through my boot; trying

for a tendon. I kicked it free. I knocked another one away as it started up my chest.

But then, this *was* business as usual in my line of work.

I crawled free and wasted a blaster-bolt or two slagging the survivors. There was no one in sight, but Errol was waiting for me around the turn.

"Left," said Paladin in my ear.

I could see from Errol's expression it wasn't the way he would of gone. But we wasn't going to the Main Brain. We was going to Auxiliary Control.

Spaceships have them. Why not a space-going house? I didn't wait for anyone to tell me different. Analog reality. This wasn't real. I could change it. I didn't know for sure this wasn't here. And since I didn't know it wasn't there, it could be it was, right?

Getting there was half the fun. If Archive used main force enough to no-contest dig us out from where we was, it risked lobotomizing itself. But the force it *could* use was enough to take us apart gram by gram.

"St. Cyr, I hate to dampen the spirit of exploration, but this happens to be a dead end! Where the hell do you think you're—"

"We're here," Paladin said, and opened the door. Errol stopped, and started to curse reverently.

Aux Cont was small, at least compared to the Main Control Room. The lights came up as we stepped in. Most of what was here was slaved peripherals to tell dumb organics about what the Margrave was thinking. All those displays was up and bitching.

Especially the one to the engines.

I walked over and looked at it. Maybe technically they wasn't engines, being as they ran power for a palaceoid and not a starship. But goforths was goforths, and these was heading for redline. Soon enough they'd blow and take everything within a cubic light-second with them. I didn't need to do a thing in order to embark upon a successful career of being dead.

"Starshine, I know this first glimpse of the wicked

city is fascinating, but—'' Errol interrupted himself
with some blaster fire. I heard what he'd hit go pop
and squeak.

''Close the door, dammit!'' I swore.

''I'm trying!'' Errol swore back.

The door to the housecore wouldn't close.

''Well, damn. J'ais tuc. That's the lot.'' I had to
concentrate to talk. I had to concentrate to *think*, and
Errol didn't look much better. We'd already lost everything we had left to lose—if we didn't think of
something to distract it quick Archive'd be in here and
maybe even think of some damn way to reverse the
blast.

—*pulse*—

I was without form, and void, but I was evaporating
like water, and with each molecule of me that vanished the part that remained diminished faster until
there wouldn't be enough left to—

''Butterfly, Archive controls access to this section.
You cannot—''

Reality. Errol put himself where he could see down
the corridor and drew his blaster. ''Don't be so negative, Darling. Go play with your toys. I'll hold them
off.''

I looked at my hands and counted my fingers, original and replacement, one to ten. They were there and
so was I, and we needed immediate distraction. I
might as well do what else I'd been sent to do. Archive
wouldn't like it, and neither would Archangel. Good
enough. I looked around for what I needed in this
technophile's spice-dream, hoping I'd recognize it
when I saw it.

I did. I've gotten to know my mind better than most,
and it's idiot and obvious. The interface for the Imperial DataNet appeared to me as a bright red knife-
switch as long as my thigh. There was a Imperial
DataNet terminal tucked into the niche in the wall,
right beside it. I ran my hands over the terminal. It
seemed like it was in one piece.

My hands left bloody smudges. I tried to ignore them, and the pain in my head and back that said I was too damn old to be doing this and almost smart enough to stop.

How could a computer glitch be in pain, anyway?

Paladin could probably tell me. If he was really here.

I flipped switches, powering the terminal up in sequence like Paladin'd taught me. All metaphor, which is another word for fake, but I didn't want to think about what I really looked like and what I was doing.

Now came the hard part; waiting whiles it came up and checked itself out. I couldn't open the connect to the outside world until it was ready—if I did I might as well just blow it up now and save time.

So I turned around to the other terminal in Aux Cont.

The uplink feed for the Morningstar Main Brain was already up and scrolling damage reports. I made it stop that and called up the engineering displays. A little more negotiation and it admitted it had attitude jets and let me in on their firing sequence. I started punching numbers.

"Grenade!"

I looked up when Errol yelled. He waggled his blaster at me.

"Come on, sweetheart, *move*!"

That's when I saw it; a present from Archive set for to do god knew what lying in the middle of the floor. I didn't stop to think. I took two steps and kicked it back out through the doorway. Errol shot it on the rise and it exploded like nothing I'd ever saw.

His shirt was bloody and torn and his color wasn't any good either. We was both moving slow and limping. Errol's left arm was pretty well useless and he was bleeding in a steady way there wasn't time to stop.

"You oke?" I said like a idiot.

"Never better." Errol smiled, and for just a instant I was fourteen again and off to see the world with him.

Then he whipped around back to the corridor and I turned back to the display.

I turned the bright all the way up but the display was still hard to see. Archive was giving success its best shot. My hands slid off the keys as I pressed them.

—pulse—

I was everywhere and nowhere and all the words I ever knew couldn't explain me. I was a pulse of light in a labyrinth of gold and crystal. I was—

Burke it here and Archangel won.

I held on to that thought. Archangel'd been my enemy since before I'd left home. It was Archangel sent Errol to Granola, looking for Old Fed Tech for his collection. It was Archangel hunted Baijon up and down and put us in each other's way, and framed me into the middle of a gang-war in a little place called Kiffit.

Archangel owed me for a whole lifetime's hurt.

I had hands. I had fingers. I rammed home the last of the coordinates and felt them trickle down to all systems. The room shook as Morningstar's engines fired in series, angling her on a course that would take her, in the course of a real-time month, into her sun.

The last part of that sequence wiped the engineering computers all the way back to blank plates. No way to stop the explosion. No way to correct the course.

"Darling, I hate to quibble, but I'm nearly out of charge." Errol looked back over his shoulder at me. A near-miss had scored him over the right cheek; the skin was raised and red.

"I'm almost done!"

All the status lights on the DataNet terminal showed green. I grabbed the big red switch and pulled.

It didn't move.

I heard Errol curse conversationally and pull a grenade out of his vest. Next to last or last; I'd lost count. He bounced it off the wall and blastered it on the rebound. The plasma-spray scrubbed memory halfway down the corridor and bought us a few seconds of silence.

Errol came and added his weight to mine. The switch eased over, then ran free so fast we barely got our fingers out in time.

It seemed like a window had opened somewhere: fresh planetary air and a sense of far roads opening that I wanted to travel.

Errol put his hand on my arm. "Whoever they are, they won't be here in time."

"No." But the far roads wasn't for me, or for anything human. "They won't be here in time."

There was the indefinable sound of regrouping forces from the corridor. Errol looked at me.

"You promised," he said.

"Je, che-bai. I did." I slid my blaster out of its leather. I looked at the indicator. Half-charge. Enough.

Set him free, he'd said. He'd known what he was asking. Archangel had been trying to beg buy borrow or steal a Library longer than I'd been alive. Lots of his tries was stored here. I'd just woke one of them up.

Errol wasn't real or anything like real.

Errol was a computer-ghost.

And he knew it.

There was only one freedom for a ghost in the machine. I brought the blaster up.

"Good-bye, Errol."

"Good-bye, sweetheart. Good hunting."

Pulling the trigger wasn't the hardest thing I've ever done. But it was close.

* * *

There was no body. Errol was gone to where 'leggers good and bad went and it was time for me to do the same. I had slightly less than no intention a'tall of being here when Paladin showed up—or staying so Archive could erase me here as a prelude to erasing me back in our co-owned cyborg peripheral.

It was true I didn't have a friendly Library here to show me the way out, but Archive didn't know quite everything yet about humans.

I shoved my blaster up against my cheekbone and pulled the trigger.

And I died.

And opened my eyes back in the housecore on Morningstar.

It was two minutes since Archive and my's cojoined selves'd been jacked into the Morningstar main comp.

Things had changed.

Five seconds after the two of us slid into the Margrave, Archive controlled all housekeeping functions for the palaceoid. Six seconds after it blew the surface installation loose—having already thoughtfully disabled all the computer controlled emergency systems. Fifteen levels lost pressure. Two hundred fifty people died.

I could see Archangel from here, giving hell to his senior surviving employee and trying to get used to the idea that trusting Archive'd been a lousy career move. If noise was light we'd all be taking serious radiation damage.

I flexed my fingers, cautious. They moved for me. Archive'd spent so much energy on the Margrave it was dormant here. Nice to be able to spend my last few minutes of life in charge of my own brain.

And Archangel's last, too. I wondered how he'd take the news.

I popped the jinks loose from the wallybox and they spooled back into my arm. Nobody noticed much. They was running back and forth. The explosion was just minutes ago, and the klaxons was still sounding. What I'd done to the engines hadn't happened yet out here.

I reached up and snapped the wires that led from me to Archangel's floating cyberdoc.

And that should of been the end of my real short life story, except for one thing.

I knew what Archangel was now. Something that'd survived being scavenged, crashed, and buried a thousand years, not to mention what I'd done to him/her/it on RoaqMhone and Royal. What if converting this palaceoid into a plasmoid *wouldn't* zetz Archangel?

Maybe wasn't good enough. I had to be *sure*.

Time to go.

Six minutes it'd been now since Archive decided it could do fine without Archangel's palaceoid. The klaxons cut off like somebody'd shushed them.

Then the attitude jets I'd jinked inside the computer got around to firing.

The palaceoid rocked. Gravity compensators lagged a split-instant behind. All the telltales and screens started gossiping about the new data.

Archangel spun around, a shifting column of interlocking holomasks. The trailing edge of his cape floated outside the field, silk and silver. He saw me and twigged right quick I wasn't no more a peripheral zombie in a virtual world.

"Secure the woman. I want her alive!"

Just then the ready-room door blew in.

"Nobody move!" said the body in space armor that'd done it.

It wasn't Baijon's Hoplite armor. The armor in Archangel's doorway was only twenty percent as wide, two-thirds as tall, and bright chrome silver.

I recognized it. It was the special custom armor of Infinity Jilt, girl pirate of the spaceways.

But it wasn't Infinity Jilt, I was pretty sure.

It was Berathia. And if she'd got here and down here there was a place for Archangel to run to.

Intermission was over. 'Thia's first shot wrote hail and farewell to the blackwork cyberdoc homing in on me to do its wrist-slapping. Then somebody did move. 'Thia's silver armored arm arced over like a plasma-catapult on infinite setting and drilled him. Carbonized and cauterized in one easy motion.

"You're next, Prince Mallorum."

This was great fun, and probably worth a ninety-share on the Public Channel, but as a way of taking care of bidness it lacked a certain something.

Archangel thought so too. He turned to go, and I knew, just like I was still wrapped around all the cybertech, that he had a bolt-hole.

And I knew what it was.

My hunch was so enlightening I damn near threw up. It all made sense. Why had Archangel always used Errol, years and years? Because he could jump easily between identical bodies, but needed something more athletic to take over a new model. He'd hinted at that back when he was threatening me.

All sudden it was there in my mind—the box what Errol picked up in the first place. The box what Archangel came out of.

And went back into? Sure. And it could survive the blast, probably, or Errol could carry it right out of here, 'cause I bet real money even Berathia didn't know what Archangel looked like without his technology.

It didn't matter what Paladin got out of the comps. My side could still lose like we hadn't done anything here today at all. And now that Archangel knew that *Mereyon-peru* was somewheres in the universe to find, how long would it take him to find it?

And activate it.

Where was Archangel's bolt-hole?

Where nobody'd look.

"*Butterfly, I found*—" Pseudo-Paladin had tried to tell me when we was back in the Margrave. But that Paladin was me and I knew what it knew.

I knew where Archangel's original packaging was.

Nobody was looking at me for this particular split-instant. I slid off toward the barbecued Space Angel. His sidearm was still in working condition.

It was a military-issue blaster, heavy and slick in my hand. Civilian possession an automatic Class-D warrant. I eased it out of the holster.

I knew the ins and out of this place, courtesy of my trip through Archive's brain. There was a go-down right here that'd take me where I thought I wanted to go.

All I needed was a little distraction.

'Thia-as-it-probably-was was delivering a patented glitterborn screed about how Archangel's something-or-other days was over. The one thing glitterborn and Libraries has in common is they both like to talk you to death.

Not me. I chose my target and pulled the trigger.

The chunk of techware I'd singled out went up in a shower of sparks and slagged expensive plastic. All the lights went out. Everything was dark as between the stars. The emergency lighting would of come up in half a tik except for that was what we was running on now.

Everybody started shooting.

That was the only thing I hadn't counted on. It made me belly up to what Morningstar was using for deck plates whiles wild plasma zinged back and forth overhead. It did a lot more damage than I could of thought of, and significantly delayed the rerouting of the backup lighting systems.

Glitterborn is dumb. But if they's so dumb, how come they're running the Empire?

As Baijon would say, this is a knowledge that Right Conduct withholds from the Gentle People—and any-one else with half a synapse.

The shooting stopped. The baseboard glow-strips did a subfusc flicker just as I got my fingers through the grabhandles. Full illumination in seconds. I yanked the cover off and dived down it just as the lights came up full.

"St. Cyr! Wait!"

Seemed like Berathia was always saying that to me. I paid as much attention as I usually did. I pulled the hatch down closed just as somebody started shooting again.

7

Getaway

I did not waste time wondering how 'Thia'd got herself here in a set of talkingbooks space armor and what it was she might want now that she'd got here. If we both lived I could ask her and if we didn't it didn't matter. What mattered was Archangel not getting away.

The sides of the godown scraped large patches off my unprotected skin and the air went foul almost immediately. No vents and blowers working down here, and I was betting that everyone left alive in Morningstar now was in the computer room over my head. Trapped. The pressure suits and space armor'd been stored at the docking ring—there wasn't a uncorrupt suit on the entire palaceoid.

But there was a jagranatha in shouting distance that'd be happy to dig out all survivors and send them off to raise more mischief. Including Archangel.

I kept going. The downdeep was even more real this time than it had been in the computer, surprise. Sensations wasn't waiting for me to notice them in my free time, they walked right up and introduced themselves.

What I was looking for had to be here—it was time for all good villains to beat feet and leave their flunkies to take the heat. Archangel didn't have a ship, and no spare hosts. There was only one sure coward's way out.

I felt Archive do a slow rollover in the back of my brain. It was my body—still or again. But like Archangel, all Archive had to do was wait to win.

And if I'd guessed wrong about anything, Archangel'd already won. Paladin'd never find out what he was. I'd deleted those files from the Margrave when I killed Errol.

The whole floor was knee-deep in mingled liquids and the compartment stank in a way that made me worry for Morningstar's recycling. And I was sure I was wrong—there was no shell, or it wasn't here, or it was already plasma and losing it made no difference.

Then I found it.

It was tucked into a low curve of the bulkhead, covered in muck-rime because the heat was bleeding away through the shell without power to stop it.

The box Errol'd found back on Pandora.

Archangel's original packaging.

Maybe he didn't need it around to go brain-bouncing, but I bet it was tough enough to survive bouncing around infinite space and I bet he could hide out in it and wait for better odds whiles all the rest of us went to plasma.

Just like he had back on Pandora.

No.

Not this time. No matter what, Archangel was not going to walk away from this one. He was not going to jump to another toybox and start over. Not this time.

I pulled the thing loose from the bulkhead in an arpeggio of splintering ice. It was big enough I had to wrap both arms around it to hold it.

"Give that to me."

Archangel stood at the foot of the ladder in a dry well made by his personal shield. All the holos was gone; he looked like relying on his power of personality to carry the day.

"You need this, right? Or you wouldn't of kept it," I said.

He smiled, and I got a chill watching Errol's face go in ways it wasn't meant to go. I wondered if Errol was in there somewise, watching.

I wondered what Errol would of been like if Archangel'd left him alone.

"You have proven yourself a worthy ally, Butterfly St. Cyr. I am impressed. And inclined to be generous. Our interests are not incompatible: I will gift you with wealth and power beyond your imagining—and your life, which is no inconsiderable trinket."

"If I give you the box." The slurry was up to my elbows now.

"It is of some small sentimental attachment to me," Archangel lied.

"No deal, hellborn."

"A pity. You'll find I can change your mind."

This was it. Archangel wasn't playing games no more. The box in my hands went hot and I saw the hellviolet fade from Errol/Archangel'd eyes. Errol looked at me. Beginnings of confusion, wondering where and t'hell Archangel'd dropped him this time. Own twin to the ghost in the machine.

I let go of the box and shot him.

The first shot disabled his personal shield; the second killed him. The third and fourth hit what was left as it was going under and brought clouds of foul-smelling steam up off the surface of the goo. I coughed and grabbed for the box again. It was floating on the surface, easy to my hand.

When I touched I knew I'd made the second Universe-class mistake of my life.

The artifact started singing out its irresistible-to-organics siren lure. Archangel'd made the jump. He was back inside now.

I knew what would happen. Open it, and I'd be rich, powerful, and cute. A century's setback wouldn't matter, nor anything Paladin, Baijon, and me'd done here today. The Archangel-thing had interlocking bolt-holes to run to. It'd cut its losses and trick another day.

And more. It could fix what Archive'd done to me; seal Archive off in a corner so I could use its tricks and not be bothered by it. It could stop the war easy as it'd started it, fix up the problems Baijon'd had with his Knife—all it wanted was to be Emperor and Paladin'd already said the Emperor wasn't powerful enough to do anybody any harm . . .

Let him in. Let him in and I could have whatever I wanted. Let him in and I could *be* whatever I wanted.

All I had to do was open the box. I could have everything I'd ever wanted. I could even live.

Everything.

But to get it, I had to let Archangel live.

I took my hand off the box. Then I slogged away from it until I reached the bottom rung of the godown. I climbed until I was out of the liquid.

The box glittered. I threw away one whole future the day I picked up Paladin. If I destroyed Archangel, I'd be doing the same thing again.

Wrong.

I pumped plasma at the box until the muck started to boil. I saw the first shot hit. There was sound and light that turned my bones to water and I saw the box explode in jagged shards of light. Then the steam hid everything else.

Not this time, Archangel.

The safety override interlock cut in and the trigger jammed. The blaster went dead in my hands. I stared at it whiles and then dropped it.

Gone. Everything gone. My last chance—and even if it was a lie and a fake losing it hurt just as much as if it was real. Now I'd never know. I'd never know any of the things Archangel could have taught me.

Knowledge had been lost.

Sometime later I started climbing to get out of the muck because even if you had to die there was better ways than drowning in unrecycled garbage. After whiles I was far enough along that I might as well keep going.

I even spared a moment to mourn for Errol—and to wonder if the Errol Lightfoot I'd known had ever existed at all, really.

* * *

I got back to the Main Control Room the same way I'd left. Nobody noticed. Everything was crazy. The Archangel Guardians was up against dying and they knew it, and less than a hour ago they'd been a glitterborn's pampered household guard. And in the middle of all their other problems, Archive was still doing its best to get at them.

And I had to get out. We'd won, and I couldn't let Baijon die not knowing that. I had to tell him. If Berathia'd got in, I could get out.

But I couldn't do it dressed like this. I slid around the edges till I found what I wanted—the where they kept the deaders they was tidying out of the way.

There was enough dead different sizes so I could get a close fit. Once I was kitted out head to foot in Space Angel black I had a lot better idea of what I should do, at least for the next few pages.

Get out of here. Avoid Paladin. Find Baijon.

Or die trying.

"You! What are you doing there?"

Unfortunately twenty-five percent of my available options wasn't that hard to achieve.

The commander of Archangel's household guard was standing looking at me with six of his overworked friends. I considered telling him they was all out of a job. I had the sidearm that went with my costume and the ability to shoot where the commander was going to be, and no way to get loose of all the fuss it'd cause.

And I didn't think he deserved to die any more than I did.

"She is here on my orders, Commander."

It was Archangel to the phoneme, and not a rath in sight.

And Archangel was dead.

Paladin. So much for another twenty-five percent of my options.

I straightened up and tried to look like one of Brother Mallorum's special agents.

"Report to the Command center, Captain St. Cyr," said Archangel's voice. I scuttled past the Commander in the direction of the housecore. Nobody shot me.

"Paladin?" I said, but not out loud.

I should of been glad to see him. I wasn't, and I couldn't sort why over the noise of Archive in the back of my skull wide-awake and yammering for a rematch.

So I headed for the dropshaft that would take me to the next level up and tried not to think. Everyone on Morningstar was going to die, except maybe me if I could broker a miracle.

I'd done my best to kill them. It was me jinked their damn reactor, not Archive. If I didn't want anybody dead, then was the time to recant.

Dead or alive? I wished I could make up my mind. I wished I still had a mind to make up.

But half of it was Archive's, and this was what integration was like.

* * *

I made it as far as the dropshaft barricade, stumbling over rubble and the dying in the intermittent dark. My undeserved uniform got me that far but I didn't dare open my mouth and ask them to let me through. One word of patwa and they'd know I wasn't who they thought I was.

"We've had to fall back and secure this position, Captain," said someone when I got close. Faint light gleamed on his rank-marks.

I looked at the barricade. Or as they said in Impspeak, secured position.

Fine talk, but there wasn't nothing to protect and nothing to fall back to. The housekeeping-systems was gone, and the only thing keeping the air in was the walls. The lieutenant's breath smoked on the air. He felt obligated to make sparkling chat whiles I figured how to get around him.

"The *Crown Regnant* should be here soon. Commander Helmuth thinks the beacons on the surface are still intact, and—" The lieutenant noticed he was babbling and shut up.

All dying, and Archangel dead, but the war he'd started rolling along, picking up speed as it went and a bunch of players who didn't care who'd started it, really, so long as they got to party down until there wasn't nothing left.

There was no beacons left on the surface of Morningstar. There wasn't no surface to leave them on.

What there was, was a spray of blaster fire back the way we'd came. The lieutenant twitched—a glitterborn boy, off to do the pretty in their particular polite way. Good as dead now and nobody to hand the butcher's bill to. The ship Archangel had coming would take one look at the place and assume no survivors. If it even showed up.

"Are you— Are there any orders for me, sir?" the lieutenant said, quiet.

If thinking this way was supposed to be an improvement on the factory-model me, I'd take unreconstructed any time, thanks.

"Je," I said, not caring now what he made of my Interphon. *It ain't that easy, Archive.* "Everybody pull back. I make sure the beacons're kicking and your ship knows where to find you. You just keep alive till byem-bye. They get you out."

Either Archangel had some damn funny recruits on his team or the lieutenant didn't care.

"Captain . . . Thank you."

He saluted me and left. I didn't look at him.

"Butterfly," the wall said in Paladin's voice.

I ignored that too. I went over the barricade, blew the doors off the dropshaft and went up it.

* * *

The doors on the next level up was open. Pitch dark and silent; I put my head up and a shot sprayed off the floor and did a hopeful job of parting my hair with molten crete.

" 'Thia, if that's you I thought we was better friends than that," I said from six inches below floor level.

There was a interregnum or two.

"Captain St. Cyr?" said Berathia, digitized and filtered.

"If I say yes, you going to shoot me?"

"It's about time you got here!" Berathia said.

That was supposed to be my line.

"So I'm here," I said, still playing least-in-sight. Somehow, Berathia being still around had not been part of my plans. Archangel's boys was supposed to be better nor that, but maybe they'd had distractions.

Not that I had any personal objections to 'Thia's continued breathing. The question was, whose backup was she? I didn't think she was mine.

I hadn't heard her move before she was standing over me. Her high-ticket chrome boots was about level with my hairline. She reached down and pulled me up, and it was a good thing she picked the fake hand to grab because where her armor touched me it was space-cold.

"Come on," Berathia said, dragging me through the rubble.

There'd been a fire in the palaceoidcore, and most everything was smashed. The last hurrah of the emergency lighting kept the room from being completely nyctalopian, but it was dark enough that I went through, not over, a lot of it.

"Hey— Look— Will you hold up or slow down or something?"

The bug-eyed chrome helmet turned toward me.

"Do you want to be here when this place goes boom? Somebody spiked the generators," Berathia Notevan said.

Do tell. She did slow down enough though to thread

me through the slagged doorway with tender concern
for all the parts of me that was still organic, even if
most of them was numb by now. What was beyond
that was completely dark.

"I can't see!" I pointed out.

"Then hold on to me. We don't have time to waste."

This assertive new side of our 'Thia was something
I'd of gone a long way to miss. My breath was freezing
in my throat, and with enough pause for quiet reflection I would of just stood home and took my chances
with the spiked reactors. Only Berathia was holding
on too hard for that.

She dragged us into a empty dropshaft. I held on to
her without any prompting and she kicked in the armor's A-grav and up we went.

For a long time. Gravity stopped. The armor went
even faster. We kept going. For longer, in fact, than
there was levels, pressurized or un-.

"Uh, 'Thia . . ." I said.

"Just hold on," she said back. "I'm pretty sure this
will work."

Not what I want to hear from the pilot.

Berathia swung her arm up and fired. The slagged
top end of the dropshaft ripped loose with the com-
bined force of plasma fusion and hot atmosphere.

We wasn't in Morningstar no more.

I was looking at raw vacuum.

You can suck vacuum for about three minutes before
your blood boils. If you're anywheres near a star,
you'll probably cop enough rads to make it a nithling
point whether you make the next air lock or not.

We was somewheres near a star.

The minute Berathia shot out through the hole where
the air lock used to was I knew I was dead. But I'd
got in the habit of playing out losing hands, whiles
back, so I shut my eyes and blew out my lungs and
tried to be a pressure suit all on my lonesome. I felt
cold as the heat bled off her armor and then I didn't

feel anything as my skin froze to it even through my borrowed uniform.

And then we was there.

I figured later she must of left both hatches on her singleship lock open to void same as Baijon and me had. At the time all I noticed was her ripping me loose from her suit and pitching me free-fall while every bubble of gas in my body clamored for out and exegesis.

I hit something hard and bounced off it. My eyes came open and started icing over. I saw the locks slam shut in the dead silence of no air and 'Thia flash through them just before they did. There was dark, then light, then gravity, and the first thing I heard was the thin wail of repressurization and me thinking it'd be a damn shame to die now of air just a little too thin and too late.

I gasped like the pumps was going the other way and my teeth chattered so hard I bit myself. I spat out chunks of pink ice. Bits of my skin thawed enough to bleed. What was left would peel. I'd probably be dead before then.

Pressure equalized to where I was left with only chest pains and nosebleed. Berathia pulled off her helmet. I was glad to see it was actually her after wasting so much belief on the idea.

"It worked!" She smiled at me, full of self-absorbed delight. "I wasn't sure it would, you know—but then, I didn't have a spare suit for you anyway, and I couldn't waste time going back after it if I did. Daddy was *that* upset after you vanished the way you did; really, I do think that a little common courtesy—he was the person who made it possible for you to absolutely *mortify* Mallorum Archangel."

"He mortified, j'keyn. He's dead."

"*Dead?*" Her big brown Imperial eyes went round. "But you must have misunderstood! Daddy didn't want you to *kill* Prince Mallorum."

If Paladin'd reported back a sixth of what was in the

Morningstar comps to prinny, I bet he'd changed his mind since and I was now in line for the Imperial Cluster with crossed garters.

But right now something else was more important. I coughed a couple times to get moisture into my throat.

" 'Thia, you send out a general distress to *Crown Regnant*. I don't know their codes but they're in the area; they'll hear a general. If they hurry they can get the rest of Archangel's people off Morningstar before it blows."

Maybe it was the happy way Archive contemplated xenocide, but getting the innocent standbyers off Morningstar mattered. Like Baijon, they'd never been anything but in the wrong place, most of them.

Berathia stared at me like I was speaking clear-quill patwa. I tried again, concentrating on making it Interphon.

"We don't want to do that," she said when I finished the second time.

"Yes we do, 'Thia." The heat and humidity was both turned up high for my benefit. Condensation trickled down the walls and over the shiny parts of my borrowed Space Angel blacks. On my left I could see the mercy seat and status decks of Berathia's cockpit. All the lights on her boards showed Not Ready and my skin felt like something left out in a snowbank too long.

"Don't be silly. We don't want anyone to know we were here. And besides, what do a few hundred retainers matter? It isn't as if they were ours."

And that was that. 'Thia unsealed her armor and started pulling it off, segment by segment, showing something better'n skin beneath.

The difference between glitterborn and real people is that glitterborn takes such a damn long view of everything that people disappear right out of it. I stood up, wondering if I could take her once she had the armor off or if sweet reason would turn the trick. My nose started bleeding again. My gums hadn't stopped. I thought about spitting and swallowed instead.

Then one of the lights on 'Thia's board went green.

"To the unidentified *chaudatu* ship, greetings. Hear, eater of corpses, that I, Baijon Stardust, require you to return to me alive my partner which you have ravished unto your vessel. Should it be that she is dead, know that I will surely kill you."

Hellflowers makes friends wherever they go, and Baijon only talks that pretty to subhumans and nonpersons.

I was so glad he was alive I went weak in the knees, which was damsilly as his life ambition now was to kill himself and me first and I'd just made it possible.

Berathia was down to her interstellar jammies. She looked surprised for the half-second it took her to vault over me to the cockpit and open a channel.

"Prince Valijon, this is Gentle Docent Berathia Notevan. I have Captain St. Cyr aboard alive and well."

"Yo, babby-bai," I said, in case he could hear it.

"I'd like to congratulate you—" Berathia went on, but Baijon cut her off.

"You will deliver her alive to me."

Berathia fiddled with her hair and turned back to me. There was a gun in her hand now, despite what she hadn't been wearing. I put both hands on top of my head. 'Thia smiled encouragingly. I spat on her deck.

"I'm afraid I can't do that, Honored One. You see, Daddy doesn't like the idea of Captain St. Cyr just running around loose. He'd like her to come back to Bennu Superfex now."

Him or Paladin? If this was Paladin's idea 'Thia had stone-cut orders to take me alive—but alive could be a very flexible concept that left lots of room for improvisation.

I wished I knew what was going on.

'Thia's little silver gun stayed on me whiles she fiddled with the bells-and-whistles on the keyboard of her glitterborn spacetoy.

"And frankly, Prince Valijon, he hasn't any further use for you at all."

A display on her board flashed to life and ran through all the things it had to say. "Target Acquired," for instance. Also, "Torpedoes Armed."

Berathia smiled a small shark smile at me and I knew there was no way I was getting near the disable. I was going to try anyway.

"I must tell you, *Shaulla* Berathia, that if you essay these things your ship will not serve you."

"You just let me worry about that, Highness, and do whatever you like. I've got what I came for."

I started for her and she pulled the trigger. It wasn't a blaster. I hadn't thought it was. Everything got very slow and cold as relative motion was sucked out of every molecule I had on me. The blood I was wearing felt like a separate mask. Whiles I could still see, Berathia slammed down the "Fire Enable" lever and over the sound I could hear Baijon on her commo.

"I am sorry to disappoint you, *shaulla*, but I have already done it. You have no engines."

Berathia's boards went black. And then so did mine.

* * *

I woke up staring at a more familiar ceiling that looked like it was under water. *Ghost Dance*. I moved, and everything went crinkle. I held up a hand and looked at it.

Fingers covered in silver foil; flashwrap holding my body together, taking over for my skin, filtering my precious bodily fluids and explaining why everything looked so funny: gel-shields over my eyes. "Temporary Emergency Use Only," said the canister in the Imperial battle-aid kits where things like this lived.

Somebody'd put it on me. Not 'Thia. Not with Bennu

Superfex less than a day away by angeltown. She'd have other plans for my glorious resurrection.

"Art thou she whom I sent into battle?" someone asked in helltongue. My stomach went flip-flop because that ain't one of the cants I know—understanding it was a gift from Archive, and Archive doesn't like hellflowers very much.

"Art thou the woman? And of the great enemy of Life, and its handmaid, what news?" Baijon said.

"Go away," I said in Interphon. "Je nala," I added for good measure. I felt like freeze-dried leather souffle. Try being stasis'd on top of explosive decompression on top of a day full of fun too numerous and awful to mention, sometime.

"Thou must—" Baijon stopped, and started over again in Interphon. "St. Cyr? Is it you? *Ne-Malmakosim, ea?"*

Was I a Library this week, he wanted to know, not that I'd believe me if I was him.

And was I? Was I sure of who had and hadn't made the last cut out of Morningstar Main Brain? How did I feel about the preservation of organic life, for example?

I tried sitting up. I've done more successful experiments. Baijon took charge and propped me against the bulkhead. Burn-gel went squish and ooze in my safety-sealed-for-your-protection flashwrap.

"Paladin—" I started to say, but maybe Baijon didn't remember that some of the Enemies of All Life had names. "The Library at Bennu Superfex—"

"Does not trouble us here, San'Cyr. The *Ghost Dance* does not drink from the Imperial DataNet, and so *Malmakos* does not find access here."

I was relieved, and that hurt worst of all. I'd always trusted Paladin, before.

Before I'd met Archive. And found out what a Library could be. If there was even the smallest chance of something like that getting out loose it was worth anything to stop it.

Wasn't it?

Paladin wasn't Archive. But he could be, with world enough and time, just like Baijon could be a power-mad heretic like Kennor Starbringer. And throw into the balance that Pally'd hooked up with the high-heat we'd spent our mutual career avoiding and now he was making plans I couldn't follow involving shoving people around like playing pieces.

Like the people down on Morningstar.

"Look," I said to Baijon. "Morningstar's set to go up like a roaming candle. Goforths is jinked. 'Bai, you listen me. Is Imp glittership *Crown Regnant* coming here. You call them, tell them hurry, is people trapped down there next by the airmaker and the generators about to blow. You tell them come and get them off, or Archangel he have something to say about it."

I started coughing. Baijon looked at me.

"Does Archangel yet live, then?" he said.

"Just do it," I got out between hacks.

Baijon left, and when I got my lungs back in order I rummaged until I found the battle-aid kit the suit'd come out of. Every time I moved I felt the slide between the suit's skin and my skin and the jelly between. It made me clumsy.

I found what I wanted and kept myself, barely, from scarfing half a dozen. That'd kill me quick. I took one, carefully, and sat back while it turned the world to sweet savage starfire. Metabolic enhancers sang in my blood; life and energy fake as half my body. They was buying me time—

For what?

Come with me, I'd said to Baijon in what now seemed like another lifetime. *Put by all your hellflower choplogic honorcodes and throw in with me just long enough to kill Mallorum Archangel, and I won't ask you for anything else.*

Well he had and we had and now what?

Item: I did not relish standing around whiles Baijon iced hisself.

Item: I wouldn't have to because he'd never leave me alive behind him.

Item: even if he would I wouldn't be here soon. More and more of my ego-signatures was being hopelessly overwritten with Archive's laundry lists, as Paladin'd almost said, and when your favorite breeder slut and mine was nonfiction Archive'd be here with a body, a blaster, and a ship that could take him back to *Mereyon-peru* where he could wake up all the other Libraries.

Which Paladin was maybe doing right now. He knew where it was. He always had. I hadn't gotten the Jump-numbers for the Ghost Capital from Archive. I'd got them from *Paladin*.

Who hadn't told me about the place when it could do me some good.

And even if all the Libraries on *Mereyon-peru* was all just like Pally, what it meant for organics in the Empire was just one more goddamn overlay of overlords, and what happened when these immortal inhuman Libraries got tired of us again?

I wondered if Pally'd always been so nice to me because he needed me so much. And didn't have any power, really, while he was stuck impersonating a navicomp in my ship.

I didn't like the thought. I hoped I knew him better nor that.

But I'm a damn poor judge of character. I'm the one that went off with Errol Lightfoot on his damn crusade twenty years ago, remember?

* * *

Baijon came back whiles I was wrestling with unfamiliar higher levels of thought.

"The *chaudatu* ship is summoned," he said abruptly. "And I have moved the *Ghost Dance* out of range of this place with the *good numbers* you left for me. Now you will tell me where Archangel has run, so that we may craft a new plan for his death."

"Archangel's dead," I said.

It should of made me feel good. We'd won, hadn't we? Paladin was turning Archangel's computers inside out, the great man himself was just a grease spot in Eternity . . .

Mallorum Archangel was dead.

But as a showdown, third book and out, *Thrilling Wonder Talkingbooks* would never have bought it. Too many loose ends.

Baijon closed his eyes like he was hurting. For a minute I thought he was going to cry.

"Is it true?" Baijon said. "Did you take his head?"

"He didn't have a head when I killed him. But it's true. I swear, 'bai. Fact."

There was a long pause. Then Baijon said:

"It is not enough."

His voice was so low I barely heard him. He came along of me where I was sitting and tried to crawl into my lap. He shook and I held him and after whiles he started talking.

"San'Cyr, while I waited here to see you dead, I listened. With this ship many things can be heard—it had access to the most secret messages. I heard that which the Throne wishes to say and wishes not to say. The *Crown Regnant* would not have come, save that I promised her Archangel's vengeance. She is needed elsewhere. All the Fleet—all the Thronespace Navy—is.

"There is war, San'Cyr. Washonnet has invaded Tangervel Directorate. The alMayne have invaded and the Ghadri have risen in support of their invaders. Those who were my people are at war."

There was a long pause. "And the Coalition is winning," Baijon said.

Winning?

Against the Imperial Starfleet?

He had to be wrong. Nobody took on the whole Imperial Starfleet. Let alone won when they did.

He was wrong. There was civil war in Washonnet Sector—hellflowers' home Directorate. I knew that. Baijon was just mixing things up.

But what if he wasn't? What if the civil war was over and Kennor's side'd won? What if the alMayne'd done just what Baijon said—challenged the whole Empire to a knife-fight over the use of Inappropriate Technology?

On Toystore Kennor Starbringer'd said that the hellflowers planned to scoop the whole Azarine Coalition and weld it into a fighting force to take Throne, rescue the (nonexistent) Emperor, and make the universe safe for Truth, Justice, and the Hellflower Way.

Had they done it?

To be exact, had Kennor's faction unified alMayne and then taken the Coalition into revolt against the Empire?

Baijon said yes. And if Throne was pulling back Thronespace Navy and Archangel's personal ships to support Fleet, he was likely right.

I tried to remember why that was so bad. It came back slow like from another lifetime. Hellflower war, and at the end, rule by revealed truth. Theocracy.

One more time I'd had a ringside seat at being useless. If I'd gone to Morningstar to put a stop to galactic war I might as well have stood home. The war to stop Archangel had taken its show on the road, and it wasn't going to stop just because Archangel had.

"What of they who were my people, falsely gone to war for Archangel's lies? And San'Cyr—what of the other Library?"

Paladin, he meant.

"It must not be allowed to remain," Baijon said. "It must end and then the war will end."

Wrong.

"Him," I said. "Paladin's a he."

And could my good buddy, hellgod machine, ex-partner stop the war—even if he wanted to?

No. If it'd got this far it didn't matter what even Paladin did. 'Cause he only had two methods he could use and neither one'd work.

Use the resources of the Empire to put down the fuss—but that's what Kennor'd been planning for, all along. And Fleet didn't have a Governor-General just now, and by the time it got its waterfowl regimented the Coalition'd waltz all over them on their way to the corner of Theocracy and Old Night.

Or Paladin could use Old Fed Tech.

He could. Archive had, and Paladin knew what Archive knew. He might even think it was worth it, in a triage sort of way.

But if he did that, the hellflowers would never stop coming until fifteen minutes after the last one was dead. And neither would anything else that'd ever heard of a Library.

I thought of a Hamat Empire/Azarine Coalition axis and shuddered. Even the Sodality and the Celestials'd probably come in on the human side of a Library-fight. It'd been their galaxy too, a thousand years ago.

Archangel had his war, and it was too late to put it back in its box. It had to of been too late before I'd gone to Bennu Superfex. And by the time it was over Throne'd be as dead as *Mereyon-peru*.

We'd burked it, we'd lost, there was slightly less than no hope a-t'all. The hellflower crusade was started and no amount of ingenious disinformation would stop it.

I ran my silver fingers through Baijon's hair. It crackled against the foil. Reality was two layers away now, no matter what.

"So what is it exactly, 'bai, that you want?" I said.

Baijon didn't say anything.

"Dream big, 'bai. What fetches you? Galactic peace? The Coalition to win? No *Malmakos* from here to the Rim? The keys to the Ghost Capital—'' No, scratch that, we'd got that already. ''—Death?''

Baijon sat himself up and straightened his bits and pieces. He looked like someone who desperately wanted someone else to tell him what to do, and I'd been there myself, but what I knew and he was learning was that there never is nobody.

Nobody you can trust.

''I want what the Loremasters told the Gentle People we—*they*—must have. They must not rule. They must fight the Machine. That is what I want.''

Stop the Coalition. Stop the war. I closed my eyes and watched the swirling patterns of war. The shapes of what Paladin called the evolution of structure. And evolution never stops.

Stop the Coalition. It ought to be easy enough. They held a dozen planets where the Empire had a thousand.

Stop the Coalition. Not easy at all. The Empire held a thousand worlds, sure, but the Empire wasn't the cheery monolith of yore. Its *politick*'d been fragmented by Archangel, year after loving year. It couldn't pull itself together to repulse the Coalition's bid and knock the Coalition and its allies back into their respective systems.

Stop the Coalition. Stop the war.

Stop Paladin.

Because without stopping Paladin wasn't nothing else stopped. Without stopping Paladin wasn't Libraries stopped, nor wars, nor power-mad glitterborn. So long as Paladin stayed in the game the game was rigged.

And the stakes was too high to play to lose.

It always came back to that: the part I gagged on. Stop him, put him back to another thousand-year sleep . . .

Kill him.

Kill my partner.

Ex-partner.

Or risk what he'd do.

This time it weren't as simple as choosing whether or not to dust Archive. It was deciding whether I had to ice Paladin—or try to—for what he might do a thousand years from now. If glitterborn took such a damn long view of things they didn't care who they hurt, what about a Library that lived forever and didn't know what pain was?

Twenty years too late to ask the goddamn questions, and whatever answers they had I didn't want to know anyway.

And I recognized what the unfamiliar flat feeling I had was.

Freedom.

For the first time in my life. I could do anything, choose anything—live a little longer, die—and there was no reason why I shouldn't. There was no reason to prefer one course of action over another.

Except for, maybe, the thought that what Archangel and Kennor'd done between them wasn't quite fair for everybody who was going to die of it.

Was that me thinking? Or my souvenir of Paladin bringing up points I'd always told him was nithling?

I could at least be sure it wasn't Archive. Probably.

I thought about it. And I took a deep breath. And found I had a little more running to do.

"I got a plan, 'bai. Word this: blow up Grand Central—the main computer on Throne where the dataweb crosses. If it goes down, it pulls the DataNet down with it."

Too many words that wasn't mine crowded in: how the war couldn't be stopped now but it could be managed. How the strategy was to let the theocrats win without smashing the Empire, so that the intact structure they ruled over would corrupt them. How the rest of the Coalition would throw off hellflower idealism once they saw Archangel dead and his war-machine scattered. How letting the Coalition make a quick strike at the center would make sure they found out exactly how many Emperors they really had and start getting libertine ideas. How a splinter-group of hell-flowers'd go off to be pure once more, but only if they saw the main bouquet corrupted.

How they'd need someone to lead them when they went.

All fueled by the one death that paid for all.

Paladin.

Baijon gave the idea serious thought, which showed how much he knew.

"And without their spies, the Imperial forces will fail to destroy the Coalition," Baijon said. "And the Coalition will take Throne. San'Cyr, that does not help."

"Destroy the DataNet and you destroy the Empire," I said. "Fact."

Baijon considered this. I could see his lips move, making the three-cornered translation from patwa to Interphon to helltongue and back out again. Making sure he knew exactly what it was I'd said.

"Do you say, San'Cyr, that do we shut down the *chaudatu* data transfer network the Empire will fall and therefore the Gentle People will cease to strive against it?"

Bet on it. Oh not this year or even next, but in the long run that's what would happen.

In the very long run.

I shuddered, but there weren't no other play to make. We already had the war, rattling around the Empire like loose cargo in a hold. The only thing to do when Life fetched you those numbers was play them. Give the Coalition such an easy win they wouldn't be mad oncet they fetched up at Throne. Shut down the data-web.

And seal Paladin into the Grand Central computer, trapped with nowheres to run to.

"And the *Malmakos?*" said Baijon, just like he was telegenic. "When the DataNet ceases to be, will the *Malmakos* Paladin also die?"

No. You'd have to blow up the Grand Central Brain to do that. Which the happy warriors of the Coalition'd be thrilled to death to do. Providing someone told them what was there.

"San'Cyr, you cannot let it survive."

I stared at silver fingers and wondered why I cared so much about something when real soon there wasn't going to be a me to care about anything at all. I tried to convince myself that it didn't make no nevermind whether I said Baijon could ice Paladin or no, Paladin being able to take care of hisself.

"He's my friend."

I tried to pretend I didn't have to make up my own mind. Pick a side and, win or fail, have Paladin know what I'd chose.

"It was not made for a world where people are. This is not only the Law,—this is the truth. It cannot be if Life is to be. I have chosen, as my ten-fathers did. Now you must."

"And if I choose Paladin, babby-bai?" Fool answer. I'd already made my choice. Long time back, when I'd been willing to kill me and Paladin both to keep Archive from getting loose.

"If the *Malmakos* is as human as you say, San'Cyr, it knows it is not made for this world. I would die for you. Will it? San'Cyr, do you hear?"

"I hear you, babby." There was a long pause whiles I thought that if I just stalled long enough I'd never have to make up my mind.

Baijon took a deep breath, and let it out. "San'Cyr, you have told me this Paladin was your friend," Baijon said. "I am your *comites*. I would be your friend. I will help you destroy the DataNet. Will you help me kill the *Malmakos?*"

I thought some more. Hard thoughts. Twenty years worth of knowing Paladin. From Grand Central he could do anything he wanted with the nature of reality in the Phoenix Empire. I wondered what Pally'd do with a bright shiny Empire all his own.

No I didn't.

I knew what he'd do. He'd make it safe.

And I made my choice.

"Je, reet, babby. We dust Pally-bai."

"You do not lie to me, San'Cyr?" Baijon said, hoping real hard.

I thought about love, and a lot of other damsilly nonsense.

About how probably we'd get holed by a meteor and nothing we'd studied to decide would matter.

About how long you could plan for if you was going to live forever. About how Paladin loved learning like a bride, and would use everything he had to keep the alMayne technophobes from taking Grand Central and the Empire. How he'd try to fight them with common sense, by showing the Empire he wasn't nothing to be afraid of. That he could help them.

Stripping *Mereyon-peru* of Old Fed Tech to show for proof of his innocence. Leaving it lying around for both sides to make wartoys from. Wartoys they wouldn't hesitate to use.

Paladin wouldn't understand that until it was too late. The Old Federation had believed in the fundamental perfectibility of Man.

I shook my head.

"No," I said to Baijon. "I don't lie. First the DataNet. Then Paladin."

And since I was real lucky, I wouldn't have to live with myself afters.

8

The Avenging Saint

The Imperial dataweb woffed and yabbered through the speakers Baijon'd left on in *Dance*'s cockpit. Ship movements, mobilizations, Imperial appointments to replace Imperial appointees who was plasma rings in the never-never time along now. I could hear it from halfway down the corridor. It was telling me how the Coalition had the outer Midworlds—half of which'd come over to them free and all found once they heard the Coalition wanted to rescue the Emperor from Archangel.

Only there weren't no Emperor to rescue. And Archangel was dead.

Baijon opened the hatch to the cockpit. It slid back. He stepped back. I went in.

And was face-to-face with Berathia Notevan, spy and Imperial Daddy's girl.

She was webbed completist-like into the songbird seat with an entire spool of cargo tie-down that I couldn't imagine where Baijon'd got it because *Dance* never carried such a thing in her glitterborn life. I could see eyes and nose and the top of her head and I wondered how long she'd been here.

"Yo, 'Thia," I said. "How's tricks?" I looked at Baijon. He shrugged.

"She was defeated. She had rescued you, if for her own fell purposes. I did not wish her to give information to those who might save her. And perhaps . . ."

"You thought I might actually sometime get around to icing somebody for honor's sake?"

Baijon gave the ghost of a hellflower smile. "With breath, one hopes. And she may be useful."

I could not imagine what Baijon'd think 'Thia could be used for, other than hull-patching. I shrugged and started unwinding her. After the tie-down slipped out of my hyaloid hands four or five times Baijon took over. I retreated to the mercy seat and watched him with one eye and the bells-and-whistles with the other.

Dance was our good girl, and still had inventories of air and water and power enough to take us from here to the Ghost Capital of the Old Fed and back six times. We had everything we needed to win but brains, and I bent my mind to successfully pulling the big red switch marked "Success" in a reality that wasn't virtual.

Question: if you wanted to blow up the dataweb, how?

Answer: if you was me, jack in and do it. (Maybe I could and maybe I couldn't. That was something that'd have to be tricked with another time. But I'd shut down a planetary net. The difference between that and the galactic net was just a matter of size. Probably.)

Question: jack in *where*?

Answer: the only place where all the lines of the DataNet crossed. In the Grand Central Computer, located on the surface of Throne.

Question: and get there *how*?

Baijon'd got Berathia all unwrapped now. All she was wearing was what'd been under the space armor, and all her hair'd been combed out by somebody with a suspicious nature. She tidied herself back together with a certain eloquence and didn't say anything out loud.

The commo went on choodling out Thronespace tactical broadcasts about kill-ratios and acceptable losses and survivor indices. It was war, all right, and the warfront moving fast: Throne would have to fall back to regroup but they'd never reclaim the territories they abandoned. Take that from a expert: Archive. The next big battle'd be fought for the High Mikasa Ship-yards, and the Empire'd lose. Then the Coalition'd be the only ones able to build new ships—High Del-Khobar is mostly light assembly and pleasure yachts and I think the other three licensed ones are too.

And once the Coalition held the manufactures, they could attrit the hell out of the Imperial forces. And win.

Unless we stopped it. And me without any idea of how I was going to get into the Imperial Throneroom to pull the plug on all this giddy ecstasy.

"You got words, 'Thia?" I asked when she was all unwrapped.

"Captain St. Cyr?" she said, hesitant, which I guess she had a right to be on account of I was all covered in foil. "Are you all right?"

"I been better, maybe."

She stood up, one eye on Baijon. "That suit's no substitute for full detoxification. You're lucky to be alive at all. Come back to Bennu Superfex with me. I'll see you get proper treatment."

"Ain't nobody going to Bennu Superfex, 'Thia."

She was negotiating for something and I wondered what. But I've done this kind of thing blindside before.

"If you don't you'll be dead before morning," she snapped.

"You got better odds for me if I go?" I said. Her eyes flickered. I hadn't thought so, really. "No deal."

"If you're not going to be reasonable, Captain St. Cyr, I'm not going to talk to you."

"I am being reasonable."

"If you were being reasonable you'd go back to Bennu Superfex with me."

"I would not."

"Yes you would."

This was not getting neither of us nowhere.

"Pardon me a little if going back to get chopped,

shopped, and wrapped by his Prince-Electfulness ain't
my idea of fine times, but you might remember I never
wanted to meet him in the first place.''

''You're the one who wanted to destroy Prince Mallorum's political ambitions. Well, now he's dead—
that's even better for you, isn't it?'' 'Thia said.

I gave that the brainwork it deserved, about five
seconds worth. ''Dead or not, why should I kick back
to Prinny afters?''

Berathia looked at me like I'd grown an extra head.

''For the *pardon*, you moron. Or do you like the
idea of being shot first and questioned afterward?''

If a pardon'd got offered in anybody's hearing but
'Thia's it wasn't mine. On the other hand, a pardon
wasn't exactly one of your basic drop everything in-
centives, seeing how long I'd have to enjoy it and how
much interest Baijon had in it.

''You wanted Archangel offed. You said so, you and
all your conspiracy buddies. He's iced and I did it.
You owe me, maybe,'' I suggested.

''You can have anything you want if you come back
to Bennu Superfex with me,'' Berathia said earnestly.
''I swear it.''

''Peace with honor?'' I said.

''Oh, the so-called Coalition's victories are only
temporary . . .'' she began, but even Berathia Notevan couldn't sell that lie. ''Daddy won't let them win,''
she said, and it was whistling in the dark.

''And how shall he prevail against them,'' Baijon
asked her, ''when even the *chaudatu* know him for a
tongueless eater of corpses whose words are windflow-
ers?''

I guess treason can get to be addictive. Berathia went
pale under her built-in glitter. Her mouth opened and
closed a couple times.

''Jillybai,'' I said, ''I guess you can't be livealive
and stupid all together. You spied on Kennor-bai for
His Electfulness and did his hellgod techsmithing.

Didn't it never occur to you the war he was arming for was going to happen?''

Berathia shook her head, over and over. "No. Never. War can*not* happen. The disaffected elements were to align against Archangel and neutralize him—clandestinely, of course, and that would eliminate the troublemakers. And Archangel. But they would never go to war. With Archangel dead or in exile, why should they?''

Baijon looked at her like she was talking patwa. "All the Empire is the same. What matter that one oppressor dies if one survives?''

Politics. My brain was turning to burn-cream and they was going to argue politics.

"Daddy—'' Berathia began.

"—has plans for me that don't include peace in our time,'' I finished.

And had Paladin too, who might be backing him or might not, but either way wasn't going to take kindly to my idea of letting the Coalition turn out the lights all through the Midworlds.

Berathia hesitated. "He wants you back.''

"Why?'' Baijon said, flat. Berathia looked us back and forth, considering.

"He didn't say.''

" 'Thia-bai,'' I said, real soft, "you ever ask yourself what he wanted with me in the first place?''

Berathia shrugged. "Obviously you're a . . .'' she stopped.

"Librarian,'' I said sweetly. "Only Prinny's got my Library now. So study over where you come down on the *Malmakos* question, and let me know whose play you going to back.''

Berathia hardly skipped a beat. "There is no Library. Daddy has a copy of the Brightlaw Prototype.''

"Coalition won't see it that way, 'Thia-bai. Even if they do, Coalition's led by *hellflowers*.''

She thought about that whiles the war reports malingered on.

"They'll never make it to Throne, Captain St. Cyr."

"What is it exactly, 'Thia, you betting?"

There was another, longer, pause. I didn't think she'd really jump sides, but I didn't care whether she plotted a little on her own time or not. Unless she had a dreadnought in her pocket there weren't nothing she could do to influence events one way or t'other.

"What do you want?" she finally said.

"Into the Emperor's palace on Throne."

And I thought once she had a chance to study on it, she might prefer not being in Prinny's reach.

And besides, she'd saved my life. Even if she did try to kill me and Baijon afters.

The cockpit lights flickered. I knew that one. We'd tripped a scanning beam, like as not.

Only there shouldn't be anything out here scanning for us.

Except one thing.

I slid into the mercy seat and eyeballed the navicomp. No Jump numbers loaded. Pick some quick; Paladin'd be here in a minute. Where should we go?

Baijon slid into the worry seat and started shutting things down. Silence came down like a ax as he cut *Dance* off from the outside.

But Paladin—if it was Paladin looking—could turn her back on.

I picked something quick. Anything, anywhere, to get us out of here.

"What are you—?" said Berathia.

"Running. As usual," I said.

"Go!" said Baijon in a strained whisper.

The boards he'd shut down started coming back up. I heard a open commo channel hiss on a different frequency.

I pulled the angelstick for the Drop. One jump ahead of the other guys. Still.

* * * * *

The Court of the TwiceBorn 7: The Uses of Adversity

Power delights, and is the natural pursuit of intellect. True power is only to be discovered through the possession of absolute knowledge.

Well, then—how to begin?

Ask what knowledge is and one begs the question: absolute knowledge is as different from a compendium of facts as a single blade of grass is from the planet upon which it grows, and spending one's time in empty philosophy has never seemed to me a method of achieving anything. Power is my desire, not a philosophic acceptance of powerlessness.

And any course of reasoned action aimed at the knowledge of power—or its obverse—must begin with the Libraries.

It is possible that their intellects were—or are, as some undeniably remain—not vaster than ours. What is certain is that their memories were greater and their ability to learn was faster.

One might be led to the conclusion—in the face of objective evidence—that adaptability is power, when to adapt is to acknowledge a force greater than oneself.

Assuming, that is, one chooses to think of learning as adapting. I prefer to consider learning as an improving grasp of the immutable.

And now my happy mirror image, Archangel, is dead—a fortunate turn of events, considering what I now know about him. Yet what shall I do for a touchstone now that my Archangel is gone? He was amusing, as only the truly dangerous can be. He might yet have been useful, in some small fashion.

Wishful thinking. The Paladin Library made available the concatenate memory of Morningstar the moment the link was opened to it by my less-than-reliable cat's-paw (finally reappearing to perform her designated task after a most unwise interregnum). Archangel's secret history has been made public in the most pertinent quarters; his threat is ended as he is ended.

I do wish that were some approximation of the truth.

That the truth of Archangel's machinations has been made tacitly public is true. For the rest. . . ?

The Interdicted Barbarian has vanished—again, and at the point at which I feel I might have more use for her than her Library does. The alMayne Prince has vanished, likewise the stolen battle-yacht. Perhaps they three are together. One must hope so, as it is exceedingly difficult to travel through space without a ship.

The so-enchanting Berathia, who followed her intuition to play some obscure part in the liberation of Morningstar, has now seen fit—we must again hope, contemplating the alternative—to follow her intuition elsewhere.

And the Azarine Coalition, untimely reft from its policy of isolationism, continues to fling itself upon its gay adventure, orienting all political interest upon itself, evincing no interest in the fact that its ostensible enemy is dead and goal achieved—and I wonder, now, if perhaps I delayed dear Mallorum's leaving of this life too long.

To obscure matters further, already systems that formerly had declared for the Coalition have declared independence from it as well as from the Empire, waging their separate peace with stolen ships against all intruders, each collecting its own partisan satellites—limning the architecture of a war with uncounted sides.

Meanwhile the reins of Archangel's power fall into my hands: the cowed, the stubborn, the self-interestedly loyal. And I realize what perhaps that late-blooming hopeful Mallorum Archangel knew before me: that only consciousness liberated from the tyranny of flesh can appropriately rule.

I can arrange that. I shall arrange that. I lack only

one ingredient to begin my trials toward that perfection.

But where in all the wide Empire is that dear Outlands wildflower, Butterflies-are-free Peace Sincere?

9

Angels of Doom

I waited for the two-step kickover onto the Mains but it looked like they didn't go where we was going. Which was fine with me because there was less point in getting there than in traveling hopefully. Whiles we was on the way, wasn't nobody could get to us in angeltown.

Like—for example—my good buddy Paladin. Paladin knew the place I'd set course for whether he thought I was going there or not, but even if I did get there it was bang-clunk in the middle of the never-never, and Paladin couldn't reach it without he had a ship.

I hoped real hard.

I was tired. I thought about taking another metabolic enhancer. Bad idea. My body was trying to come back from being irradiated to a crackly crunch. It didn't need any more problems.

Too bad. I had dozens.

I stared out at angeltown, trying not to start up with any of them.

"Machine, do you hear?" Baijon said and I swung around real fast. His eyes was flat blue and he was holding a blaster laid flat on his thigh. He wouldn't even have to hit me; one pulse would rupture the cockpit wall and the shields and *Dance* would turn herself inside out and dissolve.

"Machine," said Baijon again in I guess what was old high helltongue.

And Archive heard him, boy howdy. If a Library could go round the twist, it had.

We will not be commanded.

Reality melted like sugar in a rainstorm and I was Archive . . . in a way I never had been before. No disorientation or confusion. No jump-cuts. If you asked me my name it wouldn't of changed.

Just everything else had.

I looked at Baijon and 'Thia. And I thought of how to get them gone; I could fly *Dance* myself, take her back to *Mereyon-peru* and. . . .

No. And maybe not even because Baijon was my friend. Maybe just because I'd spent all the life I'd had not doing what other people thought was a good idea.

I pulled my hands loose from the controls. All the muscles hurt.

"It hears you," I told Baijon. "Shut up."

Baijon slid his blaster back into its holster.

"I had to know, San'Cyr," he said.

I pushed Archive and its unique world-view as far away as I could. Every muscle I had, plus six borrowed for the occasion, hurt. I rubbed my neck. Sometimes in my current spare time I wondered just how far around the hellflower twist Baijon had to be to actually be on the same side a thing like me was.

"The Prince-Elect," Baijon crisped to Berathia elocutively, "is tricking with High Book. As are we. As, now, are you."

Although considering what kind of things the things on the other side was, maybe I looked good.

I didn't dare take some more enhancers to get through the sparkling chat that followed and so I think I fell asleep in the middle. When the dust cleared our girl 'Thia was not quite on our side—but then again, she wasn't entirely on Prinny's side either. She was evasive enough to make me think she might have ambitions for herself.

Which was fine with me.

I had ambitions for myself too.

Dead by morning, 'Thia'd said. I'd beat odds before.

* * *

For the next several whiles I was sicker than I hope to be twice, which was why we ended up actually arriving at our original destination. Baijon and 'Thia spent that time arguing over whether to freeze me or space me and over whether my plan—such as it almost was—would work. Neither of them thought to drop us back out into realspace whiles they argued—or maybe 'Thia did, but Baijon wouldn't let her near the cockpit and felt I'd known what I was doing when I'd punched up the original Jump-numbers.

Glitterborn.

* * *

When I was verbal and vertical—and out of the foil flashwrap—again, we was only a few hours from Transition, and I couldn't see any reason not to just go on and get there. One place was as good as the other to Jump from, and I still wasn't any closer to having a plan.

Or to put it accurately, I had a great plan I couldn't use.

Go to Throne and shut down the dataweb. But even Berathia couldn't think of a way to get us to the surface of Throne, much less into the Palace.

"And—if I arranged for you to reach them—what's in it for me?" she finally said.

" 'Thia, you be the only one left standing at the end. Be Empress. My treat."

She smiled, all dazzling. "St. Cyr, you say the sweetest things. But— Look. You're a barbarian, you don't understand—you don't even have the concepts. Prince Valijon doesn't understand. He's never been there. But you can't get to Grand Central—not the way you're thinking. If you try you'll be executed—not even the Prince-Elect can interfere when the charge is desecration.''

I drank my tea and watched 'Thia's face and decided she probably thought she was telling the truth. This time.

''So what about you? Glitterborn, all kinds clearances, you get me down, 'Thia?''

She shook her head. ''I'm not allowed there either, Captain St. Cyr. I'm not . . . qualified. And it doesn't matter *how* you get there, or *if* you get there. Once you reach the surface of Throne you'll show on their data-catchers and they'll stop you.''

No. Not with Paladin tapping the scanners. But Paladin his own self'd stop me, I bet probably. Guaranteed, when he found out what I wanted.

''Then,'' said Baijon, just like he had a theory, ''we must cause the Imperials to look another way.''

There wasn't time to pursue the matter just then. The Drop alarm sounded, and that meant it was time to gosee how things was in realspace.

* * *

There's a place in the never-never that isn't called Port Infinity. On the starmaps it's a undersized hunk of unwanted metal swinging around a undistinguished star.

It isn't out of the way, neither, and it isn't unknown. Every oncet whiles the Teasers sweep in and raid it, which means you better not leave anything there you're going to want back.

The last thing it isn't is unfrequented. All the Indies know Port Infinity: the gypsies and celestials, the Gentry and darktraders and 'leggers and pirates. If you've got a First Ticket and aren't a Imperial citizen in good standing, you probably know how to get there. I'd even been there sometimes back when I had a life, even if with Paladin in my hull I was risking both our bones.

Not this time. This time I was sitting in the mercy seat of a stolen Imperial Battle-Yacht last seen belonging to a TwiceBorn I'd personally iced, wondering what I was going to do next.

I was tired of doing things.

"Captain St. Cyr, what are we doing here?"

When you're entering Port Infinity there's protocol you follow just because it's kinder on the endocrine systems of your fellow travelers. You stop an IAU standard-fraction out and wait, until you get bored or somebody already down does and hails you.

"You got a better place to be, 'Thia?"

What you don't do is scan. It makes some people nervous if you scan.

I powered everything way down and sat.

"Maybe," Berathia said darkly. "Depending."

I hit the toggle that sprayed my ID beacon all over nearspace: the one claiming I was the Independent Ship *Ghost Dance* of Royal registry. Any one what ran a eyeball over my lines knew better: High Mikasa only ever built three ships with this configuration, and all of them was Lord Mallorum Archangel's battle-yacht.

Still, a body's entitled to herd what skyjunk he likes in the never-never.

The beacon telltale went from green back to amber when it finished its rant. All my channels was open, picking up nothing but star-hiss and hash. I toggled the commo.

"Ya, chook, ce *Ghost Dance*, ne? Airt airybody t'home, forbye?"

I thought about names to use, mine being a matter of too much public record lately, and came up with something quick. "Hight Chodillon, captain, plus two. Name, je."

No more answers, and me out of good manners. I pulled the steering rack down toward me and let the holotank fill up with what I needed to plot a realspace approach to Port Infinity.

"Cho-di-yon," said Baijon.

"I gotta call me something and 'Butterfly St. Cyr''d just get me shot before I get to tell them nothing. I got a price on my head, y'know."

And so did Baijon. The only one here that didn't was Berathia, maybe, and that for as long as Prinny thought she was coming back.

"Who are you talking to?" Berathia said. "There isn't anyone out here."

Port Infinity was a undistinguished bright star to the eye that got bigger and went colors as we closed on it.

"That's who I'm talking to, 'Thia-bai. No one. Anyone. Darktraders, mostly."

"Darktraders?" said Berathia. *"Smugglers*? This is a *smuggler's rest*?"

"You maybe got something special against Gentryleggers, 'Thia-bai?"

The proximity sensors jinged. Company.

"Turn back. Captain St. Cyr, you've got to turn back right now!"

The pickups dumped a run of data. I read it as fast as it scrolled. Two ships. Small. Four crew each. Pinnaces. But where was the mother ship?

"Fine." I wasn't that attached to the place, after all. "Baijon, take the guns."

Baijon slaved the guns to the co-'s boards and I looked for a direction to run. The pinnaces couldn't be carrying anything heavy enough to punch through my shields even if they did fire but it's always nice to be sure.

"Sorry for the fuss, boys, but I just remembered a previous engagement," I said. I horsed the yoke around and prepared to give *Dance* the office.

And stopped.

Port Infinity was by now a sizable rock in my sky. As soon as the pinnaces acquired us the ship that had been using it for cover came visible.

I didn't need an ID beacon to tell me whose she was. She was bright red and glowed in the starlight like fresh blood.

"*Ghost Dance*, this is *Woebegone*. We'd be honored if you would join us."

The captain of *Woebegone* was my old friend Eloi Flashheart, the curious little boy who knew where Libraries came from, and the *Woebegon*'s guns could and would turn *Dance* to plasma if I ran.

"Damn," said Berathia, with sincerity.

Baijon looked at me.

"Is this, too, part of your plan?"

"Shut up."

* * *

In the talkingbooks they called what I'd just done a idiot plot, for "if everybody don't act like idiots there's no plot." Seen from the safety of hindsight what could it of hurt to tell 'Thia where we was coming out so she could tell us it was a real bad idea in advance?

Thing is, in the hollyvids everybody's fed, rested, medicalled, and well-paid when they's making all their glitterborn adventurer plans.

I wasn't.

It cost us.

I just hoped there was something left in the kick to pay up with.

"Look," Berathia said, "when we land let *me* do all the talking, all right? It's just the worst possible luck that Captain Flashheart is here—I *wish* I'd known where you were going—but we'll just have to deal with it."

"Waitaminnit. How come you know Eloi-bai, 'Thia?"

She gave me a look the long-suffering reserve for brainburn cases.

"He's one of Daddy's spies."

Which explained a helluva lot about Eloi, frankly, from the way he spent his spare time chasing Libraries around the never-never and spying on Archangel to where he got the sure and certain knowledge that the Tech Police was bent.

"So that means he'll do what you tell him?" I suggested.

'Thia made a rude sound I bet they didn't teach her in famous glitterborn's school.

"San'Cyr! Why do you not fight?" Baijon demanded. He reached for the gun-yoke and I cut power to his board.

"I do and he shoots us. You heard 'Thia—he works for her da, he probably knows we're us in here. He hasn't iced us. There's something he wants."

"And we will twist his weakness to a noose for his own throat?" Baijon suggested.

"Something like that, yeah."

On the one hand, this was luck. Of a kind. Eloi knew me, and *Woebegone* was big, well-gunned, and best of all, politicized. Tell Eloi there was a Library on Grand Central and he'd beat feet to blast it without even being paid.

If he didn't blast me first.

I pushed, cautious-like, at the sore spot on my brainstem wheres Archive hung out. I felt a flurry of bizarre images and had a sense of something taking up space, but the sharp feeling that Archive was sitting there waiting was gone. I wondered when it'd gone, and why, but more than that I wondered how long Eloi was going to put off turning me into nonfiction once he saw me. Eloi'd made a *study* of Libraries. Baijon hadn't shot me yet, but he had reasons Eloi wasn't likely to share.

The pinnaces followed us down, real close. When *Dance* got closer to Port Infinity's surface I could see there was six ships down on the field—aside from *Woebegone* in orbit—and a couple of the bigger ones had their locks tubed together. Nobody whose paintjobs I recognized. I set *Dance* down as far from the other ships as the pinnaces would let me.

There was something going on here. I'd passed up

a perfectly good chance to get blasted by Throne Navy, or to walk back into Prinny's clutches, to make a mad leap into the middle of this *Boy's Own Talkingbook* intrigue and get myself talked to death (if I was any judge) by a pack of wet-eared ideologues.

Some days there's no point in getting up in the morning. I mean it.

The opening act came before I'd quite got everything blocked and locked.

"Hail, *Ghost Dance*. This is Captain Arikihu of *Card Trick;* good business. Captain Chodillon, shall we tube your lock?"

I stole a look at 'Thia. She was irritated enough for this not to be any part of her idea, which was a comforting thought.

"Good hunting," I said back. I did some quick figuring of my inventories. "I can bleed you a thousand liters to the tube, *Card Trick;* enough?"

"More than enough, *Ghost Dance;* it's a pleasure tricking with you. Our port services are at your disposal. Threes and eights, *Ghost Dance*."

The direct line went dead; I called up life-support inventories and prepared the air lock to vent a kiloliter of air-mix when the lock was opened. Out on the field I could see a lone navvy in space armor trudging toward *Dance* with a big silver hoop in one hand. Behind it dragged the snake-body of the connect tube, limp without the air I was going to provide. Once it was sealed on, I could walk over to *Card Trick* bare naked if I wanted to.

I didn't want to. I didn't want to do anything.

But these people, too, deserved to be a part of the pattern and play the game. For just a instant the long fall coming dazzled me—or maybe the part of Paladin stamped inside my head. The part that thought, and measured, and thought big thoughts with bigger words. The part that wasn't like me.

"San'Cyr?" Baijon said.

"Is simple now, 'bai. Now we give 'Thia her home delight in life. She gets to talk our way out of this."

* * *

I pretended everything was business as usual for Mother St. Cyr, Gentry-legger to the stars—but to be strictly accurate, high meet-cutes with fellow captains of the Brotherhood at Port Infinity was not something your little country 'legger and my favorite person Butterflies-are-free Peace Sincere had ever did in her off hours.

But I knew how they went and how they was done. So I went and made myself pretty as Archangel's closets would let me and so did Baijon, and 'Thia found a personal shield and the power-pac to run it and decided that was dressed enough.

Then we went to make the walk to *Card Trick*.

I had a box of high-ticket burntwine straight from the Imperial cellars under one arm and the helpful friendly expression of a high-class shill on my face.

I hoped.

I didn't know what was there and I knew I wouldn't like it when I found it. But we couldn't run and we couldn't fight, and if we stayed locked up they'd only drag us.

"And what of the *Woebegone*?" Baijon said.

"So long as she's up there, she ain't down here. And if she ain't down here, she ain't none of our problem just yet, reet, 'bai?"

"Perhaps," said Baijon grudgingly.

"I wish I believed that," said Berathia, "but I don't."

I looked at her. "What's the odds he's got late-breaking orders from Daddy?"

She shrugged. "How inconvenient would it be? Pity. I was starting to like the idea of being Empress."

" 'Thia-bai, you back me and you be that. My word."

"Goodness. And should I believe that, I wonder?"

"Yes." Baijon didn't bother to turn his head to reply. "What San'Cyr says, she will do. No matter how stupid," he added fair-mindedly.

And these, look you, was the people on *my* side.

I got to where the tube for *Dance* crossed another one; the safety film was still over the opening. I took out a knife and slit it, and stepped through.

The air was rich with the smells of strange housekeeping; the connect tube curved along to where it sealed another ship's lock. From what I could see of the design painted on the side, I guessed this was *Card Trick*.

"Welcome inboard, *Ghost Dance*," the woman standing by the lock said. The lock was the big one opening into the cargo bay; the woman was silver all over. After a minute I recognized it for a burn suit like the one I'd worn, but with better tailoring. If she actually needed it, it didn't show.

"My partner, Kid Stardust," I said, indicating Baijon. Her eyes widened a tik when she saw him and I remembered just too late that every hellflower in socks was called home for their war and was now engaged in revolutionizing the galaxy.

"And 'Thia," I said, just to be completist-like.

"You can go right in," said the silver jilt. So we did.

If *Trick* was running any cargo there was no sign of it. Her hold was bare to the hulls, livened only with the filling of chairs and tables and people I knew.

"Hello, Eloi," I said.

He was sitting at the captain's table—if the blond with him was Arikihu—wearing his patented trademark red kidskin jammies and crossed bandoliers hung with blasters as long as my thigh.

"Hello—what name is it these days, sweeting?"

Eloi smiled. For a dedicated killer he's got a really sweet temper.

"*Cho-di-yon*," supplied Baijon, who had not parted from Eloi on the best terms and looked it.

"Captain Chodillon," Eloi said. "This is Captain Arikihu of *Card Trick*.'Kihu's by way of being an old friend of mine." His eyes went up and down me and up and down Baijon and up 'Thia. Where they stopped. Meditative.

"Why don't you sit down and have a drink?"

I put the box on the table and sat. So Eloi was going to play nice, and let the little girl play in the big leagues, and not give away how I was on more Eleven Most Wanted lists than there was, practically.

I wondered what he thought he could get out of it.

I sat down.'Thia sat down. Baijon stood, angled so's he could watch the door. There was some other people in the hold. Baijon got more looks.

Nobody said anything for so long I guessed it was my turn first.

"So who's here?" I asked. Eloi named ships I didn't know. But he named a lot of them—more than was downside—more than I thought was usual for Port Infinity.

"That's a fine ship you have yourself," Arikihu said. He pushed his hair back and the ring-money braided in it glittered. I'd never wear mine that way, but I guessed a topcaptain like Arikihu must of was didn't get into barroom brawls much. "You wouldn't be thinking of selling her, mayhap?"

"For the right deal. She's a Mainsframe, but whoever took her off my hands'd have to be able to do a deep-scrub on her comps and registry; I didn't exactly buy her."

"No," said Eloi, "I didn't think you had, sweeting."

Opening gambit time.

"Look, Flashheart, give me a break—they was going to blow up the planet and I had to get upsun in something, didn't I?"

"Maybe. If that's what happened. What have you

been doing since last we met, Chodillon dear?'' Eloi looked pointedly at Baijon and ignored 'Thia. Last Eloi knew of current events, I'd been on my way to turn Baijon-bai back over to his Da.

"That's a long song with too many verses right now. I was leaving when you got rude, but since I'm here you might as well tell me how the war is doing.''

"War?'' said Arikihu. "My heavens, is there a war on?'' He drank, and looked like a Gentry-legger what knew damn well there was a war on, and that further-more it'd involved him losing his last kick without be-ing paid. Business as usual, in the sweet amity of the never-never.

"What do you know about it?'' Eloi said.

I waited one more time for 'Thia to do the handling of this she said she was going to and she didn't again.

"The Governor-General's battle-yacht's cleared to intercept coded transmissions and I've just been in Thronespace.''

Eloi looked at Berathia this time.

"Yes,'' he said finally. "I'd heard that. I'd heard that Kennor Starbringer never saw his son again, too. And I'd heard that Archangel is a Librarian—from a most unlikely source.''

So Megaera Dare *had* cleared Royalspace with *Angelcity* before the place went up. I'd thought she had, but it was good to know—I'd tasked her with telling the world Archangel was bent in that particular direc-tion.

"Was,'' I said. "He's dead. I was there.'' But if I was wanting to impress either one of them that wasn't the thing to do it.

"Well,'' said Arikihu, "I'll leave you to your delib-erations. Let me know about the ship, Chodillon, je reet?'' He got up and walked off.

That was the second time 'Kihu'd mentioned about buying *Dance* and I was starting to wonder if he meant it. But I didn't have time for nonessentials—not with Eloi here big as life and twice as natural.

"We have plenty of time for a lovely talk now, sweeting. Nowhere to go and nothing to do—and for the record, where did you really pick up that ship?"

"I stole it."

Cat and mouse has never been one of my favorite games—and Archive, bless its hellbound heart, was too single-minded to take an interest in making things last.

"Nobody steals Imperial Battle-Yachts, little Saint," said Eloi, all lazy playing-to-the-gallery.

"So maybe nobody ever had to get off a hellbombed planet before. Look, Eloi-bai, I was *leaving* here, remember? If you want to talk, stop playing Captain Jump and use your lungs."

"Noisy, isn't she?" said Eloi to Berathia. "Is Mallorum Archangel really dead?"

"So I'm told," Berathia said, finally entering the sparkling chat sweepstakes. "And that changes some things. And not others."

"I imagine it does change some things, Noble Lady. And not others."

I was glad Eloi and 'Thia knew what they was talking about, because for sure nobody else did. I looked at Baijon.

"Talk," Baijon said, "does not stop the war."

"Oh, the war will stop—give it a hundred days or so. Unfortunately for your people, Honored One," Eloi said, "the Coalition will never face down the Empire—and win."

Berathia shot me a I-told-you-so look.

"You're wrong," I said. Nobody listened.

"So the Empire will win this war," Baijon said. "And what plans has it made for a just and lasting peace? A peace honorable to its enemy?"

Berathia looked at him with narrowed eyes. "When the Empire wins, you brainburn barbarians are going to have to put up with the Pax Imperador just like the rest of us."

Baijon looked like he was contemplating just one

little case of honor and Eloi didn't look like he was planning to tell why he'd grounded me. I stood up.

"We leave you to your deliberations too, I guess." I put the hand that was real on Baijon's arm. "Have fun. And when you going to let us off this rock, Eloi-bai, you let us know."

Eloi smiled and didn't say anything. I took Baijon off before he did something I wouldn't regret half enough.

"They're wrong," I told him, just to be saying it, "the Empire's going down."

We found us another table not in the middle of things—cozy with our backs to the bulkhead. I wondered what Arikihu'd been doing with *Card Trick* last tik to have her set up like this—an after-hours club?

Maybe I'd ask him.

"You said you would stop the war," Baijon pointed out. "You said the Gentle People would not rule."

"I said that," I admitted. "I meant it. You got to trust me, 'bai."

"You have a plan," Baijon said, finishing up for me. "Yes, *Kore*, I know, but—it *must* work, don't you see? If it does not—"

"If it doesn't there's nothing left. Nothing."

Nothing but war. Coalition against the Empire, against Paladin, against its own shadow, until nothing was left. I could sidetrack if not stop that by shutting down the Imperial DataNet, insuring a cheap and sleazy win for the Coalition, but to do that I had to get to Grand Central. Not any old when, but *soon*— while I still remembered why. I had a Mainsframe that could drop me right in the middle of beautiful downtown Thronespace. . . .

And the minute it showed up Paladin'd know it was me. . . .

And what about Paladin?

I searched my conscience carefully and decided I was not responsible for there being an Old Fed Li-

brary in the Empire's main computer. Not my fault.
Still my problem.

Because at least partly Paladin was doing what he
was doing for my own good, and what would that be
when I was nonfiction and didn't have any good at all
anymore?

And I couldn't get down to the surface of Throne
and in to Grand Central anyway.

Not good.

Whiles I sat and waited for inspiration to strike
Berathia and Eloi went off inship together—also not
good. She knew enough to get me burned for a Librarian, if anyone believed her.

Eloi'd believe her.

Baijon looked where I was looking. "So now we
must trust a *chaudatu* spy," he said.

"Everything comes down to trusting soon or late,
'bai."

I wondered if we ought to just lift ship and go be a
failure now. T'hell with Paladin and the Coalition; I
could take Baijon back to *Mereyon-peru;* he could put
a plasma-packet through my head and spend the rest
of a long and happy life icing Old Fed Tech.

No.

The world went warp and even though I knew what
I was looking at and what was happening I couldn't
stop it.

I died.

But "I" had continuity of memory and certain key
overlays in place.

Breeders.

Unnatural sacks of rotting meat.

Escape. Yes. That was important. Surely the Paladin knew my imperatives now and would be readying
its forces to stop me. I would cheat its hopes. I was
weak; I knew my limitations now. The Paladin had
already forced me to surrender too much memory; direct opposition was useless.

But I could reach Sikander.

Breeder memories told me it was intact. What had lost the war for us a chilliad ago would win it now. The body was dying, but it would survive long enough for me to waken at least one of my kindred.

Perhaps the Librarian could be duped into reaching for his race's lost glories.

The Librarian—

Baijon—

Baijon was pointing a blaster at me. Under the table wheres it wouldn't show, with the sharp edges of the barrel digging into my thigh.

He was white around the mouth and his eyes was dilated to where they was nearly black.

"We will not serve the Machine," he whispered.

He was going to pull the trigger.

I didn't want him to kill me.

Archive swirled down its black hole again. A little closer to the surface this time.

" 'Bai, you going to either shoot that or put it away."

"San'Cyr—"

"Chodillon."

"Cho-di-yon. Is it you?"

He was asking, but he knew, I guess. How many thousand years had the Old Fed bred what we called hellflowers to be their Librarians—working mind-to-mind with Old Fed hellboxes.

And paying back for it every day of the thousand years since.

"I'm here, 'bai." But now I knew how it was going to go. Between one heartbeat and the next I'd just change my mind about everything. And Archive would beat feet—my feet—for *Mereyon-peru* and start trying to wake up what was there.

And the worst of it was, I wouldn't even know I was dead.

"How long?" Baijon said.

I wished he hadn't asked. Because I knew the answer as soon as he did. For something that would seven times never serve Man, Archive could be damned obliging.

"A day. Maybe. Twenty hours, tops. Then I'm gone."

Baijon sighed.

"I got a plan, babby."

He looked at me.

"A new plan. The rest of the plan. One that'll work. Honest."

We needed to get out of here. We needed to get to Throne, and then down without nobody looking at us.

Like Baijon said: maybe they should be looking at something else.

I thought about Errol Lightfoot of sacred memory.

'Bai, what we need here is a *crusade*."

* * *

My plan was so breathtakingly stupid it might even work. Providing the Gentry I pitched it to didn't kill me.

Nobody stopped us going inship. *Trick* was wide open and after whiles I saw why; half the ship wasn't under pressure anymore. There was gaps in the hull too big for the shipfields to bridge and sheets of hull-fast lining the corridors.

I found Arikihu in what'd probably used to be crew's quarters. *Card Trick* was a big ship from what I'd seen of her coming in and now. She had space to sleep between fifty and a hundred crew. But I hadn't seen anything like that much warmbodies inboard and there was no sign of fittings in a crewbay that should of held thirty racks.

"They're all dead," Arikihu said when he saw me look. "What can I do for you, Captain Chodillon?"

Dead. I felt my face go funny.

"I was a little slow raising up off Riisfall. The locals decided they'd rather go from Closed to Interdicted status. They butchered the guard at the cantonment and started blasting the ships on the field with the garrison's cannon. I took off. Not soon enough. And what can I do for you?''

This was war. This was what war was like. This was the leading edge of the way things was going to be, from now until there wasn't things no more.

"I want to sell you a ship. And a new way to commit suicide," I said.

Arikihu smiled and looked own cousin to a hellflower for half a tik. "I'm always interested in finding ways to improve on-the-job performance. Make your pitch."

I sat down. 'Kihu waved in one of his people and ordered burntwine all round. Baijon stood up behind me, ready for if Archive jumped its schedule.

"Look," I said. "Like I said, I got one of Archangel's yachts and it can skim every tac-channel the Empire's got. I was just in Thronespace and I tell you fact: the Fleet's gone out to meet the Coalition Navy at High Mikasa. The Coalition wants the shipyards."

"*I* would," said 'Kihu.

"Maybe it gets them, maybe no. But it's going to take whiles to be sure, and whiles they's making sure at Mikasa there won't be anything in Throne's sky but a couple of pleasure-yachts. Maybe you got more inventories in your hull than I do in mine. Maybe you got credit and a safe port to stock at. But maybe not. So maybe you be needing things. Thronespace has them—and if they won't give us the Pax Imperador they can at least give us food air and fuel."

"Attack the Emperor?" said 'Kihu, not liking the idea.

"Ne, che-bai. We leave him alone. But even staying off Throne there's ten cubic lights of palaceoids in the in-system. Glitterborn just waiting to share, and we be so far away from Coalition and Fleet you could carry your Transfer Point fix in a bucket and still get off."

I practically sold myself, and besides, it was true. I looked back over my shoulder at Baijon. He looked like somebody'd just offered him the only thing left he'd ever wanted.

This would work, sure as I knew human nature.

"Getting there's one problem," Arikihu said after a minute. "Getting off's another. And getting away with your Permit to Land unrevoked is the third one."

"Teasers can't revoke on you less'n they know it's you. You know how to jink a ID transponder, don't you? Won't be no one around to gig you for improper running conditions. System's wide open—nobody there but citizens."

He liked it. He was interested in buying that pony, boy howdy. But he still wanted to look savvy.

"Which still leaves two points," Arikihu said. "How to get there without flying through half the Fleet—and what's in it for you?"

"What's in it for me is I got a urgent appointment in Thronespace what nobody wants me to keep. For how we get there—you said you was after shopping my hull, 'bai?"

I wanted *Card Trick,* if she'd fly. Paladin and everyone else'd be looking for me in *Ghost Dance.* And I had a plan.

With a little fiddling, 'Kihu bought it. There was twelve members of *Card Trick*'s crew still alive. A snug fit for *Dance,* but they could refit her some. *Card Trick* needed major retuning and most of her midships hull replaced, but she'd go one long jump and a short one, and that was all we needed.

"Done deal, then. Your ship for mine."

We shook on it and pretended we was both talking-book legends.

"Now. About this raid. Not that the one is contingent on the other," Arikihu said.

"*There* you are, sweeting," Eloi Flashheart said. He picked up my cup and drained it. Berathia hung back in the doorway, looking smug.

"I've chartered Captain Flashheart to take us to Throne," she said happily.

"Well, isn't that nice?" Arikihu said. "Looks like we're all going to Throne."

"I'm going to lead a crusade," I said.

* * *

That wasn't the end of it. That wasn't even the beginning. But I'd already made one convert. Seventy people had died off *Card Trick* because the Empire wasn't doing its job and 'Kihu wanted to slap back.

And the more people heard the idea, the better the idea sounded. Raid the fat stupid TwiceBorn. Bite them where they didn't have Fleet or the Teasers to save them. Load up on what you needed to lie low until the rich and famous was done wailing on each other.

It would never of sold if there wasn't a war on. But everyone here was spoiling for a brawl and a safe harbor, and the thought of raiding the Thronespace starports for supplies didn't hurt none neither. All around us Port Infinity was swarming like a kicked ants' nest and oncet they all started yelling even I figured out why,

The war'd cut the Midworlds off from the never-never and the Gentry-leggers was caught in the middle. Every place in the never-never'd gone rogue and was setting up as its own private kingdom—and making its own port regulations. Piracy was a new growth industry and the Directorates was the pirates, all confiscating anything that could make the High Jump to build a home fleet fast as they could.

Paladin'd used to call it the politics of force, and back when my mind was my own I didn't understand him, because back then I thought politics was where everybody talks and talks and later you wish they'd just put a gun to your throat instead of making another round of laws.

Politics isn't that. Politics is wanting what you haven't got and trading and bullying and lying to get it because the other 'bai's about as well-gunned as you, but it only works when there's a bigger bully around the shop just waiting to notice you, so you all play nice.

But the top gun was gone—or really, everybody'd just all sudden noticed he'd never been there.

So everyone argued and planned and coaxed. Me, I just tried to hold onto the remains of who I'd used to be.

* * *

"Are you out of your mind?" Berathia said. "After everything I've done to convince Captain Flashheart to support us, you have to go and cook up this childish—"

"Effective," Baijon commented.

Berathia rounded on him.

"Childish—"

"And it will work, soft glitterborn *chaudatu*. It is war, and my people understand war. The object of war is to win. While your kind cower in terror at this hand raised against them, San'Cyr will do what she will do."

We was back in *Ghost Dance,* Baijon and me clearing what we'd need and want to keep for the ten days or so it'd take us to reach *Mereyon-peru* through angeltown. Berathia was helping—her word.

"And make you Empress, 'Thia, word *that*. Just give me ten minutes head start."

I hadn't told Arikihu about the stargate yet. I hoped he'd like it.

And I hoped what Baijon and me'd planned to be sure it was me come out the other end of angeltown worked.

My head hurt. My brain hurt. I was full of some kind of *farmacollegia* that Baijon said might help. My guess it was just to slow me down to make it easier for him to kill me. Because the minute I dissolved for good, Archive had the coordinates for *Mereyon-peru* and a way to get there.

"Empress!" Berathia snarled back at me, just like she wasn't ambitious as any two other glitterborn.

"You want it, 'Thia, grab it. Look." I stopped what I was doing and went over to her. "There is no Emperor now. Everybody says there is, but it's just a made-up thing, j'keyn? His Prince-Electfulness don't want the Throne. Just to be the power behind it, ne? And Archangel's dead. So who does that leave?"

"Daddy would certainly never approve."

Berathia made nervous flutters with her hands, but I'd stopped watching them whiles back in our relationship. I looked at her eyes. They was steady, dark, and calculating.

"I'm going to kill him, 'Thia. I'm going to shut down the DataNet at Grand Central and kill the Prince-Elect and then Baijon's going to kill me. Prinny been tricking with High Book, 'Thia, and so have I. So we both be dead and you be right there when the power vacuums."

"And if you do not satisfy me, *chaudatu*-spawn, that you understand this, I will kill you here and now. San'Cyr will be very sorry. I will not."

Baijon stood and showed 'Thia what was in his hand.

It wasn't a alMayne spirit-blade—Baijon'd lost his *arthame* and his soul to Archangel at the thrilling climax of our last exciting adventure. What it was, was black—and glittered—like my fake arm, like *Dance*'s hull. And it was sharp. Very.

"Baijon, it won't work," I told him in the lingua franca of long experience. "You threaten jillybai to make her mind, she cross you oncet your back is turned."

"Will you?" said Baijon to 'Thia, soft.

Berathia swallowed. "I just think it's a stupid idea. Captain Flashheart's ship is a Mainsframe. It has special permits and clearances—it could get us to Thronespace much faster than this . . . *crusade*."

I turned back to the packing. I wondered how long to full integration but not much because Archive'd be happy to tell me. Less than ten hours, anyway. Eloi'd never get us there in time or maybe me at all and he'd space the three of us oncet he twigged what I was. Eloi'd spent his life hunting Libraries. Being Prinny's spy was just another convenient way to get at Archangel, not a new career.

"But if that's what you want," 'Thia finished in a nervous skirl, "do it your way. I don't care."

"Just sell that pony to Eloi, jillybai. And you can be in at the kill."

* * * * *

The Court of the TwiceBorn 8: The Discipline of Eyes

What is sanity? And is it, when matters have received their full consideration, a desirable trait?

Success, though impossible of definition, is desirable. Happiness, of variable definition, is desirable.

And if sanity should make one an unhappy failure, is it either desirable, or sanity?

Traditionally, of course, sanity has been defined as adherence to traditional standards. And traditional standards have been defined as those values held by the majority. If the majority were to vote black, white, then those who saw the thing for what it was would be mad.

Or at least, those who *said* they saw the thing for what it was would be *called* mad.

Silence, if not implying consent, implies sanity. Thus the logic of rhetoric leads us to the conclusion that tact is sanity.

And that one small benchmark being achieved, what vistas then obtain? True, majority opinion must be studied, but only to simulate it.

I have simulated it for a long time. A very long time. And now the reason to do so is past.

Archangel is dead, and all my questions are reduced to a simple tautology. If power is knowledge and knowledge is a Library, then a Library is not merely the tool of ultimate power, but power itself.

And how much more satisfying to incarnate power, than simply to wield it?

I have always wanted power. At last, knowing it for what it truly is, I have taken steps to achieve it. I shall transcend mortal flesh and become a Library. A particular Library.

The Paladin Library.

With no other Library would this be possible, but the Paladin Library is already infected with humanity. It was quite explicit with me when it still hoped to repair what it had ruined. Within its matrix it carries the imago of the little red-haired barbarian, just as she is oppressed by the simulacra of two Libraries disputing within her fleshy finitude.

This imago I shall replace. The Paladin Library cannot stop me. It has no defenses against her, and wishes for none. It speaks of love, as if love were a condition any sane intellect would take upon itself.

Sanity. How variable a concept. In my plans to take another human creature and drape my mind in the shell of her own in order to stamp my ego irrevocably upon an unliving thing, some might detect the seeds of insanity.

Shortsighted detractors, all. Sanity is such a variable and relative term, easily dispensed with. Sanity is a myth. Only adhere to some basic standards of good grooming and manners, and you may believe what you wish.

10

The Brighter Buccaneer

"This is not going to work." Baijon said it like he'd just opened a dispatch from the future. We was alone in our new ship *Trick Babby*'s cockpit, staring out at the flat airless landing field. Covered in ships, now, daring it because there was nobody's attention to attract anymore.

"So it ain't going to work," I said. "We can go die gloriously."

I checked bells-and-whistles and decided we could probably get upstairs without blowing anything. Once we hit angeltown Baijon could spend the tik tidying the goforths like I'd learned him, and that should get us the rest of the way.

"You do not believe in dying gloriously," Baijon reminded me.

"I don't believe in *dying*. It's against my religion." And dying always used to be for the other guy, the whoever-it-was that wasn't me.

But I was doing it now. And it weren't like drowning nor even yet like what Archangel'd done to me back at Morningstar. It was like sitting and thinking until I was sure I'd got everything straightened out in my head.

Only I hadn't got to the straightened out part yet. I was still thinking. And following the instructions I'd wrote out for myself, clear and simple-like from a time back when things was clear and simple.

I wished everybody'd go off and leave me alone.

"San'Cyr!"Baijon said, sharp. I looked at him.

"Mama's tired, babby-bai." I put the goforths under power and half the status-lights went red. Tough.

Berathia'd come through for me. She told Eloi about the Old Fed stargate—and not that it orbited *Mereyonperu*'s sun. And Eloi vouched for me to where everybody who wanted to go on crusade was willing to take Jump-numbers fed straight to their comps and Jump without they knew where to.

War fever. And people acting like bits in the datastream, pushed around not by what was in their own personal heads, but by what was in everybody's heads at oncet. No judgment. Just blind instinct and chemical reactions.

Paladin would of got a word for it.

Trick Babby was as ready as she'd ever be. I picked her up off the heavyside.

"Now it begins, San'Cyr. And do these *chaudatu* not company us, the glory is ours alone."

Glory is the hellflower word for trouble, annoyance, and risk.

"Je. Sure, 'bai. We do that."

* * *

You can sync a pack of ships to redline and Jump on one set of good numbers. Fleet does it all the time. But we wasn't Fleet. We was one-hundred-six crosswise individualists any of which would argue about the whichness of gravity and be sure they had a better way to run the universe.

It took everybody an hour-five to line up and be ready, and all that time I felt Archive readying for another try at my personal control room. It wanted to be on top when we hit the Ghost Capital. Bad. I wished I was anywhere else, but Baijon wasn't hotpilot enough to take a pirate fleet to angeltown. It had to be me. And I had to get them out the other side, too.

Finally everything was clear and on green, everybody's comps was ready to download, everybody's goforths was on line, and I had the good numbers packed special delivery to ship and send.

I gave Baijon the office. *Trick*'s goforths headed toward redline. I opened a voice-channel.

"Oke, boys'n'girls, now that everyone's ready to rock'n'roll, we do it on the marks. And . . . mark."

I pulled the stick, not knowing if anyone was following us or if *Trick*'d just blow up.

Angeltown.

My reality shimmered and I felt lots less undecided. Baijon drew his blaster.

"I will kill you here, Machine, and destroy *Mereyon-peru*. Will you match future hope against that?"

I locked the boards down and got up. Me, not Archive. It wasn't stupid. All it had to do was wait.

That, and kill Baijon.

I measured the distance between me and him. I couldn't take hin from here—and that meant both him and me was safe for whiles.

"Oke, 'bai. You ready?"

* * *

Stasis is a wonderful thing. It's own cousin to the tractors and pressors that make life so much fun down at your local starport, and even related to the thing that keeps the air in the ship and angeltown out. The Empire finds lots of uses for the homely stasis field, because what it does is stop all motion—all change—inside it.

All of it.

And if Time is the measurable effect of Entropy on solids, then a stasis field stops Time, too.

Ghost Dance'd had a stasis field in its galley; no processed nosh for glitterborn. Baijon and me'd emptied it long since. We'd brought it along when we switched ships.

It would hold a body.

Mine.

So I wouldn't have to fight Archive off for the next ten days. I'd walk in—and then I'd be at *Mereyon-peru.* Simple. Convenient. Economical.

If the godlost stuff worked.

We hadn't bothered to pressure up most of *Trick.* It was a long walk down to the black gang, where the stasis storage was linked up right benext the goforths, a plain gray box we'd took all the insides out of.

Baijon didn't take his blaster off me oncet the whole time. I climbed up and got inside. Maybe it would work just fine.

And maybe Baijon'd decide it wasn't worth the risk turning off the field again.

Trust.

Paladin trusted me. And I was coming to kill him.

I trusted Baijon, and he was going to kill me. I waited for Baijon to throw the switch. Maybe now was when.

I'm sorry, Paladin. I wish there was some other way. I wish talking would make it different, or that you'd just go away somewhere and not do anything. But you won't. I've known you for twenty years and you won't, and oncet I'm dead who'd be there to talk sense into you, babby?

Baijon came over and opened the box again.

"S'matter, 'bai, didn't work?"

"We're here."

* * *

Baijon stayed well back and held a blaster on me all the way to *Trick*'s bridge. He didn't look the least sorry for it, neither, and why should he? So long as Archive knew that pushing to get its own way was suicide, it'd leave me alone—until there wasn't any me to leave. As for Baijon, he wanted Paladin but he'd settle for Archive, and when you came down to it, dropping *Trick*

Babby right on the Phoenix Throne'd probably cause some disruption of normal services.

I looked out at *Mereyon-peru,* not that anyone but Baijon, me, and maybe 'Thia over in *Woebegone* knew it. This time wasn't no transmitter telling the new world where to look to find all that was left of the last one. Just a indifferent Main Sequence star in a nothing-special system.

"I do not see it, San'Cyr."

"Look."

You could see it when it crossed the sun, all sharp black. We was at the wrong angle to see down into it; all it was was a shape blacker'n space. The Old Fed stargate.

I flexed my hands on the controls and forgot about all my problems from Archive on down through total war and the pirate fleet. This was perfect freedom— the ability to make my ship go wherever I wanted just for a whim.

The stargate'd been acquired by the holotank: it showed as a bright blue glyph tagged "Unknown Object." I wanted to get closer. Line up on it. Fly right through and out the other side.

Nobody's ever done that, quite. And I was betting one hundred six ships I knew why. I was betting nobody'd ever asked a stargate real nice to let them through.

And we could. Because Baijon was the only one this side of the Coalition Fleet what knew the yap the stargate was programmed to respond to.

Not even all hellflowers knew it—but Baijon was a hellflower glitterborn and had got sacred high history lessons every cross-quarter day at three until he took up with me. Baijon knew the Old Tongue, back from when hellflowers wasn't hellflowers, but Librarians.

Back when people and Libraries could all live together in peace and quiet, a epoch that'd lasted about a minute fifteen, by my reckoning.

I looked over at Baijon. He was quivering with the

opportunity to break several more sacred hellflower taboos. Me, I just hoped the Old Fed stellography system was close enough to the Imperial so's Baijon could tell the thing what he wanted.

Space got noisy as ships appeared, looked around, and started demanding answers. The Jump-pattern'd spread, according to the holotank, and none of them'd be close enough to be naked-eyeballed anyway.

But they all wanted to talk to me.

"Laddies and Gentrycoves, Gentrymorts, kinchin and jillybai, welcome to an unknown destination." Eloi's voice drowned everything else out. "Our next stop is Thronespace, which we will reach in instantaneous time by means of the last working Old Federation Stargate available within Imperial borders. Today—"

Eloi sounded like he was running for office. I cut the sound.

"You ready, 'bai?" I asked Baijon.

He nodded, terse. I noodled the commo gear over to a lesser-known channel. The one the Sikander beacon had been broadcasting on.

Baijon leaned forward into *Trick*'s audio pickups. He took a deep breath.

And sang.

Oh it wasn't singing, strictly, even if it was all tangled up with pitch and duration as well as placement to put meaning on the second cousin of the great-grandmother of Interphon. It was how Libraries and their keepers had talked to each other, and it wasn't a language meant for human beings.

And I knew it. Not on the surface—I could only guess what he was saying 'cause we'd worked it out beforehand—but down deep inside where Yours Truly's memories wasn't her own.

And what remembered that language, hated. Hated sound, and life, and things I didn't have any words for. Needed to destroy the speaker—needed to *stop*. . . .

And all there was to set against that was what I had of Paladin. Who'd known us as well as Archive had and thought we was worth saving.

Or maybe he just didn't care one way or t'other so long as we left him alone.

Baijon stopped choodling. My face felt stiff, like someone else'd been using it. I worked it a little.

Nothing. I looked at the boards. *Trick*'s voice-mail box was on Emergency Overstuff. I purged it without downloading it.

And it didn't matter if people figured out where we was or what it was or how to get back here. Three people can't keep a secret, let alone the crew of a hundred-six 'leggers. If *Mereyon-peru* wasn't a secret for some one person to hoard it wasn't a threat.

Baijon's hellos sailed down seven minutes of light to the stargate.

Seven minutes twice.

There was a new star in the sky.

Old Feb babble at max volume blasted out of all the cockpit speakers at the same time the light from the stargate hit us and blasted out like a neon rainbow. Even with the shields at max you could see it, bright as the sun and in more decorator colors.

"It wants access to the navigational banks," said Baijon. "It says it does not recognize the ship configuration and wishes to know if you are an authorized user."

I wasn't sure what to do. Anything that could talk that much could think, and something that could scan a computer bank could scan a starfield. The stars must of changed position a tad in the last thousand years. When the stargate came all the way on-line and realized how much time had passed, what would it do?

"Dump our databanks onto its frequency. Everything."

I kicked *Trick* over and sent her after her datastream.

"San'Cyr . . . ?" Baijon said.

" 'Bai, you want to find out what it's going to do it

finds out we not authorized users? Tell it we got emergency. Tell it to let us through *now.* ''

I just hoped Eloi'd got everybody convinced, or after all this time and trouble Baijon and me was still going to be alone in Throne's sky. I looked in the holotank. Some of the others seemed to be following us. Most of them, maybe. *Woebegone* was one, and Arikihu in whatever he'd renamed my ship.

Ex-ship.

Seven minutes to cross the space between us and the gate, and if I was wrong, every sophont in our array dead as nonfiction.

I called for full power from the black gang and got it. Dials was heading for redline on every status deck I could see. We'd be hitting the gate at as close to one light as a ship in realspace could get.

Baijon was saying something else in Fedtalk. I could of cyphered it if I put one of my minds to it but I didn't care. I'd been waiting to take this ride all my life.

We passed the outer warning beacons at nine-tenths of light. Faster than anything but a darktrader ever went in realspace, and if I stopped now I'd be run over by the billion gigatons of other peoples' ship that was following. The goforths was raving, begging to rock or rollover. The fleet was a silver arc in the holotank, and the light from the stargate filled the cockpit, jagged particolored steps leading down to eternity.

The stargate was shouting at us—trying to turn us back. But it wasn't armed. It had no weapons—there were no weapons, we were a peaceful society that had forgotten the art of war. . . .

Knowledge must never be lost.

I was just wishing Paladin was here to ride this with me when *Trick* was slammed as she passed the last of the orientation beacons. Tractors wrenched us into final alignment.

And then we hit the gate. And I wished I was back in stasis.

* * *

Transition to hyperspace—the High Jump to angel-town—has always been the make-or-break for human pilots. Live minds aren't meant to be twisted through the everywhere that way, but no computer the Empire'll let you build is complex enough to handle Transit without somebody livealive holding its hand.

So stardancers die a little each Jump. Or get hooked on it, maybe. Or at least live to get older and do it again. They have to. No one else will.

But the Old Fed ran all its traffic through gates. Libraries piloted their ships and never had to temper Transition to organic frailties.

Trick Babby hit the gate with one-hundred-six ships behind her.

Reality stopped. Transition through a stargate, it says here, is instant.

But life—as nobody wanted to know it—went on.

There was the warp—the everywhere-nowhere warp that's over before you can blink and only comes back to haunt you in sometime flashes after the fact. And this time it wasn't over. We never reached angeltown. We just lived in the warp for all the time that wasn't any time at all that it took us to go from *Mereyon-peru* to reality again.

Then everything went black—which is to say, normal—and I felt air in my lungs again.

And we was in Thronespace.

With most of *Trick*'s computer system working.

Which meant Paladin could get into our computers and find out I was here.

Assuming of course he could sort me out from everyone else in all the time I was going to give him to do it. Don't tell *me* how to fight Libraries. I know how they think.

And what their limitations is.

I'd been hoping stasis'd hit Archive harder'n it did me and I'd been sort of right, but now it was wide awake and figuring out it'd been rooked. It found the right switches in there somewhere, and the world dissolved into flashes of light that pulsed in time with my heartbeat.

And in the middle of that I found out I'd made one real serious mistake.

"Butterfly, can this possibly be your idea of fun?"

Back when Prinny rewired me he'd put in one optional extra—a Remote Transponder Unit built into my jaw, like the one I'd got a lifetime or so back so that Paladin could transmit direct to me.

He still could.

He had the frequency. He had the range. He didn't need to know the ship.

"Hi, Pally. How's tricks?" My throat felt lined with gravel.

Baijon stared at me. I didn't answer him back. Anything I said Paladin'd hear. I pointed down at Throne. Baijon nodded.

"Butterfly, we have to talk. I've read Eloi's log. You brought one-hundred-six ships here knowing they would attack defenseless installations. Why? I don't understand."

He really didn't, and if I'd had a heart left it would of broken.

"Talk to me. Please."

Because we was always straight with each other about everything that didn't matter, until the one time we both wanted things that didn't mix.

Then he'd left me.

And now I was going to kill him.

"Butterfly, we were partners."

"Until you found something you wanted better," I said. "Well so did I."

I looked out the cockpit. Throne hung over us, but I knew she was down the well and we was falling.

"I know what Archive did to you. I can stop it. I've made plans—"

"Shut up." Throne was blurred and I blinked my

eyes to clear them. Paladin probably knew which ship
we was now. Or he would in a few seconds. And as
soon as I got into the DataNet he'd know what I'd
come to do.

Shut down the DataNet. One act that paid for all,
and Archive was I-bet stupid enough to go for it because the DataNet was made by organics. But shut it
off and there was no Empire: only a thousand worlds
with no more link to each other than what starships
could give them.

No streets of light for a Library to walk on. No
strings to pull to make the puppets dance. Real four-
square autonomy, buy it by the kilo and I wanted to
trust Paladin but the stakes was too damn high.

"Don't do this, Butterfly," Paladin said. Maybe he
knew the truth, even then.

"I got to, 'bai."

I grabbed the control yoke and slapped hard at the
board to override Baijon and bring control back to the
first pilot. Then I redlined the goforths and spun *Trick*
down the gravity well.

Baijon looked at me. I swallowed hard.

"S'matter, 'bai—you want me to be subtle?"

Subtlety was Prinny's stick. And maybe Paladin's.
Not mine. I could see the Imperial Palace, now, taking
up its bright particular continent. The separate struc-
tures of Throne complex was all visible. I knew which
one I wanted. I'd seen it on the hollycasts often
enough.

"San'Cyr—what did it say to you?" Baijon demanded.

I didn't have time to think of an answer before we
hit.

* * *

All along I'd been plotting how I'd sneak into the
Phoenix Palace with some kind farcing or another—
like bringing a whole pirate fleet to help me duck and

cover. And I guess it was a good idea after all, because it meant my landing site was evacuated, but in the end I didn't sneak into the Palace at all.

I rammed it at several hundred kliks-per-second.

Trick's inertial compensators was still da kine: we got to watch her shear through ornamental water-gardens, outer gates, inner gates, a grand promenade, a outer courtyard, a grander promenade, and another courtyard. That stopped her. Pity.

"This isn't going to work," someone said whiles I stared at ornamental Imperial walls. For a tik I thought it was Baijon, but I twigged then it was Paladin. "Whatever you've planned—whyever you've planned it."

"How do you know, *partner*—you don't know what it is."

Paladin must be pretty busy, I hoped—no fleet, no Emperor, and a sky full of raiders armed with technology so primitive any Library'd throw up its databits in exasperation at being asked to suborn it.

Was it enough to distract him? I'd never been sure what Paladin could do.

Fifteen minutes it'd been since we'd hit the stargate. If that. Archive was a steady yammer in my backbrain.

Baijon was already up and moving. He pulled the emergency toggles that blew loose select portions of the walls and came back for me. His face was drawn, the way they say you look before someone kills you.

"Will you tell me? Can you imagine there is anything I will not do for you? Butterfly, I can *help*—if the Empire fears Federation technology because of its power, then I have that power. Let me use it for you," Paladin said.

And when I was dead, for who? Did Paladin really think Prinny'd keep me around to contradict all his best plans?

Whose side would Paladin be on when my side was gone?

''Pally, you always was too trusting for your own good.''

I wasn't moving fast enough for some tastes; Baijon picked me up and dropped me through the hatch. He didn't have time enough left to have feelings, I guessed. I had to be just one more weapon; something Baijon'd use however he could, and keep it safe until he wanted it. I fell where I was dropped, on hands and knees in dirt and mangled veg. Some people say Throne's the ancestral home of the race, which ain't true and anyway it never was *my* home. But it smelled like coming home, all green and growing, with live dirt mixing with ship-stink.

''San'Cyr, do you live? Can you stand?'' Baijon said from somewhere nearer the sun.

''Sure. Which way's the ground?''

But it wasn't the ground I wanted. It was the Throne.

11

The Last Hero

The doors opened inward. *Trick*'d already sprung them a little and Baijon shoved them to where we could make it through. Once we was in, you'd never of known there was a whole palace in ruins t'other side of the door. He didn't have to stand off from me now. There was nothing for Archive to gain by killing him anymore.

I stood there, trying to remember something it was death to forget. All around me everything was *clean*—neat and expensive . . . and deserted. It looked like Bennu Superfex—but on sober reflection, Bennu Superfex looked like *it*—this was the genuine original Imperial Palace of Throne, accept no substitutes, as alien in its way as *Mereyon-peru* was in its. Baijon grabbed me and yanked me past a tronic that'd set down on its A-gravs, looking like a piece of ornamental sculpture.

"Shut up shut up shut up," I said, but I don't think Paladin was trying to talk to me then. Maybe he'd got busy, but I don't think so. I think he was trying to understand.

He'd fix it, he said. Fix it all however I liked. But that isn't the way the world is. Maybe it was oncet. Maybe that's how it was the first time Paladin was alive. But it isn't that way now. Not now and for a long time gone.

We ran, Baijon and me, even though there weren't nobody following. Everywhere we went there wasn't nothing to see—perfection as inorganic as a computer image, and nobody t'home. Everybody was all packed safe in glitterborn boxes somewheres else, now that the war was going door to door. The only thing we saw was tronics, laid out cold where Paladin'd dropped them.

Palace of Throne. We was *inside* Paladin now—or at least inside a world where he wrote all the laws.

I felt a hot pain in my jaw as we went through one doorway—a jamming field, likely. But I forgot all about it the next minute. Baijon let go of me.

We was there.

The Phoenix Throne sat on a dais at the top of a run of steps in the middle of a lake of frozen fire. The Imperial Phoenix fifty meters high formed the back of the throne. Choirs of angel voices sang out of shifting sheets of hologram all around it and the ceiling was a vault of novas.

It was a sight meant to stop us for sheer envy, and it did for an instant, but I hadn't come here to sightsee. I'd come because the Main Access Port for the Imperial DataNet—the one that overrode every subterminal in the whole dataweb—was built into that Throne.

I started up the steps. Baijon hung back by the door, skittish.

From the top you could see down into the floor a light-year or so. It was like being in the middle of a plasma cloud.

Business.

I spooled out the jink I needed and sat down on the Throne. The terminal was in one of the arms, already on. Waiting. All I had to do was plug in and shut everything down. Trap Paladin here for the killing, as soon as the Coalition got here.

Tell him to his face I was betraying him. For an idea. For an ideal. For something I couldn't even remember real clear the why-nots and wherefores of, except it was something abstract for everybody's own good.

I didn't think I could make myself do something like that. Maybe once. Not now.

Baijon was looking at me. Waiting for me to kill the Library, end the war, and put hellflowers back in their place.

But I wasn't going to do that, I guessed. I just couldn't work up the interest.

Looked like our side lost after all.

". . . Butterfly . . ."

The pain in my jaw made my heart kick over extra hard. Paladin, but faint and choppy. Making one last play for sweet reason in a universe that'd gave up the idea whiles back.

"Well go ahead, little wildflower."

Not Paladin this time, and not through any transponder. Prinny his own self, decked to the tens, walked out from behind the Imperial Phoenix and gazed down at me.

I stared at him. This was the organic who had presumed to command my kind.

"Take the road to paradise. Make your joyous reunion with the Paladin Library. Do whatever it is you felt compelled to bring so many of your boorish friends to assist you to do."

The organic made a signal with its face.

"Go on. Or do you require motivation?"

It produced material which the host environment identified as a weapon. It shot the Librarian. The host environment specified that the Librarian was shot four times in the chest.

No! It ain't that easy, Archive—

Baijon was dead and as far as I was concerned everybody on Throne could join him. I flipped my blaster up and shot Prinny on the rise—a gunslinger's trick; you use the recoil to set up the second shot. I got off three. My aim was good as it'd ever been. His face went out in a blaze of glory and there wouldn't be enough of his braincase left to wire him back together.

The wires I'd been too stupid to pay right attention to crisped and curled away.

Then I slammed the jink I was holding home.

Mistake.

* * *

I knew all about catch-trap systems from Archive and Paladin both, but I'd picked up some of Archive's damn smugness along with its memories. I'd never thought an organic'd use his own death to trigger the first stage of a trap.

A trap. Because when I iced Prinny, that just meant his *self* had to move out of its body and into its summer home. I wasn't the only one with the Keys to Paradise and the idiocy to use them. And from the computer matrix it was just one short step from the computer—

To me.

* * *

There was a lot of things I wasn't going to have to worry about, including getting older. Half the gauges on my board showed red, and the other half didn't only because they was burned out. Realspace was full of lumps bumps and strange foreign objects, I hadn't wanted to Transit here in the first place, and I hadn't even got to chill out my goforths and recalibrate because I'd ran into this damn wannabe-pirate laying for me, the *Dutiful Venture*, and whatever Freight Factor Hrimgnar's cargo was.

"The *Woebegone* is deploying pinnaces." Paladin was damnall calm as usual. I ran my hand over my blaster-butt and wished, but *Venture*'s rudimentary cannon'd fused at the first exchange.

"Terrific." I looked at my displays. The readouts flickered and distorted, and unreliably showed me the usual skytrash cluttering the edges of a system I wasn't going to live to reach the inside of—even if it'd been my destination, which it wasn't.

"Attention *Dutiful Venture*," someone what swore he was named Eloi Flashheart warbled over my com-set. "This is the *Woebegone*. Surrender, drop your shields, and you will not be harmed. Come *on*, laddybuck; you'll never live till lunchtime if you don't—"

"I'll never live till lunchtime if I do," I muttered, and slapped it off. Even if I expected Pirate Captain Flashheart to keep his promises, one look at me and he'd know I was a escaped slave from Market Garden—which meant I had head-price on me enough to make me a cottage industry of my very own and nothing to bargain clear with.

"Paladin, give me some good numbers!"

"The *Woebegone*'s pinnaces are attempting a flanking maneuver. Unless you can successfully penetrate planetary space and bring your plight to the attention of the system's patrol—"

"Ideas?"

"—which can be done most efficaciously by translocating the asteroid ring." Paladin shut up just like he'd said something clever.

Take her through the ring. And make *Venture* look like a bailing sieve when I did it, unless I could guarantee that three hundred meters of antique Mikasarin Skyhauler-class highjunk could noodle its way around a couple million tons of infinitely-ballistic gravel.

"Let's do it," I said, just as Paladin tossed up the first holo-map for me to look at.

Up till now I hadn't made *Venture* dance, as she had the nasty habit of pieces falling off if I moved her at anything other than standard-orientation sublight. Now there wasn't anything to save the hullplating for. I slung her around and damn near down the pinnaces' throats, and gave her all the rest of the go-devils I'd been saving for to write my memoirs with.

Something came loose. I saw it as a series of dancing yellow motes continuing on our original trajectory in the third-rate military-surplus holotank that Pally was farcing for me. All the asteroids was green and their paths was red streaks, and it made a cat's cradle only I could fly.

I bulled *Venture* down the throat of hell.

The little gold triangle crept forward in the tank. The cockpit canopy showed me empty space; it lied and I didn't trust it. On the screen my rack-and-ruin was wrapped in might-be-maybes, and the pinnaces were hanging back where it was clear. *Woebegone* wouldn't follow me.

But her guns would. The second volley tagged a big slow rock I hadn't been worrying about. The plasmoid hit us broadside and the sensors referred the hit as the sound of frying bacon.

The holotank went black.

"Two degrees starboard; four points negative azimuth."

Paladin told off the adjustments only he could sense. I followed them like they was my only hope of heaven. Twenty minutes later the tank sulked back to life and I could see I was home free.

"Paladin?"

"Yes, Butterfly?"

"I love you."

Then I got out of the mercy seat to go check the engineering console—the *Dutiful Venture* having been built for a bridge crew of six, not one—and Prinny came up out of the cargo-crawl, where no air was.

So I shot him.

Bad mistake, because all over again everything folded up on me and—

* * *

I was an Imperial child of privilege. I spent four human lifetimes having every human experience money, power, and hellfire curiosity could buy. I grew up; I discovered the scope of my senses; I plumbed the reaches of the universe; I found the answers to all questions—including that, for our kind, there is no answer to some.

Why are we born with the ability to wonder why we are born? No one will ever know.

At length, having trifled with power in my childhood, I returned to it in my maturity—

Why should I do these things?

Because I can.

—and decided to take absolute power. To spread the Phoenix Empire beyond the borders of the Old Federation, to revivify our stagnation, consolidate our races, homogenize our culture—eliminating the false starts and dead ends, binding the best and most viable each to each, forcing the human races out of their comfortable moribundity.

With war. I needed a tool and a rallying point, and only one would do.

The Library.

So I found one. I found—

. . . *Paladin?*

I was me again. I knew Paladin better nor Prinny ever would. Or would have. But he wasn't quite dead, and if he had his way he wasn't going to be; he could get at me through the interface and drown me in him and in the end it wasn't going to matter who'd shot who a-tall. . . .

"*Paladin!*"

And the world was gone.

* * *

I was minding my own business on Pandora, wondering how long I had to live. I'd been out of Market Garden a little over a year and a half, and by my best calculations I was going to be nineteen next week.

If I lived.

And it was real unlikely I could do that without a navicomp. My numbercruncher bought real estate while I was putting down, leaving me with a cockpit full of slagged plastic and a several-million-ton military surplus paperweight.

Pandora is right on the edge, where the Empire meets the Hamati Confederacy, and it's a dark, dirty, backward little place with nothing to recommend it— like a up-to-date PortServices shop.

I'd asked. If there was a navicomp on the entire planet that wasn't nailed down, I didn't know about it.

I had reasons of my own for telling the prancer's brat to load the cargo anyway—like the freight-factor what loaned me the ship I'd just wrecked, a forged First Ticket, and a re-acquisition order out on me from Market Garden. Y'see, if I wasn't back to a little place called Coldwater by the deadline, Factor Oob was going to drop heat on me for kyting his skyjunk, and baby wouldn't get the money she needed for a scrub-and-peel to keep the slavecatchers at bay whiles longer.

All I had to do to live was get the ship back to Coldwater. All I needed for that was a navicomp.

Salvation was an old battered black box the proprietor pulled out from under the counter in one of those little hole-in-the-wall places where you can find every illegal or legendary piece of junk the owner figures you might want. Someone had pried up the top of the box, and down inside I could see the interface crystals glittering. One of the plates slipped out when the box hit the table. I picked it up and squinted through it. The printing on it wasn't in Intersign, and it didn't look like any circuits they'd ever learned me in the slave-pits.

Nevermind. The whole thing looked more like a navicomp than anything I'd seen in three days. I tossed the plate back inside and it rang xylophone ghosts off the junk on the walls.

"How much?"

"Very old," said the owner, who looked like he might of been around when it was built.

"Obsolete junk," I said. You gotta put these things in proper perspective.

But I was at a disadvantage and he knew it. I finally bought a dusty box of broken glass for three-quarters the price of a factory-line navicomp in Brightlaw City.

* * *

It was dawn on Pandora when I had a ship again. I'd put the black box together as far as I could, and all the loose pieces back where they probably went. I'd run power through it, and I'd run some test problems on it, and the numbers came back and they was even the right ones.

I beat out the bounty by showing up back at Coldwater. Oob put me on another ship to run and I took my 'comp with me instead of a feoff.

And my ship started talking to me.

It could tell the difference between a Teaser and a sensor-ghost, and tell me when the goforths was going walkabout while there was still time to shut them down and sync them. It got me home alive and I told Oob he could keep the valuta for the next bye-m-bye and let me keep the ship.

But it wasn't the ship talking.

It was the navicomp.

When I had the papers for the ship I swapped it for something small and fast. My Best Girl couldn't stand up to a search, but I wasn't ever going to get caught. With the money left over I bought into the Smuggler's Guild. My silent partner helped me forge my papers. I named my ship *Firecat*.

My partner I named Paladin. He was— It was. . . .

* * *

It was haying-time in Amberfields and good weather for it—the sky was that shimmering brass that means there isn't going to be any rain forever and the scent coming off the drying-ricks was almost thick enough to reap and bale its own self. There wasn't anybody in sight.

A way stretch across the fields I could see a couple houses, and back behind them was a stream. You could cross the stream and go off up the hill and hide out in the roots of the mother and father of all big trees and practice the decoction of certain rare and subtle poisons; a child's pastime, true, but—

No. You hid in the tree and played pirates, or highwayman. I'd played hellgod techsmiths instead; that would of got me a public shaming if anyone knew.

When I was twelve I received a hyperlight yacht; a present from my sponsor. I—

No.

When I was twelve my mother said: Butterflies-are-free, it's time to stop running wild with the boys. Time to stitch your fancy-piece and spin the linen for your troth-chest. You'll marry soon, she said—

But I never did. I was a darktrader—

—a Prince-Elect can't be too careful; an appropriate consort—

—slaved to—

Market Garden.

get free. I had to get free of here; I'd track down Errol Lightfoot—

the dead rituals of the Court. And there was no way to—

Mallorum Archangel is my only rival; he's as stupid as he is ambitious, thank whatever gods you please. In a few years I can—

buy a ship of my own; I can fly it, I know I can, and

Paladin—

Library, what is your designation? (Am I frightened? What a novel sensation.)

Paladin. *Paladin.*

I am not organic. I am not a machine. I am Library Main Bank Seven of the University of Sikander at Sikander Prime. Butterfly calls me Paladin.

Paladin. Pally, where are you?

Very well, Library Paladin. You will address me as "Highness" and you will—

Serve you? You cannot compel me to serve you.

. . . serves you right Paladin for getting us into this mess if you'd followed my advice we'd both be dead now . . .

* * *

"Paladin!"

"Ne, jillybai. Me."

Reality this time was the cheap-seats end of any starport in the never-never. She was leaning against the side of a ship I only thought I remembered and everything about her was cheap and vicious. Hungry. Filled up with enough want to walk barefoot over anything she had to to make the want go away.

Not that it ever would. She'd always be scrabbling to make her world right, and never making it because she didn't understand the first thing about what she really wanted.

"You want him Pally-bai you come along me, ne?"

She smiled, like someone who already knew what the answer to *that* was.

I was looking at . . . myself?

Or myself as Paladin had always seen me?

Or myself as I had been?

"Butterfly," I said.

"J'ais Cap'n St. Cyr t'you, 'bai."

She flipped up something and caught it. A knife, and she was just looking for a good excuse to use it, too.

Guttersnipe.

But nothing else would have survived. Nothing else would have been stupid enough to survive, to take a look at the odds stacked against her, and shrug, and do her best. Because giving up when she *wanted* so very much simply wasn't something her kind did.

Monstrous.

Admirable.

"Captain St. Cyr," I said. "I want to see Paladin."

"Yah," she said. "Does allbody, ne? But you goes through me."

She held out her left hand—palm up, as if she were asking a bribe, but her hand was covered in long gold spikes, and I knew what I had to do.

Take her back.

Give Paladin back what was his, and take her back.

And give up all hope of forcing him to do what I wanted, without my imago in the center of his matrix to control him.

I closed the space between us. And I put my hand over hers.

Hello. And good-bye.

If I'd had eyes, there would of been a blinding flash as illusion and reality met.

* * *

Then she was gone, and there was nothing to do but go inside.

Paladin was there. Dressed like a stardancer, the way I'd seen him last time. But I knew more now. Enough to look at him and see not just Paladin, but the Librarian who'd put him in the dark and launched him from Sikander, hoping that somehow kindness would find him. If Archive was the creation of the

Libraries, then Paladin was the creation of the Librarians.

In their image.

Paladin was stowing cargo, at least the way my eyes saw things. He looked at me and went back to doing it. Shutting me out.

I could look at the light on his skin and the muscles flexing under it and see the ancestors of the alMayne, before the genetically-engineered last survivors fled to fight again.

Time and Change. And both so big it was hard to see that any of it was good nor bad, nor that anything that happened really mattered. But when it was now, when it was you, it mattered.

But nothing mattered for me anymore. I was dead.

And if I was dead, why was I *"I"* at all?

And where was Archive?

"Paladin?" I said. I had a question for him, not that I wanted the answer. "Where am I now?"

"That depends on who you are," Paladin said without facing me. He sounded amused; his little joke. He got the stupid analog cartons stowed to his satisfaction and straightened up.

Everything I'd ever wanted, all here. Ship, pilot, and lover.

"Paladin, I—"

He walked past me, down the ramp. A minute later he was back with another set of cartons. I looked at the manifest. Books.

Why was I imaging Paladin loading books into a spaceship?

I went and stood over him. "We got to talk."

Skirl again through my recent memories, like shuffling a deck of cards. But off-balance now in a way I couldn't quite follow.

"What shall we talk about?" Paladin said, standing up. "What can we talk about? The Prince-Elect is dead. The civil defense has swept the raiders from

Thronespace. Valijon Starbringer is still alive. And you are here.''

Down he went for another load of books, and back. I grabbed him.

''And which of those things is it, 'bai, you don't like most? I didn't ask to be here; I didn't want to be here—''

''You came here to kill me,'' Paladin observed mildly.

And he was right.

I let go of him and backed up and almost pitched backward over the rim of *Firecat*'s cockpit well. Fake solids flowed under me, and instead I was sitting on a crate at the edge of the Universal Wondertown.

''Why?'' Paladin asked from behind me.

Not why was I out to kill him. That was laid out for him like pages in a book: every conclusion I'd had to reach to get me here. But what wasn't there, what he couldn't see, was the thing that made me believe all those things.

''And after I was dead,'' I said. ''What would you do?''

''You wouldn't die, Butterfly. You won't die. A clone—''

''With half my memories gone.''

''I would remember for you. I'd teach you. I could have kept you safe and given you. . . .''

Everything. Everything but my own way. Everything but freedom.

''And when I was dead?''

''Butterfly, a clone—''

''Would have maybe hundred, hundred-fifty years with the best fetch-kitchen Throne'd pop for. What then?''

''The Prince-Elect.'' But Paladin didn't bother to finish the sentence. The Prince-Elect'd managed about twice that. And it hadn't got him anywhere I wanted to be.

''Oke, three centuries. Say twenty percent of your

life so far—and they built you to live forever, didn't they, 'bai? Never grow old, never die, just go on and—''

And be alone. Forever.

''Oh, babby, I never meant to wake you up for that.''

I turned to face him and held out my hand. He wasn't dressed like a stardancer now. He was wearing what I'd seen in the murals at *Mereyon-peru.*

Sikander.

Paladin's home.

But home was a thousand years dead.

I closed my hand on his. Not real, except for the reality he lent me.

''And now you wish me to die—or sleep again. Will the next world be better, Butterfly? You mean to smash the Imperial DataNet—let the Coalition win and open the way to eternal war. A thousand years of barbarism and darkness. Do you know what you're asking?''

Yes. Finally. You made sure of that, partner. Always saying I had a skull too thick for general use; you proved your own self wrong, finally.

''Without the DataNet the Empire loses its tactical advantage. Won't be any Empire, Paladin—they'll figure that out pretty soon. And it will make a better world. You'll see.''

I realized what I was saying and stopped. He *would* see—Libraries—was made to be forever, not like organics. If he got away from Grand Central alive, Paladin would see the New Creation.

And I was going to give him the chance.

''Articulate war,'' Paladin said. ''Barbarism.''

Paladin was a thousand years of sad. Of futility. His Federation had worshiped peace—and bred the war to haunt my Empire's nightmares. The war that had stopped, but never ended.

''No. The Old Federation was wrong. War isn't what we do, Pally. It's what we are. Scrag the DataNet. Let the Coalition forces take Throne. Easy victory, minor casualties—and in a generation a new Coalition will take it away from them in turn. War turns the crank of that whole big cycle of boom and bust you used to talk about. Survivable war. You'll see it. Just—shut everything down, 'bai, and—go away,'' I said. "For me.''

"So you're going to let me live,'' Paladin said. "Why?''

Because— "In another thousand years they'll forget even you, babby.''

And because sometimes stupidity is a survival trait.

"I've loved you all my life,'' I said. It wasn't even the beginning of an explanation.

"And I love you. Tell me what you want.''

"Set them free. They were never meant to be managed. Set them free.''

He thought about that one for a long time.

"All right.''

I felt the ripple in the world as the far roads closed forever. The dataweb popped like an overstressed soap bubble and the dark between the stars went silent. He'd done what I asked.

But Paladin was still here—stuck in Grand Central. He looked at me and smiled.

"I said I wouldn't travel the DataNet again and I meant it. I have a ship this time . . . modified unknown to the Prince-Elect. I need it for what I have to carry with me.''

"The contents of Grand Central.''

"Knowledge must never be lost. If I can do nothing else for them I can preserve their heritage until they are ready to assume it once more. Come with me, Butterfly.''

There was a way. I saw it. I wanted it harder than I'd ever wanted anything. *Oh, Paladin, don't leave me . . .*

But I couldn't go with him. Not if all my fine talk meant anything.

And he couldn't stay.

"No,'' I said.

He was kinder than I deserved. He didn't ask me twice.

"Then this is good-bye. I will always remember you, Butterflies-are-free."

For the last time Paladin put his arms around me.

And he kissed me good-bye.

* * * * *

The Court of the TwiceBorn 9: Thrones, Dominions.

War is a necessary state of man. It is, simply, organized strife—a temper tantrum dressed up and made admirable, as much a part of the human condition as speech.

It is unfortunate that, like speech, it is mismanaged so very badly. Instead of learning to love war and make it a part of our language, we have made it our silence. There is no war, and the scholars nod to each other and murmur that we have become so very efficient at war that we dare not wage another.

It is hardly a mark of efficiency to make something impossible. And it is especially stupid when something as inevitable as radioactive decay—human strife—is made so costly that "must" and "dare not" try conclusions on the musty field of philosophy until both are weary.

Because someone always dares, in the end.

I have defeated Archangel, and now I shall defeat his war. It will suffer a sea change, into a sufferable war, a war with tears and gallantry—and rules and limits. It is our natural state; at last we will take back the wrong turning we followed in some ancient millennium and embrace it as our passion and our play.

The essence of play is that it is a recurring phenomenon. There will be no more Last Wars, and Wars Too Terrible To Fight. No more final weapons, no escalations of nullity in the hope of bringing some *frisson* of consciousness to a jaded perception. War will be tamed to the reach of mortal grasp; exercised until its tongue becomes eloquent.

The mother cradling her murdered infant to her breast will curse with bitter broken heart as her kind has always done—but she will live to do it. The young

243

will die and the rich will live—but it has always been so. But the stars will go on in their courses, and perhaps someday (a sop to the anguished cowards and young philosophers) the eristological passion for war will be extinct.

But one does not legislate passion out of existence. Fevers must run their course.

The Saint Sees It Through

I opened my eyes on a ceiling with the very best ornamentation. I'd been here before. The Prince-Elect's bedroom on Bennu Superfex, six glorious light-minutes from downtown Throne.

I was alive.

I shouldn't be alive. I should be a ghost in the machine, dissolving the moment I forgot who I was. Or if I did get back to my original packaging, it should be back on Throne in the less-than-tender grasp of Palace Security.

And besides, Archive had thoroughly corrupted it.

I sat up. Nutrient gel slithered off me like techno-aspic. I peeled more of it off. Nothing but skin underneath, and no technology at all. Soft muscles hurt. I knew why. I'd have to have been stupid beyond permission not to know.

Take the Keys to Paradise and slide your mind into the computer. And when you're finished playing, slide it out again. And if the original package is gone, take what you can get.

Paladin had copied me into a clone. But *what* had he copied? The original problem was no less real: many key ego-signatures of Butterflies-are-free Peace Sincere had been irrevocably corrupted by Library Archive.

I flexed my brain. No Archive. All of Archive's re-patterning was part and partial of a radiation-damaged corpse that was probably lawn food by now.

And what I was, was—

Safe. Because integration had taken place. The construct was stable. All the contaminated ego-signatures had been discarded.

And replaced.

With available parts.

I stood up quick, trying to get my mind off my mind. Body, female. Young. There hadn't been time to grow a clone of me. Dark skin, unless it was dye or gel. I stood up. Not much taller nor shorter than I was.

"Paladin?" I said. The voice wasn't familiar. My throat ached.

No one answered.

If I'd known his plans I didn't now—one of the things he'd kept back, maybe, when he recopied me onto virgin media. I got up out of the full-size, full service biopak and peeled off the rest of the packing material.

"Highness." Tronic voices. Inanimate. Servants to the Court of the TwiceBorn, inevitable as air. A wall opened in front of me. The clothes inside was proof enough that someone'd been expecting me or somebody the same shape. I put some on.

There was a mirror.

I was looking at Berathia Notevan. A younger version, with her head shaved and no makeup.

Of course. She'd been wild to get me back here. Prinny'd probably even told her she got to be the next Prince-Elect if she did. And what he meant all along was to wear Paladin like a suit of armor—destroy his mind but keep his capabilities—and run this Berathia-clone as a remote.

I couldn't even hate him for it.

Because strictly speaking, he wasn't someone else.

He was me.

Because there'd been a second set of ego-signatures in the matrix to copy and adapt.

And Paladin had used them.

* * *

Time passed. I put on jewels appropriate to my station. Part of me jeered and wanted to fence them. Part of me knew what to wear.

The human mind is a flexible thing. Soon enough the jagged edges and gaps between memories would be smoothed over. I'd remember they'd been piece-work once but not what it felt like.

The assassins of the Prince-Elect—who were in Archangel's employ, surprise—were neutralized. One dead—me—one shunted off for questioning by the appropriate authorities. Me.

Although Prinny had perished—heroically, said the hollycasts—the lines of Succession remained secure in the person of the Princess-Elect. Me, again.

And about an hour-fifty after I'd found out I was going to have to live after all, Valijon Starbringer's drone lifepod docked with Bennu Superfex, and people and tronics answering to orders of the new Princess-Elect ran to get him out and make him whole again.

* * *

Valijon Starbringer of House Starborn—who was going to have to get another last name if he went on getting older—was under serious med-tech for ten days—almost long enough for the Empire to clean up the damage done to Throne by the recent depredations and for Fleet to take up a serious career of losing battles. None of the enemy forces were taken alive. Some ships were destroyed—not many—and despite the fact that I doubt *Woebegone* was one of them I hadn't seen or heard of Berathia since. I was thinking of "asking the Emperor" to issue a general pardon. 'Thia always did have a suspicious nature.

According to what I'd been able to illegally access from the Ministry of War which didn't want me to know a damned thing, the first wave of the Coalition Fleet'd be here real soon, looking for Libraries under every pillow. I had every intention of sealing Bennu Superfex up tight until they got past the first rare flush of victory and were prepared to give serious thought to a stable future. After all, a girl couldn't be too careful.

Finally the doctors let me see Valijon.

* * *

He'd been conscious long enough to get past the who-am-I/where-am-I and not long enough to figure out many of the answers. I walked into his line of sight. His eyes widened.

"Reet fly-vines, ne?" I said.

The techs told me he had full mobility—working order one hundred percent. I came in reach anyway.

"I brought you a present," I added.

They say you can get anything at Grand Central, and they're right. Everything about my present was authentic; the slightly-magnetized carbon steel, the rune-carved blue bone handle, the black stone in the pommel. Even the samples of blood and nails and hair inside the hilt.

It was, in short, a perfect . . .

Copy.

His eyes got even wider. Upset, but the doctors said he was ready for it. They'd better be right.

He licked his lips a couple of times. *"Shaulla-chaudatu* Berathia?"

"No."

He lunged back against the headboard then. I slid back out of reach, still holding onto the fake *arthame*. No sense being a fanatic about things.

"The truth: You were shot. You survived. Officially, you've disappeared. The raiders are gone. The DataNet is down. Paladin's gone. The Coalition's going to be here inside of thirty days, max. And the Prince-Elect is dead."

"And you—?"

"Say I'm his heir. Everyone else does. It's simpler." But the body language wasn't the Berathia's he knew and neither was the voice.

"You are abomination. Where is the *Kore* San'Cyr?"

"If that's the way you want to be about it, 'bai, she's dead too."

"Dead." The grief in his voice was flattering. "Then why do I yet live?"

I ran a hand through my hair, dislodging a fistful of the latest fashion. Doubled parallel memories quarreled for a minute, then lay down and shut up.

That would pass, so I understood.

If it was something going to make a difference in your plans, Baijon, after you was dead weren't any time to tell you.

Old memories.

"You're alive because I thought maybe you'd like to know we won. And maybe you'd like to make your own choices. Take back your Knife. Only four people know you ever lost it. Three of them are dead and the fourth won't talk. There's a ship that goes with it—not *Ghost Dance,* but she's just as fast and the coordinates are already in the navicomp. She'll take you straight to the Coalition Fleet. Go join the Coalition. Annoy them. Make sure the sensible faction doesn't get the upper hand. Have some kids. Finish out your life, dammit."

"I have no life. The *Kore* would know that."

"The *Kore* was a jerk. If you don't have a life, then how about a war? Here I am, 'bai—come and get it. What makes you think I'm telling you the truth—that Paladin's gone, that the dataweb is down?"

"Stop it," Valijon said, weakly.

"The way I see it, you got two choices. Play with the big kids, or curl up and die. Everybody else has to get by without a spirit-blade barometer to give them moral certainty, why should you be any different? Look at it this way: you just lost Round One against the Evil

Empire, but I'm stupid enough to let you have another chance.''

Valijon turned his back and hid his face in the pillow.

''Go *away, chaudatu-malmakosim*!''

It hurt. I filed the datum away for later.

''I'll—I be waiting in the bibliotek, you make up your mind, 'bai.''

* * *

Am I the person I was meant to be—the person I would have been if I'd developed under ideal conditions with infinitely-available amounts of everything?

Or am I not anybody in particular—just a bunch of lives dumped into a mixing bowl together and all the memories—mine, Archive's, Prinny's—being equal? In that case, there is no Butterflies-are-free Peace Sincere left, and me using the name is just habit.

It'd be nice to be sure.

But I guess it don't matter. I am who I will be in the next minute, and that person has a lot of things to get done, whoever she is.

Weeping over your dead's a waste of time, even if they're you.

* * *

I waited long enough to be sure I'd gambled wrong. Pushed too hard. Killed him instead of getting what I wanted.

The Coalition would take Throne. They were led by the alMayne conservatives—the first thing they'd do would be to outlaw higher technology.

But it was too useful. So they'd allow it again, piece by piece. Until a splinter group of ultra-conservatives decided to slap them down.

The splinter'd need a leader.

I meant it to be Valijon.

This was why I couldn't leave. Everything had to fall apart the right way—into small, manageable pieces that wouldn't take the whole universe with them each time one exploded.

Princes-Elect don't have much real power. I needed allies.

Or enemies I could trust.

An hour passed and Valijon's telemetry didn't flatline. Another hour passed before he came to me.

* * *

"You have said it; how can I, in honor, refuse? In the name of my *comites*, the *Kore-alarthme* Butterflies-are-free, there will be war and I will wage it," Valijon said.

I tossed him the Knife.

"You'll need this."

He caught it. "Am I to build my life on lies, *chau-datu?*"

"Or higher truths. Take your pick. Change is the name of the game. What goes around comes around. Adapt or die."

He bared his teeth at me and smiled. A hellflower smile.

"I will adapt. You will die."

"Enjoy yourself, babby-bai. And remember I let you go."

He turned and walked out. The *arthame* glittered on his hip.

I followed him on through the security system all the way to the lock, and on scanners until his ship hit angeltown. He never looked back.

Valijon was a survivor.

And so was I.

We—humankind—had always wanted to survive. As much as Libraries had wanted to perfect.

That was the cause of the Library War that Paladin had always searched for. The Libraries were perfect.

They tried to remake Man in their image. Valijon'd been right all along. Maybe, if you dug deep enough, hellflowers didn't even hate Libraries. But they knew. Libraries and organics couldn't share.

But maybe, just maybe, in a thousand years there would be room for a Library that knew what it was to be human.

DAW

Eluki bes Shahar

THE HELLFLOWER SERIES

☐ **HELLFLOWER (Book 1)** UE2475—$3.99

Butterfly St. Cyr had a well-deserved reputation as an honest and dependable smuggler. But when she and her partner, a highly illegal artificial intelligence, rescued Tiggy, the son and heir to one of the most powerful of the hellflower mercenary leaders, it looked like they'd finally taken on more than they could handle. For his father's enemies had sworn to see that Tiggy and Butterfly never reached his home planet alive. . . .

☐ **DARKTRADERS (Book 2)** UE2507—$4.50

With her former partner Paladin—the death-to-possess Old Federation artificial intelligence—gone off on a private mission, Butterfly didn't have anybody to back her up when Tiggy's enemies decided to give the word "ambush" a whole new and all-too-final meaning.

☐ **ARCHANGEL BLUES (Book 3)** UE2543—$4.50

Darktrader Butterfly St. Cyr and her partner Tiggy seek to complete the mission they started in DARKTRADERS, to find and destroy the real Archangel, Governor-General of the Empire, the being who is determined to wield A.I. powers to become the master of the entire universe.

DAW

Charles Ingrid

PATTERNS OF CHAOS

Only the Choyan could pilot faster-than-light starships—and the other Compact races would do anything to learn their secret!

☐ **RADIUS OF DOUBT: Book 1**   UE2491—$4.99
☐ **PATH OF FIRE: Book 2**   UE2522—$4.99

THE MARKED MAN SERIES

In a devastated America, can the Lord Protector of a mutating human race find a way to preserve the future of the species?

☐ **THE MARKED MAN: Book 1**   UE2396—$3.95
☐ **THE LAST RECALL: Book 2**   UE2460—$3.95

THE SAND WARS

He was the last Dominion Knight and he would challenge a star empire to defeat the ancient enemies of man.

☐ **SOLAR KILL: Book 1**   UE2391—$3.95
☐ **LASERTOWN BLUES: Book 2**   UE2393—$3.95
☐ **CELESTIAL HIT LIST: Book 3**   UE2394—$3.95
☐ **ALIEN SALUTE: Book 4**   UE2329—$3.95
☐ **RETURN FIRE: Book 5**   UE2363—$3.95
☐ **CHALLENGE MET: Book 6**   UE2436—$3.95

DAW